SOMEBODY ELSE

'You were some dish,' says Betsy Thornhill's boyfriend on seeing an old photograph of her. A casual remark, but Betsy, a fifty-one-year-old American living in London, finds herself conscious of age. She goes in for a 'little work' on her face and comes out looking marvellous, younger by fifteen years. She goes back to New York, where she has not lived for thirty years — to a city devastated by the aftermath of September 11. A few days after she arrives, Betsy is accused of murder. She looks at the police sketch. 'It isn't me,' she says. 'It's someone younger.' 'Look in the mirror,' says the cop. Betsy is trapped by her own face . . .

Books by Reggie Nadelson
Published by The House of Ulverscroft:

HOT POPPIES

SPECIAL MESSAGE TO READERS

This book is published under the auspices of

THE ULVERSCROFT FOUNDATION

(registered charity No. 264873 UK)

Established in 1972 to provide funds for research, diagnosis and treatment of eye diseases. Examples of contributions made are: —

A Children's Assessment Unit at Moorfield's Hospital, London.

•

Twin operating theatres at the Western Ophthalmic Hospital, London.

•

A Chair of Ophthalmology at the Royal Australian College of Ophthalmologists.

•

The Ulverscroft Children's Eye Unit at the Great Ormond Street Hospital For Sick Children, London.

You can help further the work of the Foundation by making a donation or leaving a legacy. Every contribution, no matter how small, is received with gratitude. Please write for details to:

THE ULVERSCROFT FOUNDATION,
The Green, Bradgate Road, Anstey,
Leicester LE7 7FU, England.
Telephone: (0116) 236 4325

In Australia write to:
THE ULVERSCROFT FOUNDATION,
c/o The Royal Australian and New Zealand College of Ophthalmologists,
94-98 Chalmers Street, Surry Hills,
N.S.W. 2010, Australia

Reggie Nadelson is an American journalist, travel writer and documentary film maker who divides her time between London and New York. She is also the author of the thriller *Hot Poppies*.

REGGIE NADELSON

SOMEBODY ELSE

Complete and Unabridged

ULVERSCROFT
Leicester

First published in Great Britain in 2003 by
Faber and Faber Limited
London

First Large Print Edition
published 2004
by arrangement with
Faber and Faber Limited
London

British Library CIP Data

Nadelson, Reggie
Somebody else.—Large print ed.—
Ulverscroft large print series: mystery
1. Women photographers—New York (State)—New York—Fiction 2. Surgery, Plastic—Fiction
3. Mistaken identity—Fiction
4. Detective and mystery stories
5. Large type books
I. Title
813.5′4 [F]

ISBN 1–84395–357–9

Published by
F. A. Thorpe (Publishing)
Anstey, Leicestershire

Set by Words & Graphics Ltd.
Anstey, Leicestershire
Printed and bound in Great Britain by
T. J. International Ltd., Padstow, Cornwall

This book is printed on acid-free paper

For David Miller

PART ONE

1

When he called again that Saturday, Betsy Thornhill bought an answering machine and wondered why it felt defensive somehow, like buying a gun. The endless phone calls that had come since she got to New York rattled her.

She thought: all the guy did was give me a ride in from the airport Thursday, then call and want a date. All he wanted was a date for dinner. There was nothing threatening about him, either. On the phone she was cool at first, then chilly. He called anyway. Maybe it was just that she was out of practice with guys asking her out, but it got under her skin and not knowing why it did made it worse. Maybe it was the newness of being away from home and back in New York.

She was making a fuss about nothing, she said to herself as she entered the store on Sixth Avenue where the owner in a yellow turban surveyed his dusty empire of toaster ovens and video players. He winked at Betsy and gave her a deal on the answering machine, batteries included, and a cell phone, cheap. By now her anxiety had subsided and she was laughing at her own melodrama.

What people saw, as she walked down Sixth Avenue, was a youngish woman in a red duffel coat, pretty in an unconventional way, arms too long, carrying a bulky plastic bag, smiling to herself; it made people who passed notice her and wonder what the secret joke was.

What Betsy saw in the store windows she passed was her own face. She stopped in front of a deli. She gazed at the Danish pastries with gooey yellow centers and sugar glaze glistening on the dough. Surreptitiously, she examined herself, still surprised by the reflected encounter with the younger Betsy.

The feeling she was detached from her face that she'd had after the surgery was beginning to fade. She still wanted to touch it, though. Feel the smooth skin under her fingertips. The way it fit her bones. Cut to fit, she thought. My bespoke face.

It excited her, being in New York where she hadn't lived for thirty years. Before, when she came to New York, she'd come for a few days for work or to see a friend. Now she was here for six months, on her own, starting over. With the new face, she felt like a space traveler, ungrounded, free as a bird, turned on by this dizzying sense she was herself and not herself.

The September before, just after her fifty-first birthday, she'd gone in to have some work done. Of course, she was scared. She was frightened of knives, it seemed trivial and vain, the surgeon could screw it up and, anyhow, four hundred years ago, you could be damned for going to God with a face not your own.

It started when Tom saw an old photograph of her in the house in London where they lived. He whistled and said, 'You were some dish back then.'

Suddenly every magazine she saw was offering holidays where you could get fixed: warm places, new faces; like the Spanish explorers in Florida's swamps, you would discover the fountain of youth. In restaurants, pretending to rest her face on her hands, Betsy found herself covertly pushing up the skin around her neck and cheeks. She began seeing the relationship between her face and the food she photographed for a living, the decay implicit in both and, for the first time, thought about death. I'm old, I'm going to die, she thought, waking up in the middle of the night in a tangle of sheets soaked with her sweat.

Then she was looking in too many mirrors. Boy oh boy, Narcissus only looked in a pool, don't be a dope, she said to herself. For months she forgot about the whole thing. So when she finally went for a consultation, it was on a whim, it seemed.

'Most women I can give five years, possibly ten,' the surgeon said. 'You,' he added, fingering her face lightly with the soft hands, commenting on the texture and structure and elasticity of her skin, 'you, I can give ten, even fifteen.'

And then, when was it? A few weeks after she saw him, she was in the hospital, wheeled in to surgery, her mind lazy with drugs, the surgeon hovering over he, his creamy hand holding hers. Aftershave that smelled of grapefruit. His small, well-shaped head with the embroidered cap he wore in surgery, bobbing like a nodding doll.

'It's going to be just fine,' he said. 'Squeeze my hand, Betsy,' he said.

Tom was away in Hong Kong on a job when she had it done. He came home for Christmas. She drove impatiently to the airport, wearing her new red coat, fixing her hair in the mirror, the rain pinging on the roof, the London afternoon so dark it shut out everything except the head-lights and the cars in front of her.

He came out of customs, the battered raincoat over his shoulder, shoving a trolley loaded with presents. Tom never came home without presents. She leaned against a wall and waited for him to notice. She fussed with her hair and put on more lip-gloss that tasted of strawberry and fixed her leather skirt but Tom just passed by, just passed, not seeing her at all.

Tom? Tom?

It took him a week to tell her how much he hated the face.

'You said I was a real dish in that picture when I was younger.'

'It was just a stupid remark. I loved you the way you were,' he said. 'I don't know you now.' And it was days before he added, 'OK, since you asked, it's because you look like somebody else.'

⋆ ⋆ ⋆

Now she went into the deli and bought one of the pastries with the yellow jam in the middle and ate it as she walked. It surprised her when she passed the Waverly that the theater was shut up, the place she had happily seen hundreds of movies. She could smell the sour lobby and feel the plush seats, some of them unhinged and broken, taste the fake butter on the oversalted popcorn. She sang the words from *Hair*. 'I met him in front of the Waverly . . . ' she warbled and a raffish old black man tipped his fedora hat at her. She was singing out loud and off key.

Ketsen's phone calls didn't mean anything; it was jet lag, the tiny finger of anxiety that tickled your calm. All he wanted was a date. It was all he ever wanted from the time he offered her a ride at the airport, so the unease was vague, like a shred of meat between your teeth you couldn't pick out with your tongue.

* * *

The plane had been late Thursday afternoon when she got in from London and pushed her bags through customs into the terminal where a couple of soldiers with sad-sack faces and guns, one chewing gum, the other picking his acne, patrolled the lobby. A wall of noise washed up over Betsy. Passengers, families, sky caps, drivers, the limo guys in suits with printed signs, others with names scrawled by hand on ragged cardboard, all jammed up together in a waiting area in the lobby that was under construction. Dust was everywhere and wires hung loose like bundles of weeds.

Gypsy drivers in shiny suits prowled the crowd, looking for passengers who needed a ride bad enough to take a chance on traveling the long way while the meter ticked.

Someone screamed in Russian. Spanish. Hindi. Over here. Here!

A couple of Hasidic Jews with six kids dragged two suitcases on wheels towards the door, hurrying. They had a connection to make. It was Thursday. The Jewish Sabbath began from tomorrow. If they missed the plane, they'd have to sit it out here at the terminal. Would they sit on the floor and wait? The thought distracted her.

The woman's wig slipped and she muttered with fury, clutching her head. A suitcase rolled away from her. One of the boys, a gawky teenager with ringlets and a cell phone, chased it. Hurry.

Betsy was used to airport chaos, but normally she traveled light; now, shoving a tower of luggage, she felt like an immigrant. After twenty minutes, she saw a driver signal her.

'Coming,' she shouted. 'I'm over here.'

'I think it's mine,' he said.

That was how she met him, her heading for the car she thought was hers, Bobby Ketsen coming out of customs and claiming it. It turned out it was his. When Betsy called the car service she used, no one knew anything about her.

He wore black jeans and a black T-shirt and a leather jacket and had a curly mouth, greenish eyes and an expensive carry-on. He was tall, six one, she thought. A few inches taller than her.

He said, 'Can I give you a ride?'

'I'll get a cab. Thanks, though.'

'There's a taxi strike,' he said and turned to the driver. 'Hold on a minute, will you? You're sure about the ride?'

In London, she had seen him at the airport, her standing in line, waiting to board, him sitting until the last moment the way business-class passengers do, sure of a place at the front of the plane and enough space to stash your bags.

Now, not thinking, she said, 'Are you following me?'

'Yeah, I am.' He smiled. 'But I'm harmless. No, I mean, I saw you at Heathrow, and you just looked like somebody I once knew, for a second. I'll help you get a cab if you want but you'll wait forever, this place has been a mess since 9/11.' He looked sheepish. 'I'm probably talking too much.' Her overloaded luggage cart wobbled and he reached over to steady it, then put out his other hand. 'Bobby Ketsen,' he said.

'Betsy,' she said. 'Thanks.'

'Let's go,' Ketsen said to the driver, tossed his bag on top of hers, put his hand on her cart and took possession of her.

* * *

On the way into the city, he talked into a cell phone for a while and she looked out of the window. The frenzy at the airport faded and she relaxed against the seat and watched the lovely marine light just fading over the cemeteries off the Expressway.

Ketsen snapped his cell phone shut and turned towards her.

'So — you're here on business?'

'Yes,' she said.

'I saw you trying to get an up-grade at the airport and I thought, now that takes real style.'

She shook her head. 'I didn't get it. I was ritually humiliated then exiled to steerage in the back of the plane.'

'I feel for you,' he said and asked what she did.

'I shoot fruit,' she answered like she always did, and he laughed and said it was odd, them meeting up, because he was in the business, more or less. He ran an on-line photo-shop. He bought and sold photographs, he said. Art stuff, mostly. Wasn't it a coincidence, he said. For a second, half a second, the frame froze, then the feeling disappeared.

'Could we take the Brooklyn Bridge in?' she asked.

'Sure we can,' he said.

The driver protested; it was a lousy route, he said. Bobby said, 'Just take it, OK?'

'Thanks.'

'You've been away long?'

'Almost two years.'

'So you need to see it.'

'Yes.'

They crawled onto the bridge and she put her face against the window. The twin towers were gone. The skyline was diminished. Teeth ripped from the gums. It didn't matter how you put it, she'd read it all, it was different, seeing it: it made you feel battered. She had watched the attack on TV on September 11; it was a few days after the surgery and she saw it from the sofa at home in London and felt lousy.

In the late afternoon, light spun off the cables of the bridge and the faces of the buildings were gold and brazen, but all you saw was empty space on a fragile island. Sliver of concrete. Easily smashed.

'You want to put your arms around it, don't you?' he said, reading her mind. 'Where were you?'

'London.'

'I was home. I live nearby. I went on the roof and I thought, when the second plane hit, they're making a movie. My eyes wouldn't connect to my brain. It's what everyone thought. We all felt dysfunctional.'

Ketsen took another call and Betsy leaned back against the seat. There was a traffic jam on the bridge and they were silent for a while and then he made some small talk and they discussed photographers. It turned out he knew her agent. Everyone knew David Sellers.

It was like that during the ride into the city, no menace, no drama, no feeling this ride would change her life, just small things: the feel of the leather car seat, the sound of Ketsen's cell phone and voice, the smell of his pear shampoo.

'How old are you?' she said.

'Why?' he said.

'I'm nosy,' she said.

'Thirty-one.' He put his arm along the back of the seat behind her. 'What about you?'

'Actually,' she said, tentative, trying it on, 'I'm thirty-five.'

He glanced at her and nodded. He said, 'You have a place in the city?'

'My aunt's, in the Village. Cornelia Street. She left it to me.'

'Lucky you.'

'You said it!'

'You're here for a while?'

Betsy looked at the crowds pouring into the subway and the imperious buildings around City Hall. As they cut across to the west side, the red sun dropped into the river and the magic hour settled on Manhattan.

'Yeah, I am,' she said. 'I think maybe I'm here to stay.'

The car pulled up in front of a loft building and stopped and he opened the door.

'This is me,' he said. 'The car will take you wherever you want, OK?'

'Thank you. Really.' She held out her hand. 'Bobby, right?'

'Right.'

Again, for a split second, something about the way he looked at her made her wonder if the meeting was really accidental, but he just gestured to a bar on the ground floor of his building. The Tribe was spelled out in curly blue neon over the turn-of-the-century door.

'They do pretty good burgers, if you ever feel like it. Betsy, can I ask you something?'

'Sure.'

He stuttered slightly and finally he said, 'Listen, how do I ask if you want to come up and see something I know you'd like without it sounding like a come-on?'

'Is it a come-on?'

'Yeah, it is,' he said. 'But there's like five people working up there.'

She said, 'What's this thing I have to see?'

'You said you take pictures of fruit. Vegetables, too?'

'Absolutely.'

'You won't be disappointed. The car will wait and then take you where you want to go. Come on up.'

She had followed strangers down back alleys to restaurants in Bangkok in search of fish to photograph, bummed around Morocco taking pictures of tagine, and here was a good-looking guy waiting for her and wanting to show her pictures so she climbed out of the car and followed him into the vestibule of the building.

In the dim hall with its peeling gray walls and harsh fluorescent light, she waited next to Bobby Ketsen as he pushed the elevator button. The old freight elevator shuddered to a halt. Ketsen heaved the gates open. Betsy got in.

* * *

The green peapods were like jewels, but also alive. You could feel the fleshy texture and wet surface, as if they'd just been washed. All the photographs on Ketsen's wall were by Irving Penn, some she'd seen in books: a hand in a latex glove holding a hammer and smashing a bright red lobster; a sandwich with ants crawling over it; wormy apples. There was also a pearl onion and a spoon heaped with caviar, the fish eggs like oily ball bearings.

Penn was her hero. He took pictures of food the way the Dutch painted it so you always saw it alive, in motion, the egg cracking, the viscous yolk slowly spreading, the slick of sweat on a slab of salmon.

Shooting food, you had to catch it and keep it fresh before it went bad, before it rotted, and if you were good, you trapped it fast, the look, taste, smell. You could make it nostalgic or erotic. What was it Penn said? 'Photographing a cake can be art.'

Ketsen said, 'You like them? I had to take out a mortgage to get them.'

'Yeah I like them — I mean, they're sensational.'

It made her interested in Ketsen, that he would go out on a limb to acquire these pictures. He took off his leather jacket; the sleeves of his T-shirt were rolled up over heavily muscled arms. A show-off gesture, the sleeves, she thought. Otherwise he seemed almost diffident: she liked him.

He stood beside her in front of the pictures and put an arm lightly over her shoulder.

'I'm glad you see it,' he said.

He took her elbow and showed her around

his place; there were white walls and a wooden floor and a row of industrial windows. Parked near one of the windows was a vintage Harley, the chrome glittering.

'My toy,' he said.

'You live here, too?'

He nodded and pointed beyond the studio to a stripped wooden door. 'Back there.'

At a long white table, two girls were hunched over computers. Crouched on his heels on the floor, a boy sorted some prints. Somewhere, through hidden speakers, Miles Davis played 'Sketches of Spain'. A faint odor of pot clung to the air.

The kids were in their early twenties. Age was the first thing she noticed these days. Get over it, she said to herself silently. Give it up.

At a separate desk, a black girl with a curly pony tail talked into the phone and Ketsen gave her a high five and held out his hand and drew Betsy in.

'This is Betsy,' he said. 'She picked me up at the airport.'

'Sure, Bobby,' the girl mocked him. 'Hi, Betsy,' she added and shook her hand and went back to the phone.

'You want a drink?' he said.

'I ought to go.'

'Right.'

On a plinth near a window was metal

twisted around a piece of concrete the size of a man's hand and covered in dust.

Betsy said, 'What is it?'

'It's a piece of Ground Zero,' he said. 'I keep it to remember. I got terrific pictures down there.'

'You took pictures?'

'Wouldn't you?'

Ketsen walked her to the elevator and pressed the button and smiled, pulling a card out of his pocket. 'Here's my number.' He held the card out to her. 'You only shoot produce?'

'Other stuff. I do a brilliant muffin.'

He pulled open the elevator door, waited until she got in, closed it, then banged lightly on the gate and pushed the card through the metal bars.

'So call me,' he said. 'If you want. Please.'

On the street, before she climbed into the car, she looked up. Suddenly, he was standing at the window, looking down at her, watching her, palms flat against the glass, smiling, a quizzical look on his face so brief she barely caught it. She got into the car and slammed the door.

2

Betsy tossed the remains of her Danish into a garbage can, licked the powdery sugar off her lips, wiped her sticky mouth with the back of her hand, went home, unpacked the answering machine, plugged it in and recorded a message. Without waiting for another call, she ran out again and walked north.

I should be tired, she thought. David, her agent, always asked if she was tired after a trip. She had crossed the Atlantic, her legs folded up in the economy seat like a pair of pretzels, she was up late unpacking her first two nights in New York. But the adrenalin was high, she felt wide awake. Now she was at the Greenmarket in Union Square where fishermen in rubber boots sold fish from upstate rivers and farmers laid out potatoes and parsnips. Tomatoes, too, including Heirlooms like little grotesques, though it was the wrong season for tomatoes and Betsy wondered if they were engineered. Scientifically fixed. Like me, she thought.

At a stall where cheese was turning soft in the sun she paused and reached into her pocket for her camera. Decay was her subject.

The cheese oozed, she looked through the lens at it, she heard him. A hand grasped her arm.

'Hey, Betsy?'

Ketsen's voice. He had followed her to the market, furious she never returned his calls. She turned around. He was holding a camera.

'Say cheese.' He laughed and took her picture, then slipped the camera in his pocket. 'It's only me. Bobby. I thought it was you. So how are you?'

'Fine,' she said coolly.

'Did I scare you? Hey, I'm sorry.'

'Don't be ridiculous,' she said.

'Isn't this weird, us meeting up here?

'Is it?'

'Yeah, of course,' he said. 'So what about lunch? I know a guy who can get us into the Union Square Café. My treat.'

'No.'

'OK. Sure. So see you soon,' he said and stuffed his hands in his pockets and walked away.

She called out, 'Bobby,' and he turned around and she asked, 'How did you get my number?'

'I got it from David,' he said and disappeared into the crowd.

★ ★ ★

The warm weather was freakish, she thought, carrying bags of fruit home. Headlines proclaimed it the warmest winter on record and there was the threat of drought. The streets were thronged with people, but, in spite of the weather, the city seemed subdued as if the good times were over, shattered and blown away like fragments of glass and paper the morning the World Trade Center fell.

'You settling in OK, hon?' Marie Tusi called out from her window on the ground floor.

Ground floor? First floor? What did New Yorkers say, Betsy suddenly wondered and felt foreign. They said both, she remembered, but one up was always second.

Marie added, 'You need anything, you let me know, OK?'

Marie and her husband, Dev, had lived in the building for years. The way she always did, she sat in her window, framed by it like a skinny, middle-aged Madonna with a cigarette. She coughed and waved at Betsy.

'No, thanks. Thank you.'

'I'll make my short-ribs for you, OK?' Marie called.

On the buzzer, the strip of paper with Betsy's name had come unstuck and she put it back. Putting it up was the first thing she did when she arrived two days earlier.

Upstairs, still astonished it was all hers, this place she'd inherited from her Aunt Pauline, Betsy set the bags down in the kitchen. The three-story tenement was built in the 1920s. Pauline's apartment had been an afterthought, a fourth stuck up on the flat roof so the landlord could make an extra buck. You climbed three flights to her front door. Inside, another six steps led to the living room that looked out over the street. So did the narrow kitchen. In back, the bedroom and tiny bathroom had windows over a triangular cement yard where garbage cans were chained to the wall. A rusty tricycle with two wheels listed on its side.

Betsy had lived here during her senior year in college when Aunt Pauline was still in New Jersey. Thirty-two years ago. A precocious kid who graduated college at nineteen. I was nineteen once. She left New York the year the World Trade Center opened.

Before she took her coat off, Betsy called her agent, David Sellers, at home in London, but there was no answer. She left a message. As soon as she put the cracked brown plastic receiver down, the phone rang again. The machine picked it up. It was Ketsen.

His voice was low and warm and raspy, a

voice that said this was a guy who liked a smoke, a few drinks, but who paid attention; there was self-mockery and he sounded abashed, a boy wanting a date.

Had it been an accident, them meeting? What was it he said on the way in from the airport that caught at her like a fishhook in the flesh? Betsy couldn't remember and she got a Diet Coke out of the fridge, gulped it down, tossed the can and landed it in the garbage. The phone rang again, but by the time she snatched it up, he was gone.

Later that night, she ordered sesame noodles from the take-out on Bleecker Street and unpacked some of her bags and called her mother on Long Island, but there was no answer. Betsy was whacked now. The next time the phone rang, she picked it up and held it to her ear and knew; the quality of breathing had become familiar.

'This is Bobby Ketsen,' he said. 'How's it going?'

'I'm fine,' she said evenly.

'I thought we could do some business, if you want, that's why I called your agent. I like your pictures. You feel like a drink tonight? We could go for a beer or something.'

'No,' she said. 'No thanks.'

Seeming not to hear, he said, 'I might pass by your place tomorrow, see if you're OK.'

'Look, I don't think that would be a great idea. OK?'

'I'm sad you feel like that,' he said. 'But I understand. Have a good weekend. Call if you feel like it.'

'I have to go.'

'Promise you'll call?'

She was silent.

'So, talk to you soon, Betsy.'

He used her name; it made her skin crawl, as if he'd touched her uninvited.

Betsy slammed the phone down, then picked it up and tried her agent again, but there was still no answer and anyhow she knew David would never give out her number.

I like your pictures.

Maybe all he wanted was her work. I like your pictures, he'd said, but where had he seen them? I like your work. I like you. Betsy poured some vodka into a glass, added grapefruit juice, and got a cigarette. She turned on the TV.

Vertigo was on and she lay back against the striped sofa that sagged on one side. The drink made her drowsy. She watched as Jimmy Stewart cajoled Kim Novak. Please me, he said. Do your hair this way, color it like that, wear these clothes, he urged until he made her into an immaculate facsimile of his dead wife. Carbon copy. Dead ringer.

When Betsy looked up, the movie was over. She had fallen asleep. She glanced at the answering machine. There were no more messages that night, and Betsy, exhausted, went to bed, and woke up Sunday tense, listening for the phone.

There were no calls on Sunday, but the possibility that he might come by, that he might somehow know her address, made her angry. There was something insidious in Ketsen's pursuit, the watching her from his window when she got in the car, the phone calls, the meeting at the Greenmarket in Union Square.

In London, Betsy inhabited a whole house, but it was up for rent now. Her whole life was stashed for six months in this tiny apartment like a ship's cabin perched on the top floor of the building. It made her feel light and clean. In New York, though she missed her friends, she felt unencumbered, free. Except for Ketsen. Ketsen's calls cluttered things up. He scratched the smooth pleasure she felt at her return to the city. He got in her way.

3

The next morning, wearing a pair of faded cut-offs and an orange sweater, she was eating half a toasted bagel with black cherry jam when the buzzer went. She would remember for a long time that the clock on the wall said 9.10. Piled-up copies of the *New York Times* lay on the kitchen table. A jumble of headlines — drought, terrorism, Enron, the death of *Wall Street Journal* reporter Daniel Pearl — caught her eye as she spoke into the intercom.

'Yes?' she said, then pushed the window open and leaned out.

On the sidewalk below a man walked backward from the building to the curb and looked up, shading his eyes with his hand. He wore faded jeans and a brown leather jacket and a light blue scarf. Then he walked back to the building. Again, the buzzer sounded.

'What?' Betsy shouted.

'Is Betsy Thornhill in?' the voice said. 'I'm Detective Dolce.'

She buzzed him in and heard him lumber up the stairs and knock. She opened the door. He was six two, six three and had a paunch and beefy shoulders, a drinker's nose and half a day's stubble. His blue eyes were bloodshot, the brown hair speckled with gray. He was probably forty, but he looked older. He looked worn, she thought. Worn down, worn out.

'I'm Detective Frank Dolce,' he said, repeating his name, pronouncing it with two syllables. Dol-che. 'Sorry to bother you.' He held up a badge and wiped his shoes on the mat.

'Come in,' she said.

It occurred to her there was something wrong in the building. Maybe someone had reported the broken stairs that led to the back alley or the bums who slept on the stoop. A bar nearby had spilled its drunks onto the stoop at four Sunday morning and she'd heard them yelling and the bottles break.

Betsy went into the kitchen. The cop followed her.

'You can sit down,' she said.

'Thank you.' He sat uneasily on the edge of a kitchen chair.

'I was having coffee,' she said. 'Can I fix you some?'

'No. Thanks.' He folded his hands awkwardly and looked at them, embarrassed, as if he was expecting someone else.

She sat, too, aware suddenly of her shorts,

and her bare flesh. Casually, she picked up a green and white dishcloth from the table and draped it over her naked thighs.

'What is it?' she said.

The cop smiled awkwardly. 'Do you know a man named Robert Ketsen?'

'Bobby Ketsen?'

'So you know him?'

'He gave me a ride from the airport Thursday. There was a taxi strike.'

'That's it?' the cop — Detective Dolce — asked. 'Are you sure?'

'Pretty much. He called me a few times.'

'Why's that?'

'Dinner. A date. You know.' She felt herself, idiotically, blush. 'He asked me out.'

'But you didn't go?'

'No.'

'You two talked a lot?'

'No. He called, I didn't want to see him. Actually I bought an answering machine. I only talked to him once after that,' Betsy said. 'Maybe twice.'

He took off his jacket. He was planning to stick around, she saw.

'You bought an answering machine so you wouldn't have to talk to him? Isn't that a little extreme?' Dolce asked.

Betsy got up and, irrationally, started for the living room.

'I needed an answering machine. I'll show you. I just got this place and it didn't have one,' she said.

He called after her, bringing her back to the kitchen.

'Could I have some of that coffee after all? If it's not too much trouble,' he asked.

Turning around, wondering what he really wanted, Betsy fumbled with the espresso pot and filled it with water and coffee and put it on the stove, and tried to smile. She wanted him on her side.

'My dad was a cop,' she said.

'In the city?'

'No, on the island. Rockville Center.'

His sister lived in Rockville Center, he told her, and repeating herself, she said again that her dead father had been a cop. He went to law school and became a local politician on the island, she added, but he was always a cop. She told him how she loved going to the station house where the guys rode her around on their shoulders. The story made Detective Dolce smile. Betsy was nervous and it made her garrulous.

'Anything in the coffee?'

'Black's fine,' he said.

When the coffee was ready, Betsy took the pot off the stove, poured some in a mug, watching the thin stream of black liquid. She wanted him to go away now. The coffee dripped down the side of the mug, she wiped it up hurriedly with a yellow dishcloth; the coffee stained it. The smell of coffee was acrid. Burned.

She said, 'I hope it's hot.'

He drank some coffee. 'It's good. So, he annoyed you? He threatened you?'

She shook her head.

'He seemed like a nice enough guy,' she said. 'It's just he kept calling and then he turned up in Union Square, at the Green-market — I forgot to tell you that; it was probably an accident. It just got on my nerves, the sort of begging, you know?'

Dolce ignored her question and swallowed another mouthful of coffee 'This is really great, thanks. You think he was stalking you?'

'I don't know,' she said and poured herself some coffee.

'You never saw him after that?'

'No.'

'What about Saturday night? You didn't see him and forget?'

'How could I forget where I was Saturday night? Of course I didn't see him. I was here, unpacking and eating take-out.'

'Alone? It's just routine for me to ask.'

'I ordered some Chinese that I didn't eat most of. I probably have the check that came with it. I don't know if they put a date on.'

'What time?'

'Around eight. What's going on?' She kept her tone light but the back of her throat was dry and ashy like old cigarette butts.

Dolce put out his hands and stared at the palms as if he could read them. 'You didn't see the news this morning?'

'No.'

'Robert Ketsen is dead.'

Betsy drank out of her mug, trying to clear the bad taste and said, uncomprehending, 'What do you mean, dead? You mean he had an accident?'

'He was murdered.'

She looked at the wall over the stove where the robin's-egg blue paint had puckered and blisters formed. The iron radiator hissed. Through the partly open window came the background buzz of the city, the sound of traffic along its arteries, the noise more ferocious than she remembered.

In the kitchen with the humpback old fridge, she saw Dolce at the table and it seemed surreal, as if he'd come to see her about a TV show. It was a cop show, and this soft-spoken guy in a leather jacket was here looking for a location to shoot an episode.

Can we shoot here? Can we talk with the director about it? Would you mind very much if we changed the furniture around? We would pay, naturally. Of course, she'd say, change the furniture if you need to. Are there any stars in this episode?

'What happened?' she said.

'That's what we have to find out.'

Betsy reached over and pulled open the fridge and got a plastic bottle of Evian. She drank from the bottle and held it between her hands as if it were ballast.

'Did you like him?

She said, 'I didn't *know* him.'

'He gave you a ride, didn't he? I mean you don't just hop in a car with any guy who asks.' He said it gently. 'I mean you're a cop's daughter. Your dad probably told you, never ride with strangers,' he added. 'That was a stupid thing to say. I'm sorry.'

⋆ ⋆ ⋆

There was a disconnect between her brain and her hands which were freezing so she put the water bottle on the table and sat on a chair, her hands under her.

She was a middle-aged white photographer. Mostly, her world was a pretty benign place. She didn't know dead people. She didn't ride around with people who got murdered on Saturday night. Friends got cancer and died sometimes; once, briefly, she had dated a cameraman who got killed, years later, on an assignment in Bosnia. After the Trade Center attack, there were dead people, but they were on TV, the news, behind glass. The cop in her kitchen waited patiently, hands folded.

'The airport was crazy, and I saw this limo guy I thought was for me and it turned out it was his and mine never showed, so he offered me a ride. I took it.' Her words came out garbled.

'He came on to you?'

'Why do you ask?'

'You said he called you. He asked you out. He was obviously interested.'

'I guess. Yes.'

He leaned over the table and touched the sleeve of her orange sweater lightly. 'It will be OK,' he said. 'So he gave you a ride into the city.'

'Yes.'

'You talked.' His tone was unagressive.

'Sure.'

'What about?'

'What happened to him? You don't know or you don't want to tell me?' she asked. 'When did you find him?'

'Yesterday afternoon. It was Sunday but his secretary went in to help him clear up some paperwork. She was there Saturday night, too. She left late, and he was still alive. When she got back Sunday, he was dead. You were saying what you and Ketsen talked about,' Dolce said and added, 'Could I have some more of that coffee? I didn't get much sleep.'

Betsy said, 'I'll make some fresh. What about the phone?'

'What phone?'

'You could look at phone records, couldn't you? I mean. I talked to some friends in London Saturday night. Late.' She saw him suppress a grin and said, 'You think I've seen too many cop shows?'

'Maybe a couple. But, no, that really helps. You call your friends at night? I mean at night New York time? Your friends stay up late in London?'

'Yeah, sure, depends what night it is, it depends how late,' Betsy said. 'What difference does it make? Look, we talked about photography, Ketsen and me,' she added. 'I'm a photographer. I shoot fruit.'

'It's your hobby?'

'I make a living at it.' For the first time, she was irritated.

'Of course. Who do you work for?'

'Magazines. I'm free-lance. In Europe mostly. I mostly shoot food. I did a book last year.'

'Can I see? The book?'

Betsy went into the living room and got a copy of *Fruit* and put it on the table between them.

'It's big,' he said.

'Yes.'

He cradled the heavy book carefully in one arm and turned the pages slowly and examined her photographs.

It seemed to her that he was settling in. He had accepted the coffee, now he was looking at her book. Betsy tried to ignore the sensation he was circling around, waiting to catch his prey.

The blood flowed back into her hands and she lit up a cigarette and smoked it with as much bravado as she could manage. She was good at rearranging reality, it was what she did for a living. A friend said the way she greased up yellow peppers with lubricants she got at sex shops, you felt like you were up inside them, could practically fuck them. For *Fruit*, she had written the text and taken the pictures; it had been successful. The publishers commissioned another one. She would call it *Tutti-Frutti*. Or maybe *Veg*.

In her mind, she assessed the situation for its anecdotal potential. So, she'd say to friends over some red wine, so I'm in New York my first week and this detective shows up, and, you're not going to believe this, I swear to God, but he says . . .

Dolce flipped the pages of her book. 'This is good. So you talked about photography with Ketsen. Anything else?'

The coffee dripped slowly. Betsy listened to it and watched the stripes of light that came in through the Venetian blind. He didn't ask if she'd been to Ketsen's place and she didn't tell him. She'd only been there briefly on Thursday. It was only to look at Ketsen's photographs. It didn't mean anything.

'How did you find me?' she asked.

Dolce extracted a nest of crumpled paper out of the pocket of his jeans and fished a scrap from it and gave it to her. 'Your name was on Ketsen's desk along with the address and a London number.'

She looked at the number.

'My agent,' she said. 'David Sellers. Ketsen said he called him to get my number. Then I realized David wouldn't give out my number ever — unless he was stoned, and even then.'

'You didn't ask him, this agent guy?'

'He's out of town.'

He nodded. 'Ketsen couldn't have gotten your number that way?'

'Probably not. Unless he managed to con someone at David's office, but I doubt it.'

'You have a cell phone?'

'I bought one Saturday, but I didn't give him the number. I only gave it to a few people in London.'

'Why London?'

'I live in London.'

'You don't sound English,' he said.

'No? I try not to. I always hate it when people go to England and come back sounding like Masterpiece Theater or something. Anyhow, I'm not English. I've just been there a long time.'

Carefully, he put her book on the table and got up. 'Thanks for the coffee.'

He put his jacket back on, nervously now, his thick fingers fumbling the zipper.

'That's OK,' she said.

'You're going to be around for a while?' He reached in his pocket, gave her his card. 'If you think of anything, just give me a call.'

'I'm here for six months.'

'Working?' he said.

'I'm doing another book and some magazine pieces.'

They left the kitchen, him in front, her behind. In the living room, he gazed around, then reached for the front door.

'One other thing,' he said. 'Your voice was on Ketsen's answering machine.'

Betsy was confused. 'But I never called him.'

'He recorded his phone calls to you. You sounded mad as hell, tell you the truth. The way it looks, at least to the experts, he played that tape over and over. He saved your voice.'

4

The cop, this Detective Dolce, left, and Betsy stayed where she was, holding his card and leaning hard on the doorframe. Bobby Ketsen was dead and her voice was locked up in a box on his desk. He gave her a ride in from the airport and called her and she bought the damn answering machine because he called so much, but he kept her voice anyway. Stole it.

There wasn't much that shook Betsy, not outwardly. She was scared of escalators. Horror movies. Getting old. In spite of her effort to see the humor in a dead guy who wanted a date and a visit from a New York cop at 9.10 on a Monday morning, it got to her.

She tried to picture it, Ketsen in the loft, someone coming in, shooting him, slitting his throat, the cops finding her name on his desk, her voice on his machine. The detective didn't say how Ketsen was murdered. The texture of the whole thing was wrong. It was unreal. Then she heard the voice from the stairs below. Bel was back.

Bel Plotkin lived on the second floor, was

in her late seventies now, a short, slight, durable woman; she struggled up the stairs, clutching her battered doctor's bag, and exploded into Betsy's arms.

'Cara Betsy. How the hell are you?'

She hugged Bel and said, 'Yeah, I'm fine,' and went back into the apartment.

Bel followed and threw herself into a chair and smoothed back her wispy white hair.

'Give me a cigarette,' she said.

'You're still smoking?'

'Kiddo, I am seventy-eight years old. I got a right.' She looked around.

'You fixed the place nice.'

Betsy found cigarettes in the desk drawer and gave Bel one and lit it for her and held off telling her about the cop. Bel would worry and there was nothing to worry about.

'Listen, sugar, I'm so sorry about not being here to welcome you,' Bel said. 'But I was with the idiot who is, by birth at least, my sister, though it's bloody hard to believe. It wasn't bad enough when she was here, now I have to go to Brooklyn.'

'Is she OK?'

'Sissy is very stupid.'

Betsy said, 'Wouldn't know if bats flew out of her own ass, right?'

Bel laughed. 'I guess it gets to you when

you have diabetes and they want to chop off your foot.'

'Yeah, no more tap dancing for Sissy, right?'

Bel guffawed and took a deep drag on her cigarette.

'You're almost as tough as I am, aren't you?' Bel said. 'I forgot about Sissy's tap-dancing lessons, and you went with her . . . what were you, eighteen, nineteen?' she said. 'Anyhow, the whole week's been a bore, but good came of it, I mean you're here, so that's my reward.'

'You must miss Pauline.'

Bel Plotkin and Pauline Thornhill had been best friends from the day they met as nursing students on the steps of St Vincent's in 1940. They moved to the tenement on Cornelia Street together. There were Italian families on the block and it was known that if you were a young girl and had trouble, one of the local guys would take care of it for you.

Later, Pauline moved to the top floor. She married and left for Weehawken, New Jersey, and Betsy used the apartment. Pauline came back before she died and left the place to Betsy, her brother's daughter.

Bel stayed on the second floor and never left at all except for her time at medical school in Rochester and the trips to Venice and Rome. She loved Italy, opera, politics, reading. She still worked three days at week at a clinic in the Village.

Bel rearranged her hair and leaned back in the chair and smoked, the cigarette held between her thumb and forefinger.

'It must be a year since I saw you, right, cara? Before the bastards hit the Trade Center. Jesus, Betsy, we waited at St Vinnie's all day and after the first rush, nothing. Everyone was dead.' She leaned forward and crushed a cigarette in the ashtray on the low table in front of the sofa. 'Let me look at you. Marie Tusi, she says to me, I think Betsy did some stuff to her face, so I tell her she's jealous. She didn't like that. She thinks she's a sexy Italian woman but she's just a big skinny *gavone*, sixty years old with those lousy bones. She sprained her wrist last week, second time this year, and messhuga that I am, I help her in the kitchen making tuna casserole for Dev's church group.' Bel inhaled more smoke.

'You're a good woman, Bel.'

'Not to mention the lousy asthma she has and still smoking like a chimney — I should talk — and obsesses about going to Rome to see that nightmare of a Pope.' Bel laughed and coughed and then said. 'What does she know from Italy? You should have seen Marie on the 11th — *I'm so scared, Bel, I'm scared.'*

'You don't like her.'

'She's territorial about people. There's a nice woman on the third floor with a kid, a sweet girl and they kept to themselves, but Marie had to butt in. They're away for a month, she comes to tell me, what's it her business? The husband left, she says. Never mind. So you did it? Your face?'

Betsy said, 'You think I was crazy?'

'Absolutely not, who cares if you look good? Anyway, you were always greedy for anything new, even as a kid.'

'I was?'

Bel looked at her hard. 'Am I smelling a problem? Are you OK?'

'I'm fine.'

'You remember I always told you and your friends, I'm a doctor, you tell me something, it's privileged. So tell.'

'Not even under torture, you always said and we couldn't figure out who was coming to torture you, but it sounded really romantic. Can I take you out to dinner?'

'Love to. Can't. I have to get back to Sissy who thinks the Arabs from Atlantic Avenue are coming to get her. Who'd want to get Sissy?' Bel said. 'You look wonderful, cara.'

* * *

Over the kitchen sink with the rust stain in the middle was a light with a chain and a small mirror. Betsy pulled the chain and a bare bulb came on.

On the kitchen table was the Polaroid she used for work and she picked it up. In the bright light from the bulb and the sun outside, she took her own picture in the mirror flat on, no dipping her chin, none of the model's habits she'd learned when she was a young assistant and worked fashion, hauling cameras and lights, going out for booze and cigarettes and dope. It killed her interest in fashion, but she knew the tricks. While the camera spewed out her picture, she watched herself in the mirror, where her eyes looked very light, a chilly blue, and the short dark hair pushed back behind her ears and the orange sweater she wore made her face seem very pale, her eyes very cold.

Betsy held the picture up to the window then looked in the mirror again. For a few more seconds, she stood in what she still thought of as Pauline's kitchen, tipping her head left, then right, making faces. I love this face, she thought, and leaned forward and kissed her reflection.

At her last appointment with the surgeon at

his office, he had congratulated her as if she'd won the lottery. Hurrying out, he turned her over to his number two, a young doctor with a little mouth like a kitten who said he rarely saw cases like hers and surveyed her hungrily as if he wanted to lick her face. She was his piece of porn.

Superb, he said in his nasal London accent. Brilliant. Softly, as if he'd come up with a brand-new idea, he added, 'Fits like a glove.' How about an iron face in a velvet glove, Betsy wanted to ask, but he was content with the glove and he was very young with a square head like Rock Hudson and not irreverent. Good hands, no sense of humor.

Younger was the point. People said, I'm going in for some work, I want to look better, not necessarily younger. But there were no standards for better than weren't about youth. Right? Better meant smoother skin, firmer jowls, plumper lips. What culture idolized wrinkles? A few Confucians, maybe, but Betsy didn't know any Confucians.

It cost her, though. Not just the money. It hurt like hell. Weeks after the surgery, her hair was still matted with blood, her skin turned yellow, she looked like a chipmunk, face puffed, eyes black. The lift, the eyes, the peel, the brows, the neck. A snip off her nose because it had become fatter with age. It wasn't what she had planned, she only wanted a bit of a lift, she said, but the surgeon offered her a deal. He looked at the old picture she gave him, the one when she was still a dish and he said, 'I can make you look like this, only better.' Turn back the clock. Fly high. Start over.

When the stitches came out she felt as if her face had been sewn up with crude fishing line, but she figured the pain was some kind of penance, a quid pro quo, God testing her, though she was over God by the time she was twenty.

Too much thinking, she thought, admired her face one more time, grabbed her coat and camera and went out.

* * *

The sides of beef, blood congealed on them, ribs gleaming white, hung from big metal hooks in a cavernous warehouse in the Meatpacking District. Men in white coats and hats slid the beef along metal rails and onto the loading platforms and into waiting trucks. You could smell the raw beef, fresh meat.

Betsy checked the location for her shoot that week in a studio upstairs from the warehouse, then went back and shot the meat for a while to limber up. Soon she lost herself in the work and almost forgot about the cop.

For a couple of hours she worked. She could take pictures that would satisfy the editors she worked for, but she could never find in herself the thing Irving Penn had. That even less skilled photographers had. She was good enough but it was only a facility, a trick, nothing more. Her pictures were never the way they were in her dreams. You see a beggar, you're too prissy to shove the camera in his face. You hurry too much, she thought. You can't stand waiting. You sail over the surface and move on to the next job. Only she knew that even her book was mostly sleight of hand. Charm.

With a face a little like a bull, a fat butcher in a bloodied white coat sauntered out of a warehouse onto the street and eyed her as he lit up a cigarette. He held out the pack and grinnned and Betsy smiled back but shook her head and instead of taking his picture, because it seemed intrusive, turned and walked away and wandered for a while.

The warehouses were disappearing, replaced by bistros and bars and galleries. Betsy wandered for a while, then stopped for a glass of red wine and a sandwich on Little West Twelfth Street. On her way home, she picked up a piece of taleggio at Murray's cheese shop on the corner of Bleecker and Cornelia. It was dark now, and yellow light spilled onto the sidewalk from the restaurants on her block.

Marie Tusi was leaning out of her window, smoking and staring. The cops were back.

5

A big maroon Crown Victoria was at the curb and in it a guy worked on a paper carton of coffee with a Greek frieze around the edge. Emerging from the other seat was Detective Dolce who asked if they could come up. We have a picture, he said. Do you mind if my partner comes up, too, the heater shut down in the car and it's getting chilly. She nodded, but it wasn't cold.

Dolce was all spruced up. There was a razor nick on his chin, he had a fresh haircut. He was an ugly man with a sympathetic face. He reached for her bag and gestured with his other hand at the car.

'My partner,' he said.

The two of them followed her into the building and up the stairs.

In her apartment, she switched on the lights, dumped her red coat on the sofa and automatically checked the answering machine. There were no messages.

Dolce's partner was a thin, stubby man with a crew cut.

'Jimmy Grant.' He put out his hand. 'How ya doing?'

'Hi.' Betsy shook his hand, then went into the kitchen.

'Frank says you make great coffee,' Grant followed her and sat on a chair and after that was silent, watching her, not talking.

Frank Dolce sat on the same kitchen chair he'd used before.

'It was really good,' he said. 'The coffee.'

She was aware of the sounds in the building, a TV, a vacuum cleaner, her own heart. From the street, other noises distracted Betsy: a woman yelling, someone rolling a garbage can to the curb, an ambulance somewhere.

'So,' Dolce said. 'Coffee?'

Betsy looked for some cigarettes and Dolce held out a pack and she took one. He lit it for her.

'I'll make some if you want,' she said. 'But you didn't come over for my coffee so just be straight with me, OK? Please?' She put her cigarette on the rough edge of the sink and looked at the rust stain. 'Maybe I can help. But I'll make the coffee anyhow. There are some cookies on the table if you want.'

Frank Dolce took an oatmeal cookie off the plate, examined it and ate half. 'You went up to his loft, didn't you?' he said. 'These are good, the cookies.'

Not telling him she'd been in Ketsen's loft

had been a simple mistake. There was no reason, it just happened that she didn't. But he knew.

'I stopped by for a few minutes after we got into the city Friday,' she said and tried to explain about photographs, heard herself chatter about Irving Penn.

The cops didn't care about her taste in photography. All they heard was her lie: it made her sweat.

Jimmy gobbled a cookie, and, except for the chewing, kept his mouth shut. They were both silent and she could hear the clock.

'Someone saw you go into Ketsen's building Saturday night,' Dolce said finally. 'Tall woman, dark hair, red coat.' He glanced towards the living room where she'd left her coat. 'You have a red coat, don't you, Ms Thornhill?' He turned away to his partner. 'Jimmy?'

As Jimmy reached into his pocket his sleeveless argyle sweater rode up over his green polo shirt. There was a gun in his waistband.

Betsy had never seen a gun close up, and she watched it while Jimmy pulled out a piece of paper and handed it to Dolce.

'Why don't you sit down?' he said to her and unfolded the piece of paper on the table between them. 'The witness who saw a woman go into the building — we got her with a computer artist who worked this up for us.' He pushed it across the table in Betsy's direction. 'When I saw it, I thought: that looks kind of like Ms Thornhill.'

The image was printed in color on cheap paper. Instinctively, her hand went to her face as she looked down at the picture.

In it was a woman with short dark hair and a wide mouth. Betsy's nose and eyes and chin. The eyes, like hers, were set wide apart and very light blue. Then it blurred and all she saw were marks on paper and a cop chewing oatmeal cookies, and she thought it might be a hallucination. A psychotic break that made her separate herself from herself. All of a sudden, as if it was stapled to her skull, her face felt too tight.

The cops waited.

She had the impression they were waiting for her to drown, like a fish she'd seen in a Chinatown restaurant in a tank of water. It skittered across the tank, waiting for someone to fish it out, kill it, eat it for dinner. A dish like me.

Studying the scarred paint on the old kitchen table, she looked at the picture again.

'This isn't me,' she said.

'It looks a lot like you,' Dolce said.

'Who was the witness?'

'It doesn't matter,' Dolce said. 'So you don't think this looks like you?'

'Of course not. I mean, there are similarities, like the nose, but this woman is different.'

'How's that?' Dolce asked. 'Help me out.'

'This woman is much younger than me. I mean she could be in her late twenties, her early thirties.' she said. 'I'm fifty-one years old. I was fifty-one in August. I'll be fifty-two this year.'

Frank got up and put his hand under her arm lightly, and tugged and she understood he wanted her to stand. She held onto the stub of her cigarette and it burned her finger and she flipped it into her coffee mug where it sizzled and died.

Was he going to arrest her? Read her her rights and pull her arms behind her back, snap on the handcuffs?

He kept hold of her arm. The two of them moved towards the sink with the cracked mirror over it. Dolce pulled the chain and the light came on. He touched her shoulder lightly, she moved to the right so that she stood in front of the mirror. She could see Dolce's reflection next to her own. He held up the picture.

'It is you, isn't it?' he asked. 'Maybe you were at Ketsen's a second time and you forgot, the way you forgot you were there the day you came in from the airport? Is that what happened? It's possible you made a date with him and you don't want to say?'

Betsy turned away from the mirror.

'I wasn't at Ketsen's on Saturday,' she said. 'I keep telling you. I swear to God.'

'Well, that's OK,' he said. 'We're going to get out of your hair now. Thanks.'

'You are?' His abrupt decision to leave worried her.

'Sure.'

'Can I keep the picture?' she asked.

'Sure you can if you want. You know something, Ms Thornhill, I believe you. I can call you Betsy?'

She nodded. 'So that's OK. I mean, if you believe me.'

'Even if you were there Saturday night and you don't want to tell us, which I could understand, why would you want to kill Robert Ketsen?'

'I didn't kill him.'

'You didn't like him. You didn't like him calling you up.'

'So what?'

In the corner, Jimmy seemed half asleep, sprawled on the chair, arms folded.

Frank Dolce said, 'You got an answering machine to avoid him, and yet when we listened to his tape, you were on it. You sounded angry.'

'I wanted him to leave me alone.'

'Like I said, I believe you. I mean, why would you kill him, what's the motive?'

'I don't have a motive. I wouldn't kill some guy because he calls me up a few times.'

Dolce was silent. His cell phone rang and he turned his back to the others to take the call. Jimmy yawned again. It was like the dentist, drilling, stopping suddenly — you not knowing if he would start again, hit a nerve.

Dolce put his phone away. He zipped up his leather jacket with a brisk gesture.

She wanted to say 'Wait.' But for what? There was nothing to say. The other guy, Jimmy, struggled into his jacket. She picked up the picture without thinking and followed them to the font door and Dolce pulled it open.

'We'll be in touch, OK?' he said.

She nodded. 'Sure. Yes. If I think of anything, I can call you, right?'

'For sure. I gave you my card? Here's another one, just in case.' He pulled a card out of his back pocket and handed it to her. 'You should give yourself some credit, Betsy, you know?'

'What?'

'If you're really fifty-one going on fifty-two,

you have to admit you look pretty great for your age.' He shook her hand and, followed by his partner, trotted down the stairs and left her holding the computer image of her own face.

⋆ ⋆ ⋆

Bel stood in her doorway. She wore her winter coat and under her arm was a bottle of wine. She had arrived minutes after the cops had left.

'What's with the cops, kiddo?'

'Come in.'

Bel held out the wine. 'This is for you. So?'

'I thought you were going out.'

'I'm going. But Marie who sits in the window all the bloody time watching the street because she has nothing better to do tells me, Bel, there's cops going up to Betsy's at all hours.'

'Twice,' Betsy said.

'OK, twice. You want a lawyer?'

'What for?'

'You tell me. I could ask Mark Carey.'

'I thought Mark Carey was dead.'

'Excuse me, Mark is sixty-five and the best lawyer in New York and he's my friend.'

Betsy didn't want to give it oxygen by talking and she shook her head and answered,

'Thanks, but I'm fine.'

'I'll be at Sissy's in Brooklyn if you need me,' Bel said. 'You're sure about Mark?'

'Let me think about it,' Betsy said.

Bel turned to the door. 'Don't think too long.'

* * *

Bel left. Methodically, working to stave off panic, Betsy went to work, first unpacking food in the kitchen. She ate a couple of Oreos and pulled fruit out of brown paper bags. There were grapes the size of walnuts, oranges, tangerines, mandarins. Manet's painting of four mandarin oranges on a white tablecloth was Betsy's favorite picture. She'd get a print of it, cover some of the blistered paint in the kitchen, cheer the place up.

Orange, she had once read, was Sinatra's favorite color. She got her CD player and the mini speakers, set it up in the kitchen, put on Frank who sang, 'I've got the world on a string.'

She loved Sinatra because of her father who collected the LPs she still had, all ninety-seven in the original sleeves on a shelf in her house in London. The Ketsen business swam into her mind, but she pushed it away and sang with Sinatra: 'Sitting on a rainbow.

Got the string around my finger.' Sinatra's crackle of sexual vanity, the arrogant pleasure in owning the world poured out of the tiny speakers.

In the living room were her aunt Pauline's boxes, six brown cartons neatly sealed with tape. Betsy tried to get a picture of Pauline in her head, a real picture, not a photograph and couldn't. Too many years had passed. She should have visited more. Pauline was her father's sister, her last link with him. The last time Betsy had lived in the apartment she was a college student and he was alive. Pauline and her twin, Maureen, died within a few months of each other, Maureen in March, Pauline in May.

Sitting cross-legged on the faded kilim, Betsy opened the first box. It was packed with records, 78s in brown paper sleeves. She examined the names — Ezio Pinza, Licia Albanese and Renata Tebaldi — the stars Pauline adored and saw, when she could afford it, at the old Met on 39th Street. From the bottom, Betsy pulled out *The Freewheelin' Bob Dylan*, the cover photographed on the corner of Cornelia and Fourth. Betsy sat and rubbed the surface of the album and tried to reclaim herself at nineteen when she bought it for Pauline, and couldn't. *Go on, Aunt Paulie. You might like it. Try it!*

Under the album was a flat object wrapped in tissue and Betsy opened it and found a crisp fifty. She looked through the other records and then a box of books and another filled with clothing, extracting more bills, each one brand-new and wrapped in tissue paper, tens, twenties, fifties, carefully placed between the leaves of a book or folded into silk scarves or starched cotton blouses.

In all, there was fourteen thousand dollars. Pauline knew she'd find the money. There would be no estate tax on the cash. Have a good time, honey, Pauline always told her, have as much fun as you can, sweetie, it all goes so fast.

Betsy sat without moving among the records and books and tissue paper and cash. Pauline was gone. She wanted to cry and couldn't and tried to remember her aunt and couldn't. After a while, Betsy got up and put on a ski jacket — the red coat she loved was a liability now — and went out and walked because she couldn't sit still. No matter what she did, she couldn't stop herself thinking about the piece of paper with her face on it. The apartment seemed stifling. The cops had tainted it. Dread, like a scrap of stale bread was stuck in her throat so she couldn't clear it away no matter how much water she drank, or vodka.

'Hello, Betsy.'

Marie Tusi's door opened as Betsy passed. Marie stuck her head out.

Betsy waved. She liked Marie who had held her captive a few days earlier to talk about her asthma and about Dev who spent his days playing cards with other World War Two vets and came home late after his men's group at Marble Collegiate Church.

Marie worked at home as a travel agent, mostly booking cheap trips to Rome for the women she'd grown up with around Mulberry Street who still went to church with her at Old St Patrick's. Dev was a Protestant. Marie had rolled her eyes and said to Betsy, How could an Italian man become a Protestant?

'Dev's late,' she said now. 'Come on in.'

Betsy kept on going. She closed the front door and walked to the corner. Through the window, she watched enviously as people in Murray's bought cheese and olives and blood-red sun-dried tomatoes. She turned and walked aimlessly for half an hour. A mean wind was blowing and she bent her head against it. The streets were emptying out.

She wanted to lose herself, wanted to get away from the oppressive apartment on Cornelia Street, but where would she go? She had no experience of the hinterlands except on assignment for some magazine and then only with an assistant and contacts, and usually in aid of shooting exotic fruit. And the cops would know if she disappeared.

Anyway, even if she found a cabin on some remote ridge in Montana, someone, her friends or her agent or Bel, would find her and say, 'You seem depressed, darling.' It's not like you, they'd say. What's wrong? How about something nice to eat, a nice job, a pill, a shrink, some shopping, a weekend in Venice? Poor Betsy, they'd say, how can we help, and they'd be puzzled because everyone liked her, she was funny, impulsive, generous, a little credulous, fearless.

Her friends thought of her as someone who got on planes to crazy places to take photographs. She wasn't fearless, though. She was terrified but she did it anyhow because if you didn't the fear pulled you into its quicksand. It was an act, this bravado, but taking risks, even making a fool of yourself once in a while, was her own measure of success.

She loved the travel and she loved coming back and the crowded domesticity of her life — the friends, the parties, the company. It seemed suddenly cloying. She couldn't run away. She felt trapped, stuck. Until a few days before her life had seemed an agreeable tale, a comedy of manners, and now it was as if the new director was some film noir guy who didn't really get it that her life was fine, had been fine, and easy and terrific, new face, new city.

Come on, Betsy, she said to herself. Cheer the fuck up. It didn't help. It didn't work. She was scared to death.

Butting heads with the wind that picked up as she got near the river, she walked around the Village, past the Spanish restaurant where she had paella on her first grown-up date with a boy from Astoria whose mother smoked her own mozzarella in the basement of their house. She walked downtown, across Canal to Hudson Street. Jittery. Anxiety twitching like a muscle under the skin.

She walked hard, sucking up as much oxygen as she could and realized she was heading south to Bobby Ketsen's place.

6

It was grim but it was funny, too, her new face getting her in trouble, her skulking around New York like some overage Nancy Drew. She waited for a light on Hudson Street, then crossed on the red. What could they do? Arrest her?

Who was Bobby Ketsen? Who was the woman who looked like her who killed him? Who was the witness? Betsy got to Ketsen's building, then shied away. It looked dark and forbidding and she turned abruptly and walked in the other direction and found herself in front of the First Precinct.

Was this where they'd take her? Lock her in a cell? On the wall were photographs of cops who died in the World Trade Center, peeling now, and damp. The wind suddenly picked up a garbage can and knocked it over and she side-stepped it and started walking again. She was hungry. She wanted to stuff her misery with food.

Across Broadway was a small Chinese restaurant and she went in. There were only six tables and a counter where a woman sat reading Chinese newspapers. Betsy sat down hard on a chair and leaned on the Formica table top and pulled off her hat and gloves. She ordered hot and sour soup.

When the Chinese woman brought the soup, Betsy drank it so fast, it burned her tongue and throat. She ordered tea and spring rolls and pork dumplings. She cracked open the fortune cookie first. There was nothing inside so she ate the cookie.

A copy of the *Post* lay on the next table and she reached over and took it. There was nothing about Ketsen's murder.

WINTER OF OUR DISCONTENT, a headline read. She glanced at the paper. Bin Laden rumored to have nukes. More bodies uncovered at Ground Zero. Stock markets volatile. A guy selling snow shovels in Brooklyn going bust. Betsy scanned the gossip columns, but her mind wandered.

It was a mistake, she told herself. The system worked. She had nothing to do with Bobby Ketsen's death.

'You like?' The owner bobbed over her with pleasure as she removed the empty bowls.

'I loved the soup. Everything. It was really delicious.'

Saturday night when Ketsen was killed, she was home on Cornelia Street eating sesame noodles. She wasn't nuts. She didn't black out, sleepwalk downtown, kill Ketsen because he had called too many times.

The point was, she said half out loud, the point was to figure out what the hell really happened.

Her mind lurched. For the first time she considered whether somebody was out to get her; she saw a conspiracy. In a teabag? Cut the crap, she thought to herself.

He seemed OK, the detective, this Frank Dolce, who said he believed her. She tried to get a fix on him and the situation, give it some reality so she could grasp it and squeeze it down to size. It slipped away. A guy was dead and she was involved. It was some parallel universe she'd dropped into where a man was murdered and cops with guns showed up at her apartment and someone described a killer who resembled her.

Abruptly, the storm in her head broke. She sat up straight, smoothed her sweater, brushed her hair off her forehead, polished off her tea, felt like herself.

'Can I get some almond cookies?' she called out to the woman behind the counter.

The door opened and a man hurried in, pulled off a baseball cap and a sheepskin jacket. He sat down at the table next to Betsy's and grinned at her.

'Some night,' he said.

'Right,' Betsy said. He ordered soup,

spareribs, fried rice, scallion pancakes and a beer, then took off a thick brown sweater and the striped scarf that was wound halfway up his chin. When he was finished, she saw he was only a kid. Soft face, high forehead, spiky wet black hair like an overgrown hedge. He wore faded jeans and a blue sweatshirt. He was a kid, but he was sexy.

The kid looked out of the window.

'I hope it's finally going to snow. Big. A blizzard. That sounds weird. I guess I'm an event freak.'

'Me, too.' She was glad for company.

'Yeah, really? I know there's people that get fucked up from it, but everything looks nice and clean, the creeps go underground, there's less assholes around, you feel like you own the city, you know?' He rubbed his cheek where it was red from the wind.

Betsy drank some tea. It was as if she'd found herself in a mountain hut with the kid, a passing mountaineer, eating sticky spare-ribs at the next table.

He hesitated. 'Can I maybe buy you a beer?'

'Sure.' She was tired of feeling scared. 'Why not?'

He put the plate with his spareribs on top of the soup bowl and balanced his beer and rice in his left hand and got up and slid into a chair at Betsy's table. Delicately, like a juggler, he set the plates down, then reached behind him for his pancakes.

'Help yourself,' he said.

In a single bite, Betsy stripped the meat off a rib. He ordered the beers, and she, thirsty from the pork, drank half of hers in one gulp.

Behind the counter, the Chinese woman, glasses on, was still reading her papers.

'You live around here?' the boy asked.

She drank some beer. 'In the Village,' she said. 'Cornelia Street.'

'Cool.'

He sized her up. She didn't mind. She liked it. Yeah, she did, and she said, 'What about you?'

'I live in Brooklyn. Over in Dumbo.'

'Where's that?'

'Down under the Manhattan Bridge overpass,' he said. 'I'll probably have to get out. Real estate guys fucking us over. It sucks, you know?'

'What do you do?'

'I'm free-lance,' he said and she figured he was an artist just starting out, not wanting to admit to her he ran errands at some studio. She didn't push it. He was trying to impress her.

He looked at his empty beer glass.

'You want to go get a real drink?' he said.

This kid, who couldn't be more than half her age and had a bland, unlined face, wanted to buy her a drink and she was flattered. The encounter with Bobby Ketsen made her cautious.

'I'd love a real drink, but I have to go.'

'So what's your name?' he said.

'Betsy,' she said.

He asked for his check, put some money on the table and wrapped himself up in his sweater and scarf and put on his gloves. He put out his hand. She shook it.

He said, 'So, bye, Betsy,' and walked out and and she was alone again.

* * *

From behind a pair of sunglasses, she peered at the other passengers on the subway as if they could deliver answers, but it was late and most of the faces were shut up for business. A fat guy snored. A woman next to him lolled against the seat. A teenage girl with pink hair, reading Virginia Woolf, looked over her glasses at Betsy as if she knew all about her face. The noise of the train made it hard to focus. Think, she said to herself. Think about Bobby Ketsen and how you met him, his studio, his secretary, the others. By the time the train reached her stop, she was obsessed with the secretary.

Was she the witness? What was her name? She'd been there late the night he died, she found Ketsen's body the next day. Did she see someone and think it was Betsy because she had met her at Ketsen's studio? Betsy remembered how the secretary looked when Ketsen arrived. When he smiled at her and gave her a high five and singled her out.

Ketsen had a kind of allure. There was the easy smile, the offer of help, the way, at first, you wanted his approval. In retrospect, she saw it: you wanted him to like you.

It would have made him a natural in their business, especially if he worked with women, stylists, writers, models. You wanted him to like you. Wanted to know what no one else knew about him. He was the kind of guy who stole your interest.

She played back the scene, first in London where he watched her, then running into him in New York. The offer of a ride had been spontaneous, the kind of thing she did. But what was it he said in the car on the way into the city?

The doors opened at her stop. It was Monday night. Bloomingdale's was open late and she needed new sheets and she stayed on the train.

That day she took the ride from Ketsen,

she did it willingly. In the car, they made conversation, they had photography in common, he had believed she was thirty-five; he asked her out. She'd been with Tom so long, she had forgotten this was how people got together. It was the kind of thing that happened all the time, except for the phone calls.

In the train window, Betsy saw her reflection. The girl who stared back looked more like the police picture than she'd realized and she put her hands up to her face, then looked away and saw, as if for the first time, her hands were heavily freckled with irregular brown spots. As if her real age had forced itself to the surface of her skin.

Most of her life, Betsy had been the youngest person she knew. She liked older people, liked being the kid, the pet. Men, she realized, had wanted to help her but she always thought of them, the photographers, the editors, as mentors. As a child she'd been chubby but in college her metabolism changed. She ran and swam and in spite of the way she loved food, she stayed thin. Then the insides of her arms got wrinkled, the skin loose like chicken feet. Her neck was lined. Her eyelids felt like crepe paper.

She started lying about her age and sometimes she forgot how old she really was and was shocked when she saw it in her passport. After the surgery, she got a new passport. I'm old, though, she thought. Vain. The train rattled towards the next stop.

Betsy rubbed her face and when the train stopped at 59th Street, she ran out and up the stairs and crossed the street. She was too late. It was after nine. Bloomingdale's was shut for the night.

From her coat pocket, the cell phone rang. Plucking it out, she huddled, out of the wind, in the doorway of Bloomingdale's. In the windows, tan plaster mannequins in bikinis played under paper palm trees on a backlit beach.

'It's Vicky, darling. Betsy?'

'Hi, Vic.' She was glad to hear her. Glad to hear the effusive voice, the silvery-voiced 'darlings' that bounced off some satellite up in the mink-colored winter sky.

They went way back, her and Vicky Faraday. Met on a Freddie Laker flight going to London, Vic having been in New York looking for Bob Dylan, her going to London to cross the street at Abbey Road.

On the plane Vic was looking for a place to spit her gum and Betsy held out her hand. If I spit it in your hand, we're bound together for life, Vic said and she did and they were. The Faradays took Betsy in until the girls got their own place. Was that some kind of spell, the spitting in my hand, she asked Vicky years later, and Vicky said, no, of course not, I made it up.

Vic, divorced three times — Betsy was godmother to both her kids — was an entertainment lawyer. She lived on the phone, said pretty much what she thought and was the first person Betsy knew to get her face done. Come on, she'd said to Betsy. You'd look great, darling. It'll be fun.

'Darling, are you all right?' Vicky said. 'You haven't called or anything.'

'I'm sorry.' She heard the hesitation in Vic's voice. 'What is it? How are the kids?'

'Yeah, fine, adolescent, hormonal, you know. No, listen, there's just a teeny thing, nothing much, actually. Max hasn't rung you?'

In London, Max Blackstone lived in the house next to Betsy's.

'I haven't heard anything from Max.'

'I was sure Max would have rung,' Vicky said.

'Please, Vic, ring me about what?' she said, eyes watering from the wind on Lexington Avenue.

'Darling, Max went round to your house yesterday to check everything was all right, the agent had rung him to say that there's a couple who want to take the house for six months. Max rang me.'

'What else?'

'Don't get into a panic. Promise me. But you don't ever really panic, I know that, right? I mean you're cool as a fucking cucumber, right? Solid, as always?'

'Jesus Christ, Vic. Tell me what's going on?'

'We think someone's been in your house.'

The mannequins in the lighted window seemed to move, frolicking on the fake beach, then whispering together and watching her and moving towards the plate glass where Betsy stood. She wiped her eyes and blinked.

'What?' she said to Vicky.

'It was only an impression Max had, which is why he rang me,' Vicky said. 'I suppose I know your house better than anyone; he knew I'd stayed in your spare room those months after the divorce, right, the third one? So, we went through it together and there were little things, a drawer in your desk, in your studio, you know, not quite shut. We all know how obsessively fucking tidy you are with your work, but there were some photographs left out on your desk. A picture askew on the wall. So we got hold of Crystal, your cleaner, who said she'd been in Thursday just after you left for the airport and she'd done a thorough clean. There was a faint smell, Max said, as if someone had been smoking.'

'What else?'

'Those photos you keep in your mirror in your bedroom, and on the little dresser, the family pictures?'

'Yes?'

'I noticed because we'd shopped for those silver frames together, you remember? At the Flea Market in Paris? Remember?'

'What about them, Vicky?' Betsy felt her stomach turn over.

'Did you take them with you?'

'No, I forgot. I asked Crystal to put them away in that storage cupboard in the basement.'

'She said that she didn't have time, she was coming back the next day to do it,' Vicky said.

Even in London, in her other life — the safe, tidy, familiar life — someone was looking for her. Three thousand miles away, someone had been in her house.

'Vic? You there?'

'Can you hear me? Where are you?'

'Looking at the display windows,' Betsy said. 'Stalked by bimbos in bikinis.'

'What?'

'Outside Bloomingdale's,' she added, pulling on her hat.

'Lucky you.'

'You'd be surprised.'

Vic said, 'What do you want me to do about the tenants?'

'Just leave it with the agent, OK? Please.'

'Are you angry?' Vic said. 'You sound angry. I hate your letting the house. I thought you might change your mind and come home. We all miss you dreadfully.'

'I can't do that right now.'

'You don't sound wonderful,' Vic said. 'I've got a long weekend coming up? Shall I come and see you? I've got absolutely tons of air miles.'

Vicky couldn't help her. She'd come to New York, install herself on the living room sofa. Take over. Vicky always knew the right people and she'd see this as a project and Betsy would suffocate.

'I'm fine. I'm cold. I'll call you soon.'

Betsy slipped the phone in her pocket and stood for a moment, watching people fight the wind on Lexington Avenue. One of them — she couldn't see if it was a man or a woman, just a figure in a down jacket, the hood up — came in her direction as if he, if it was a he, knew her. She pressed herself against the store wall, but then the figure hurried by and she jogged a block to Third Avenue to find a newspaper stand. They were all shut. She ran into the subway.

In the subway she stood at the foot of the

escalator and looked up and gripped the handrail and tried not to watch the stairs as they disappeared in front of her, tried not to look at the parallel lines of metal grooves. Nausea welled up and her stomach churned and the ground seemed to slip away under her feet. She thought about the figure on the street who had seemed to know her.

The rail under her hand felt rubbery and dank and she gripped it and knew what it was about Ketsen that had made her anxious. It was the way he had looked at her as if she was familiar, as if to say *I know you*.

Somehow she got to the top of the moving stairs and onto the platform and saw the train coming down the tunnel. Waiting for the train at the deserted station, she understood what it was about Ketsen that bothered her, what made her avoid him. He had pursued her, wanted her, forced the acquaintance because she reminded him of somebody else, someone she now resembled, someone younger.

7

If I'm only thirty-five, who am I? When the gynecologist looks inside, can she tell? Do I have rings like old trees? Where was I when JFK was shot? Betsy sat up that night and drank vodka and tried calling her agent who didn't answer.

Most of her friends were on hormone replacements but not her, not yet. Collagen. Botox. Not to mention stuff for your bones, your heart, your moods. It was the essential truth of her times: that women need fixing. No one was having babies anymore. If I'm thirty-five, she said to herself, who the hell am I?

It was bullshit, but she was, deep down, a sucker for it, the promises of the utopian you. It was what screwed her up in the first place, it was the reason she was here in New York with the wrong face.

On the coffee table was the copy of her book. *Fruit* had acquired a cult following in London. People started talking TV and it made her greedy.

It was fun at first, production companies vying for her. She began wanting it, the TV, the celebrity, America, even. How sweet it seemed, this idea, that she would have, after all the years away, a book published in America, and a TV show that her mother could watch with her friends and brag. My Betsy, she'd say. Look, it's Mary Elizabeth on TV. Betsy reached behind her for the phone, then realized it was too late to call her mother. She'd try again in the morning. They got along OK now. She had made her peace with her years earlier, a crusty irritable peace. Betsy was a grown-up, her mother was nearly blind and on Long Island; she visited when she could and called twice a week.

All through the previous spring and summer, after the book was out and selling, there had been the calls and she saw producers but no one committed and in August, a hot London afternoon, it dawned on her something was wrong. She sat in the TV production office, white walls, little orchids growing out of glass pots, lines of sunlight, motes of dust like silver in it. Not silver, she thought; just dust.

That afternoon, she sat on a leather sofa and realized this was an audition. The fabric of the sofa under her thighs — she was wearing a short linen skirt — was soft as flesh and the same color. A fat, boneless sofa where she daydreamed of a cigarette, but instead made fingerprints in the leather, one two, three four. The fat, doughy fabric with its silky, stretched surface popped right out. It was like poking your finger in a fat boy's face.

No one in the office smoked, Betsy longed for a cigarette. Fag. Everything in England she got accustomed to, the style, the lingo, except them saying fag for smoke. Have a fag, darling. No one here offered, so she had a virtual smoke where she imagined the cool dry paper filter between her lips. In. Out. Nicotine in the lungs. In the bloodstream.

Looking around, she realized this room, this sofa was where people finally gave it all up, all hope, all ambition, and laughed to herself. The Sofa of Lost Souls.

She looked at the skinny girl producer who had short greasy hair and bony hips and the girl looked anxious, staring at the phone as if waiting for a boyfriend to call. She'd never have a man, Betsy thought with pleasurable malice. She'd grow old alone, the hair would get thinner, she'd be in some basement flat with an orange cat and then the cat would die.

They never said it, of course. No one said, you're too old, babe. They stuttered and made excuses. Hollywood was worse, though. She got that far because some agent approached her at a London party and she actually fooled herself into flying out to California.

At the meeting, a breakfast in a place in LA named Hugo's or Yugo's, the agent showed up in a big-shouldered double-breasted suit. He had a part in his hair that shone as if he polished it every morning.

Have something nice, he said, as if she never got a decent meal and she said, well, you have something, and he looked as shocked as if she'd suggested he shoot up in public. Still, he ordered egg whites, scrambled with hash browns and onions. He picked out the onion pieces and ate them and stacked the uneaten potatoes at the edge of his plate.

Loved her book. Saw TV syndication in a series on food, the Food Channel maybe, and asked who she thought could host it. Me, of course, she said and finished her coffee. She went home after that and he never returned her calls.

In London that hot summer day on the fleshy sofa, she sat and listened and they all said, it's fab, brill, superb, Betsy, love the book, want the TV, but, we need the demographics, the youth market, someone . . . They never said, of course. It was implied. Someone younger.

* * *

In the apartment on Cornelia Street, Betsy checked her e-mails, from Vicky and Max, both worrying someone had been in her house, and one from Tom asking how she was but formal, distant. Gossip and news and jokes from colleagues and acquaintances. She missed them horribly, this safety blanket she had knitted for herself. An only child of old parents, she had no siblings except for the baby who died when Betsy was a kid — no one ever mentioned her. Her father dead, his sisters, Pauline and Maureen, dead, childless. Her mother was the youngest of eight; Betsy had first cousins in their seventies.

There had been men, of course and Betsy had almost married a couple of them. Instead, she invented a family. In London, Betsy occupied a whole house; over the years, furniture accumulated, so did books, photographs, things she brought home from shoots — rugs and lamps and mechanical toys. The house was always full, especially after Tom moved in.

A full house, Betsy would think, satisfied. She went to bed, the way you did if you were an only child, listening to sounds in the house, listening, satisfied, to other people washing up, settling down, sleeping under the same roof.

She looked at her watch. It was midnight.

There was the job tomorrow. She picked up the phone.

'Why the hell didn't you call me? David?'

She was shouting at his machine three thousand miles away. It was midnight her time and five a.m. in England and when he answered, he was groggy with sleep.

'Who is this?' he said.

'It's me. Betsy.'

'What time is it?'

'I don't know, around twelve here,' she said.

'I was sleeping.'

'Well, get up. I've been trying to reach you for days.'

He had been in Marrakesh for a break. Yes, sorry. Something unexpected. He'd been out of town. Sorry, sweetheart, he said, but he was bushed, pooped, exhausted. She heard him fumble for a cigarette.

'I need you,' she said.

'What?'

'Bobby Ketsen.'

'Who the fuck is Bobby Ketsen?' David sounded petulant now.

'Just shut up and listen. Please. Did you give my number here to anyone at all?' she said, but she already knew. She had known all along.

She had never given David her phone

number in New York. He had her e-mail. She'd left the number of the cell phone at his office, but that was after Ketsen was dead. He couldn't have given it to Ketsen and she knew it before he told her. She wanted the confirmation. Dreaded it. She heard him light up. The match struck and flared.

'I haven't got a phone number to give out. Only a mobile — cell phone, you Americans call it. I've e-mailed you three times asking for a number, though, being me I think I've used the wrong e-mail address. I've never ever given your number to anyone and you know perfectly bloody well that I never would do.'

'David? Don't go. Not yet. Talk to me.'

'What about?' he said.

'Anything.'

'How's the new book? Everyone's tremendously excited about it. How's New York? How's the weather?'

She said, 'Tell me again. You never got a call from Bobby Ketsen. He runs some kind of on-line photo shop. He knew you.'

'Everyone knows me, it's ridiculous. Look, seriously, he might be in the files. I'll have a look tomorrow if you like.'

'Thanks.'

'You're welcome,' he said. 'Do you want some more work? If you feel you need a bit of cash, I could advance it to you. Or a different magazine? *Food & Wine?*'

She thought about Aunt Pauline's money.

'I'm all right. Thanks. Just let me know about Ketsen.'

'You've done the chicken shoot?'

'Tomorrow,' she said.

'You do a fabulous chicken,' he said. 'I have to sleep now.'

* * *

'Hi.'

The girl who opened the studio door the next morning wore black leather pants and a black sweater and she led Betsy to the kitchen which was saturated in early light from the high windows. It was the kind of pure sea light you got off the Hudson River as the winter sun came up.

Half a dozen people were at work in the kitchen. There was noise and light and the smell of food and she was in charge.

'Nice place,' Betsy introduced herself to the stylist, a large woman with thick blonde hair, red leather pants and a parrot on her shoulder.

'Masha,' she said with a Russian accent.

'Hi, Masha. Nice kitchen.'

'Yes,' she said. 'Here is your assistant,' she

added, gesturing at a thin guy in black.

He helped her with her bags and said, 'I am Kurt.'

'Hi, Kurt.'

'I love your work,' he said, fawning a little.

'Thanks, Kurt,' Betsy said and put out her hand. 'Yeah, that's really nice of you.'

'Really. So.'

'So,' Betsy said. 'Let's get going while there's still some light. Let's not lose it, guys, OK?' She looked at the windows. 'We probably need lights, anyhow.'

'Here is my assistant,' Masha said, snatching the girl in black into her orbit. The parrot flew off Masha's shoulder onto its perch, which swung near one of the windows. 'Name is also Masha.'

A man in a five-button suit from the ad agency hovered around the table. He represented the chicken people, he said.

Betsy took off her coat. She liked advertising shoots. The editorial work with younger cooks and stylists was less fun because they were obsessed with natural. If the soufflés fell or the ice cream melted or the chicken dried up, you did it again.

Betsy preferred tricks. Once, she had painted strawberries with red nail polish.

The ad people were devoted to this agenda of good looks. In the kitchen, two testers worked at the stove. Masha's assistant set up the table: roast chicken; mashed potatoes; corn bread; corn on the cob. A Fourth of July dinner. She laid the food on a red-and-white checked cloth. Sunflowers were arranged in a tin milk pail. Hidden speakers pumped music. James Brown sang 'I feel good.'

Black Masha put damp tampons in a microwave then stuffed them, one at a time, up the chicken's ass. The bird stayed plump, juicy, the steam rose. Kurt put up lights. Betsy picked up her camera.

'Get under the table now, you idiot,' Masha the stylist in red pants said to Masha in black. 'And smoke.'

She crouched near the table. 'I don't like this cigar.'

'Just do it. Come on, babe,' Kurt finally said to black Masha. 'Do it for real. Puff harder. This is an American chicken dinner. I want the steam up. Where the fuck are the mashed potatoes?'

Betsy asked for Vaseline and smeared the peas and carrots herself. She stuck her hand in the mashed potatoes and pushed them around. Someone made another batch of potatoes into ice cream that would never melt even under the lights.

Under the table black Masha smoked and coughed. Betsy got down on her knees and talked to the girl who looked fretful and green from the cigar.

'I get cancer this way,' black Masha said.

Betsy was solicitous. 'I'll be quick, I promise. You don't have to inhale a lot, but the steam looks better if it's been swirled around in somebody's lungs, OK? Look, think of it as a part in a movie. Think of yourself as a femme fatale in an old movie, and just fake it if you can.' She winked at black Masha. Black Masha looked up gratefully.

Red Masha swore at everyone. 'Get more potatoes,' she said. 'Many more. Not these instant shit, either. I want real mashed potatoes. I want.' She set her face in a conspiratorial smile at Betsy. 'You know I am right, yes? You know this instant shit is nothing. Yes?'

'Yes, Masha.' Betsy felt confident now. She was on the job. It was fine. Being at work, she was absorbed, efficient, juiced up.

'Can we please just do this? OK? Please, guys? It's just a chicken,' she said and, ignoring the horror on their faces, picked up her camera and, ignoring her cell phone that had been ringing all morning, shot the chicken.

8

It was Frank Dolce on the phone and he asked if she could come to the station house, then offered to pick her up at the studio.

Frank the cop was how she thought of him; it made him an object, made him less real. He was waiting downstairs in front of a meat truck when she emerged from the building.

He looked weary, a guy who ate the wrong stuff and screwed up and tried to do better. His mild expression conveyed the fact that if you'd messed up your life, it didn't make you a criminal. So he was apologetic when he saw her.

Fingerprints, just routine, he said; there were lots of prints in Ketsen's place, as you can imagine, people in and out all the time. The less fuss, the faster they rule you out, you know? Said it as if he, Frank Dolce, was convinced she was innocent. The system works, she thought. It was her mantra.

If she came with him right away, he said, the house would be pretty empty, late afternoon, shift change, you know, maybe she'd feel less self-conscious. Sure, she said, and reminded him she had been raised to think the cops were the good guys. She called him Frank and saw it pleased him.

'Are there a lot of cops like you in New York, Frank?'

'Sure there are.'

In Frank's maroon car, she put on the seatbelt, he offered her half his BLT and some of his coffee.

Just routine, this thing, Frank said again, no big deal. OK? He polished off the coffee and then his cell phone rang and Frank opened it and grunted into it and swore and jammed it in his pocket.

He said, half to himself, 'I have to make a stop.'

'What is it?'

'You really want to know?' He was eager.

'Sure,' she said.

'It won't take long.'

* * *

Downtown, on Broadway, the streets were thronged with people. The wind was still up but it was sunny and some of the guys already had their jackets off. Everything out of sync this year, Frank commented. The temperature hitting sixty in the middle of the winter, nothing the way it should be.

The sidewalks were packed with stalls

selling souvenirs from September 11. American flags. Fireman's hats. T-shirts. Photographs of the World Trade Center before September. Two-foot-high plastic figures, GI Joe in uniform (you could get your soldier white or black) with a little tin trumpet, playing God Bless America when you pushed the button.

Tourists coursed by the stalls and snapped pictures and bought flags. A pack of kids in God shirts offered prayers. You could get a prayer anytime, free of charge. Betsy was glued to the car window.

The fence outside St Paul's was a shrine. Candles, flowers, teddy bears, rosary beads; paintings of firemen in heaven. Stuck to the iron bars were flyers of missing people. Some were wedding pictures. Some featured height and weight and distinguishing marks, as if it would make a difference. You could feel the yearning in the pictures even after six months.

At the viewing platform, tourists lined up with their tickets so they could go up and look at Ground Zero. Somewhere she'd read it was the city's biggest attraction. The tour buses stopped so people could stare in the direction of Ground Zero — the pit, the pile, the hole in the middle of the world.

Betsy rolled down her window. A few feet away, a cop waved at a man with a camera on the wrong side of the barricade. He refused to move.

'Listen, mister,' the cop shouted, 'show some respect. You know what that dust on your shoes is? That's people.'

'I shouldn't do this,' Frank said half to himself. 'I'll leave you at the Starbucks on the corner, OK?'

'Why?'

Frank was silent. He knew it was crazy, bringing her with him; he did it anyway.

He turned a corner into a barricaded street and pulled up alongside a garbage truck. He stuck his police ID in the window and said, 'Come on.'

Along Cedar Street, everything was dusty. In front of the building where Frank had stopped was a dumpster piled with rubble, a broken toilet sticking out. The windows were covered with sheets of thick brownish plastic. From around the corner at the site, the jackhammers shattered the ground.

She said, 'Where are we?'

'Fifty feet from Ground Zero,' he said.

In the hall of the building the mailboxes were broken, doors off, bundles of mail sticking out and covered in dust and ash and powdered concrete. Wearing a protective suit made of papery white fabric, a white mask over her nose, a woman dragged an industrial vacuum towards the stairs. She nodded at Frank and pulled the mask down.

He said, 'You called. I got here as fast as I could.'

Her face was white with the dust. 'Thanks for coming, Frank,' she said.

'What happened?'

'The bastard clean-up crew came back last night and ripped out all the lights in all the hallways,' she said. 'They stole the rest of the plumbing fixtures on the sixth floor.'

'You called in the violation?'

'Yeah, but what's the point? They want us out, you know? They want to get us out and then clean up and shove up the rents.'

'I'll do what I can. I promise.' He put his arm around the woman's shoulders and she slumped against him for a few seconds, then straightened up.

'Fucking elevator's broken again, too,' she said. 'You going to check upstairs?'

'Yeah. You want help with that?' He pointed at the vacuum cleaner.

'I'll manage,' she said and put her mask back and went through an open door on the ground floor.

Betsy followed Frank up two flights of stairs. At the top was a door held in place by a thick chain with a heavy padlock. He unfastened it and pulled off the chain and put his shoulder against the door, then reached inside and turned on a single bulb that hung from a string.

The ash got into Betsy's throat and mouth and she coughed to get the grit out and couldn't, and looked around at the studio apartment. It had high ceilings and four big windows, but most of the plaster had come off the walls and the windows were gone and covered with plastic. There was plaster everywhere, broken glass, paper, crushed wood, and the ash, the powder that covered everything. It looked like Pompeii, was all she could think. Everything the way it was since that morning when time stopped.

Betsy gestured at the apartment. 'What is this place?'

'It's mine,' he said.

'The woman downstairs?'

'A neighbor.'

The table, chairs, sofa, ghostly shapes under the dust, were heaped with more glass, pots and pans, one showing coppery through the dust. Books, CDs, dishes, bottles, plants, towels, jeans, socks, a yellow T-shirt, a mangled baby crib. My nephew's, Frank said.

Part of a green plant still hung from a hook on the wall. In the kitchen, the door sagged off the refrigerator and inside lemons were encased in green mold and white dust. A piece of a gray plastic computer keyboard lay on top of a phone near a desk and the only things that moved were the loose boards under their feet, her and Frank, and the paper that fluttered as they walked.

There were photographs. On the floor, desk, sofa, were hundreds of snapshots. People looked out of them through the dust and Betsy bent down and picked one up. It was a picture of Frank at a wedding. He had on a tux and a frilly shirt and his thick hair was stuck down with gel. She held it out.

Frank said, 'Yeah, me. My brother's wedding.'

'You were here on the eleventh?'

He shook his head. He'd been lucky, he said. He was already at the station house when it happened. But the place was wrecked. The place he got when his marriage broke up and he couldn't stand the suburbs anymore. He had come down here when the rents were cheap and the lofts spacious and only artists and weirdo cops came to live before it got fancy. It got him into the city and out of the burbs and he loved the place. He fixed it up. Almost fifteen years he lived in it. Now he was stuck in the spare room at his mother's house in Bay Ridge.

She listened to the stories, heard Frank talk, it made everything else small. For a minute, anyhow. Then her own trouble opened its trap and pulled her back. She was sorry as hell for Frank Dolce, though.

'Let's get out of here,' he said and tossed the wedding picture back onto the floor and switched off the light.

★ ★ ★

At the station house, she followed Frank into a small room with the technician, a dwarfish Hispanic woman. He got her some coffee while the woman pushed her fingertips one at a time onto an inky pad, then pressed them on paper. Frank explained everything, even showed her the computerized prints, the way they matched the swirls, how they looked for individual detail.

Betsy did what she was asked and tried to listen to Frank who explained how everything would be digital soon and gave her a pack of Handi-wipes to clean her fingers.

'You don't have to worry, you know,' he said. 'There were a dozen different sets of prints at Ketsen's place.'

'So you said.'

'You'd be surprised how many people get fingerprinted, you know? I mean not just criminals,' he laughed. 'Anyone in law enforcement, for instance. Security guards. Schoolteachers.'

'Really?' She smiled. 'I think that makes me feel better.'

Frank leaned towards her.

'I know you didn't kill Ketsen,' he said softly.

Frank told her there had been two other deaths in the area recently, one domestic, probably an accident, the other an outside case. The locals were up in arms. They were mad and scared. The neighborhood was already traumatized from the Trade Center attack, he said. It was a place where people had paid five million for a loft, businesses went bust, and now the killings. Everyone was edgy, he told her, and some of them baying for blood. He leaned towards her while he talked and he was earnest and made a temple of his thick hands. He was going to help her because he believed her.

She said, 'You are?'

'Yes.'

It was stifling in the station house, though. He talked and she felt claustrophobic. People pissed off because their condos that cost them five million were unsafe, the cops coming up empty except for her. When the papers got hold of her picture, everyone would know she had done it. She corrected herself: They would believe she had done it; they would believe.

She felt herself listing in his direction; she felt safe around Frank; she liked his face. He was big and solid and his thick flannel shirt was red-and-green plaid, like Christmas.

For a minute, she sat on the edge of a steel desk in the little room and looked out through the grimy panes of glass. In the main room, detectives in plain clothes milled around and sat at computers and drank coffee. The place smelled of stale coffee and the stables around the corner where the mounted cops kept their horses.

Frank followed her gaze.

'Most of us are trying to just figure out how to keep everyone happy and deal with stuff, you know? There's still a lot of people without any place to go. You want me to get someone to run you home, Betsy? It's all right if I call you that?'

'You already asked me. It's fine. I like walking.'

'If you want to hang around an hour, I could drive you myself. Betsy?'

She wanted to please him and she said, 'Yes, OK. Thanks. Frank, Ketsen's secretary found the body, right? I met her, what was her name? Was she the witness?'

'Don't play detective,' he said. 'I swear to

God I'll try to help you, but if you start messing around, it'll just look worse for you. And me. Let the system do its thing.' He smiled and patted her shoulder awkwardly. 'You'll wait for me?'

'Yeah.' She smiled. 'A ride home would be nice.'

'Come on and I'll show you a place where you can sit.'

Frank led her into an area of the station house where there was a row of gray chairs that looked as if they were torn from an old movie house. A water fountain and Coke machine were the only other objects in the area, except for a table, a dead poinsettia with a frayed red ribbon on it and a cup with a half-eaten Milky Way on the saucer.

From the gray chair where Betsy sat she could still see the cops at their desks under the fluorescent lights that gave everyone a sickly pallor. Across the room a guy carried a stack of speckled cardboard boxes that wobbled as he walked. There was something familiar about him. The boxes hid his face. She watched and wondered if he was going to drop the boxes. He set them down on a desk and she saw his face and her stomach churned. It was the kid from the Chinese restaurant who bought her a beer and asked her out. He was wearing the same blue sweatshirt.

A woman who sat at the next desk looked up and smiled at him and he laughed. It was him, the kid. The meeting at the Chinese hadn't been accidental. The shared spareribs were a ploy. He was a cop. He was on her case.

Clutching her bag, Betsy sidled towards the exit sign, crouching a little, crab-like, so Frank Dolce wouldn't notice. She hurried out and down a flight of stairs to the street and only stopped running when she slipped and fell on her knees and the pain slowed her down. She got up and punched a number into her cell phone.

'Bel?'

'What's that, cara?'

'I found a lot of money in Pauline's things. You packed her stuff?'

'Yes.'

'You knew?'

Bel said, 'What's in there is for you.'

'I wish you'd take it.'

'What do I need? I got everything, I call the car service when I want, I go by the beauty parlor twice a week, I get to the movies and theater and opera and I got my books and music and now I got you. God knows my patients bring me more food than I could eat in a lifetime — they don't have money, they bring food. Paulie left me whatever I asked for. She said, you take what you want, Bel, you get first dibs. The rest was for you.'

'Are you sure?'

'Sure,' Bel said. 'But you didn't call me about the money, did you? What is it? What's wrong?'

'I need Mark Carey's phone number.'

9

There was something self-conscious about handsome men, she thought when Mark Carey opened his front door. His eyes were green with brown in them and the gray hair was too long. It curled over his collar and he flicked it away. His green crewneck had holes in the sleeves, the denim shirt was faded, brown corduroy pants worn, brown suede brogues custom made.

'I'm Betsy Thornhill,' she said.

He shook her hand and looked over her shoulder at the trees on his block. 'Goddamn fakes,' he muttered.

She followed him into the house.

'Sit down,' he said, gesturing at a chair in the hall. 'I won't be long.'

Leaving her, he went to his office, glancing at the trees again. Fooled by the warm winter, they were showing green buds and he thought, damn trees, tricking themselves up in green in the middle of February. What was the poem? On his desk, paper was piling up on the case that provoked his passions and that he simultaneously found distasteful and didn't have the stomach for. Getting soft, he thought. It involved some of the Muslim men allegedly connected to the Trade Center attack, silent, stubborn, zealous men who wouldn't talk to him and were happy to die.

Mark Carey wondered how he could defend these bastards who brought down the towers where two of his nephews worked along with a whole law firm of kids he'd taught. But that was who he was — defending the indefensible. There were plenty of people who hated him for it and thought he did it for the limelight and that he played to the jury and went on TV too often.

While the girl — Bel's goddaughter — sat in the hall of his house with the high, elegant rooms, he was distracted by the phone. He answered some calls and tidied the legal briefs on his desk while he talked, poured himself a shot of Cognac, tossed it back.

His hair fell over his eyes and he pushed it back. He had a big round head like a Greek sculpture and he hated it and kept his hair long as a disguise. It curled over his forehead and his collar. Disguise and neglect, he claimed, though Judith said the long hair was part of his vanity. Get it cut, for Chrissake, Mark, his wife always said when she saw him, which wasn't often. She stayed in the house in Maine and painted her pictures and took the photographs which lined the walls of the town house in the West Village.

A writer who interviewed him once wrote that Mark Carey was as tan as George Hamilton and had a face made for public performance, like a cardinal or an anchorman or a judge. The lines in the face, she'd written, made him look like a well-aged cut of meat and she found herself wondering, because he looked pretty good for sixty, which he was at the time, if he'd had work done. She didn't like him, but she slept with him, and then wrote the piece which he kept on the wall.

He slept with all of them. Reporters. Young attorneys. Old friends. Whoever showed up at the house in the West Village and wanted to. They were all pretty cute. He liked them all. He could never resist.

Not anymore, he said to himself. You're too old now, buster. It's all over, he thought. His fingers were stiff on the piano keys when he played.

He wasn't much good. As a kid, he had wanted to sing and act, but his father, a lawyer and medieval scholar, disapproved. Performing was frivolous, he told Mark. He never said it, but he also disapproved of his son's beauty and it embarrassed Mark, who began to stutter.

He burrowed in his books and learned

Russian and invented baseball teams from Mars. He played them in the back yard against the Brooklyn Dodgers. Later, he inherited the house from his father and plenty of dough from his grandfather on his mother's side. Criminal law cured the stutter and gave him a stage. The limelight turns you on like a blow job, his wife once said to him.

Then he remembered: the girl was waiting.

In the hall, she sat, waiting for him. She looked thirty-five, thirty-six, tall, pale, familiar. He remembered they had met once, years before. She must be older than she looked. Dressed up, she might have been elegant, he thought, with that Roman nose and the hooded blue eyes and long neck.

'Come on in, Betsy,' he said, took her arm, guided her to his office where she sat in a leather armchair. 'Bel thinks you need some help.'

'Yes.'

'That's what I'm here for.'

'Thanks,' she said and, for an instant, felt relieved.

At the door he had been somber, distracted. Now he smiled and the smile was explosive. It lit up his face. He was a man, she thought, who exploded this smile on you as a reward, so that you worked for it.

Betsy watched him fumble with a pair of

glasses and his hair that fell into his eyes and some paper on the desk.

She got the police picture out of her pocket and unfolded it and handed it to him and he pulled his glasses down on his nose and looked at it.

'It's you?'

'A cop brought it over and said a witness saw this woman leaving Ketsen's place and they found my name on his desk and I said it can't be me.'

'Slow down. Let's start from the beginning. Who is Ketsen?'

'I got in from London last Thursday, a guy at the airport offered me a ride, his name was Bobby Ketsen. He asked me up to his studio to see some photographs and I went and then I left and he kept calling me so I bought an answering machine.'

'He threatened you?'

Recounting the events of the last few days, Betsy made the story as plain and dry as possible. No hysterics. No hyperbole. Shrink the events, drain the terror, make jokes. Tell me it's nothing, she thought, looking at the man on the other side of the desk. Tell me I'll live. It was like cheating on symptoms at the doctor's office when you were scared of the diagnosis.

'So that's it,' she said. 'This cop — a

detective — comes over and then he comes back with his partner and they tell me someone saw me.'

'They didn't mention who this witness was?'

'No.'

'Any ideas?'

'I think it was Ketsen's secretary,' Betsy said. 'One of the cops mentioned she was there late working that night. I met her when I went up to look at the photographs.'

'You think she might have seen someone and remembered you and reprocessed what she knew.'

'Yes.' Betsy gestured at the picture. 'I told them it wasn't me. It can't be.'

Carey looked at it.

'You see why?' she said.

'Tell me.'

She pushed at her cheeks with her hand. 'I had work done to my face,' she said.

'You must feel trapped, then,' he said. 'You must be thinking, people think I killed a man because I look like someone who might have killed him. Is that it? Do you feel trapped?'

Tears of frustration gathered. Betsy rarely cried. When she was little, she had believed the souls of dead people lived in milk bottles on the front stoop. It made her mother furious. This is nonsense, she said and one evening she took the bottles into the kitchen, put them in the sink and broke them with a hammer. Betsy cried all night. She was about eight. After that, she hardly ever cried.

He said, 'It will be all right.'

'I'm not even sure it was an accident, me running into Ketsen like that at the airport, I'm not sure about anything. I just don't fucking know what's going on, and I think it's because I did my face. You understand?'

'You're Pauline Thornhill's niece, aren't you?'

'Yes,' she said.

'Eva Thornhill is your mother?'

'Yeah.'

'So you think God punished you, is that it?'

'You know my mother?'

'I met her with Bel. Bel was Pauline's friend and she was your father's sister.'

'Yes.'

Carey came around the desk, knocking some papers off it and took off his glasses and reached down and patted her shoulder.

'There isn't any God. Millions of women have cosmetic surgery every day. Right? So listen to me. There's no reason you should remember, but we've met before, did you know that?'

'I didn't. I'm sorry.'

'It was when you were living on Cornelia Street, you were at Barnard, I was visiting Bel and you came tumbling in with some marvelous news, I can't remember, you'd won a prize or had an exciting date, but you were completely delicious, off to conquer the world.' He smiled. 'But why would you remember, I would have seemed an old man to you then. Now I am an old man,' he muttered. 'Look, obviously this is a mistake. The police didn't pressure you, did they? No one read you your rights?'

'No, except they did my fingerprints.'

'Too bad. But never mind. You want my advice? Go about your business. Do whatever it is that you do. What do you do?'

'I take pictures of food,' she said.

'Food is good. You're not hungry, by the way, are you? My housekeeper left some lemon tart.'

'I'll pass,' she said. 'Thanks.'

'Take your photographs and keep your mouth shut. What's the name of the cop you talked to?'

'Frank Dolce.'

'You have his card?'

She pulled it out of her pocket and gave it to him and Carey said, 'Wait here a minute,' and left the room.

For five minutes she waited, listening to the

sound of his voice from the other room. When he returned, she saw he walked an old man's walk with a stiff leg.

It was a knife, he told her as he sat down. The killer hit Ketsen with a small hammer and then slashed him with a knife. Ketsen had been drinking, it would have been easy. The police were working on a make for it, but the knife wounds were unusual. Mark Carey reported all this to her with a small, triumphant smile.

'How did you find out?' she said.

'I have friends,' he said.

Betsy looked at the wall of the office where there were framed photographs of Carey with Nelson Mandela and Carey with Martin Luther King and Malcolm X and Bobby Kennedy and Warren Beatty. Bill Clinton.

She said, 'I remember my father talking about you once.'

'He told you I defend a lot of guilty assholes?'

'Yeah, but he was a cop,' she said.

'He was a good cop. You were crazy about him?'

'Yes.'

'Any jerk can get the innocent off. It's my motto, you see. Would you like a cigarette?'

'No,' she said, feeling somehow petulant,

not wanting anything from Carey, wishing he hadn't told her about the knife. Why did he tell me? He told me to prove that he could, that he's connected. I don't want to know about knives.

The whole encounter shook her up, she wanted to run away, wanted to stay, didn't want to think about the knife, couldn't think about anything else.

'You're a virtuous girl,' he said and lit one and held it the way Bel did between his thumb and forefinger. 'I have to go soon, but what about a drink first?'

There was a makeshift bar on a table near the desk. He poured the wine and while they drank, talked on the phone. Watching him, she felt stranded. He finished the call and turned to her.

'There's one other thing you can do — because you'll want to do something. Won't you, Betsy? I mean you won't just sit around no matter how often I tell you that's the best thing. So try to think of anyone you've met who might have had it in for Ketsen, all right?' He got up and stretched. 'I'm going to fix it for you. I'd do anything for Bel. We've been friends a long time and I love her.'

The meeting was over.

Carey led her to the front door and helped

her on with her jacket and without any warning put his arms around her and kissed her on both cheeks.

Can I stay? she wanted to say, but he had already opened the door.

10

Betsy made her way towards the river on foot, not because it was mild, the city basking in the warm weather, but obsessively. Go about your business, Mark Carey had said, but she couldn't. She'd gone home and looked through the phone book until she remembered the name of the car company Bobby Ketsen used, and now she was heading for Greenwich Street eating walnuts out of a bag while she walked.

She passed the Film Forum. A new print of *The Sweet Smell of Success* was showing and she looked at it longingly and imagined herself in the dark theater, a waxy tub of popcorn, heavily salted the way she liked it, in her lap. In London, she went to the movies three, four times a week, alone, with friends, in the middle of the day, late at night. For her it was plain enchantment to sit in a dark movie theater and watch the show. She finished the nuts.

She kept walking, scavenging in her pocket for something more to eat. These days, she was always hungry and carried food around in her pockets — an apple, walnuts, a KitKat, a York Peppermint Patty — and the lining of her pocket was filled with chocolate and crumbs. She found a few more walnuts and ate them as she walked until in an office on Greenwich Street near the West Side Highway she found Al Kovlovski.

Al Kovlovski was a short man with a big bald head and tiny hands. He sat behind the dispatcher's desk at Crandall Cars, eating French fries and smoking Tiparillos at the same time. The small room was jammed with stuff, the desk piled with paper and files, jars of ballpoint pens and cigars, a huge ashtray overflowing with butts. On the window sill were empty Fresca cans and a dead plant, and in the corner, a TV tuned to the Weather Channel. The air was rancid with the stink of grease and old cigars, though the smell of the crispy fries made Betsy hungry.

For a while, Al looked at her suspiciously and whined. Half his drivers were stuck at home in Queens or New Jersey. A water main was bust by the Midtown Tunnel. There were delays at LaGuardia and a terrorist alert at Newark and a blizzard had shut down Chicago. Now this woman he had never seen was in his office.

'What?'

'You're Crandall Cars?' she asked.

'So?'

'I need some help.'

'You need help?' He pointed a French fry at her. 'Lady, we all fucking need some help. I got three drivers with some fucko flu bug, I got one driver in the garage who ain't got no car. Plus a pile-up on the L.I.E., what else is new, and the President is in town, who needs him? I got seven cars where no one wants them and customers calling night and day.'

'I don't want a car.'

He ate the potato and wiped his hands on the green blotter that covered the desk.

'No?'

'No.' She stood near the door.

He had a sour, round, pickled face, like a colorless tomato in a jar on the table at Katz's, she thought, but he pushed his mouth into a grumpy smile.

Al rolled his chair forward, pulled a pile of papers off a second chair and said, 'You're making me nervous. Sit down already.'

Betsy pulled her hat off, shook out her scarf and sat on the edge of the chair.

'You know a man named Robert Ketsen?' she asked.

He snorted. 'Cops beat you to it.'

'He was a customer?'

'Was being the correct terminology,' he said. 'It's not bad enough we got this shit traffic and all, I lost a good customer.'

'I'm sorry,' she said. 'It's tough losing a good customer. Believe me, I know.'

He held out the greasy carton.

'You want some fries? Can of soda? You get real dehydrated in the winter.' Like all New Yorkers, Al had medical opinions on everything. He peered at the cans on the window sill. 'I got Coke, I got a Dr Pepper, Diet or Regular, one can orange Fanta,' he said. 'And Fresca. What?'

'I love Fresca.'

Al brightened up. 'Me, too.'

'You ever notice Fresca is around again a lot?'

'Yeah. It's good.' He held out a can. 'Here.'

'Thanks.' She took a big swallow of the soda. 'So. Ketsen?'

'Yeah, OK. You're cute, but how the fuck do I know who you are?'

There was a photograph of Al with a boy and a girl on the shelf above his head.

'You got kids, Al?'

'I got two.'

'Can I be straight with you?' she said.

'You want to know why a guy like Ketsen used a shit-looking place like this for his car service?' he said. 'We was down by the World Trade Center, you know, and when it got hit, we lost the space. You should have seen the shit that got dumped on our place, so we had to move in a hurry. Only this dump is what looks shitty, our cars are brand-new, so you can't judge a book by no cover, right?' He waved his arms around the office. 'We been planning a move. Anyway, we take care of our regulars, you know.'

'I'm sure you do,' she said. 'Ketsen came in from the airport Thursday. Your guy dropped him at his place, then made a second stop on Cornelia Street. Your driver made a note of the address on the second stop?'

'Sure,' Al said. 'He has to. We charge extra for every stop.'

'Ketsen ever call you up after he got in?'

'He never calls. His secretary calls.'

'You have a name for me, the driver? Al?'

'You're a cop?' he said. 'You're working his case?'

She lied. 'I'm helping out.'

Al put a miniature hand on the grubby plastic mouse and flicked through a list of names on his computer screen. It was speckled with grease. He looked up.

'Here. It was Tony, you want me to give him a call?'

'Would you do that, Al?' She beamed at him. 'That would be so nice of you.' She tipped back the can and swallowed some more Fresca. 'This soda really hits the spot.'

He picked up the phone.

'What's it to you that's so important you come over to this fuck hole of an office, excuse my French?' Al was inquisitive.

'I just want to know if Ketsen or his secretary called Tony and asked for the address of the second drop-off. Probably he won't remember, but you could do me a humongous favor and ask.'

Less than a week in New York, Betsy was talking like she never left. She was an unconscious mimic and she could hear herself now, talking like Al, like a New Yorker. She was saying purse or pocketbook for bag. Automatically she filtered out any Britishisms, any words that would make her sound too hotsy-totsy, too foreign. A guy like Al, who was a language course all by himself, you could put him off if he figured you felt superior.

She smiled some more at Al and held out a pack of cigarettes, but he shook his head, picked up a portable phone, dialed Tony's number and got up from his chair. He wandered to the window and mumbled into the phone and walked out of the office into the corridor.

Betsy surveyed the office. She leaned over the desk and towards the computer. She nudged her chair forward some more and pretended to look for matches and scrolled through the addresses on Al's screen.

Ketsen's address was listed along with his phone and e-mail, his secretary's numbers, but before she could memorize them, Al finished his conversation and returned to the office. He hoisted himself into the swivel chair next to his desk.

'You been checking out my address list?' he asked.

'I'm sorry.'

'It's OK. I talked to Tony and Tony remembers you,' he said. 'Don't gimme that dumb look, I know it was you that got dropped on Cornelia Street, OK. He described you. A tall cute girl, he says. Dark hair. Great baby blues, he tells me.' He peered at her. 'So he remembers because he said Ketsen was coming on to you and you were a pretty tasty package. High class. Tony's words, swear to God, OK, and also he remembers Ketsen's secretary did call right after.'

'To get the address?' she said.

'Yeah. You in trouble, lady? You're not a cop.'

She glanced at the desk. 'Can I please have one of those French fries, Al?'

He held them out. 'Be my guest.'

She reached into her pocket and extracted the KitKat. 'You feel like some candy? This is your own business, Al?'

'My brother. Don't worry, he's in Florida. Condo in Boynton Beach. What else do you need?'

'I could use Ketsen's secretary's name and if you have an e-mail, a cell phone, maybe I could reach her.'

He picked up a scrap of paper, glanced at the screen and scribbled.

'I don't got her address, but I got her cell phone because she sometimes made reservations for Ketsen out of office hours. But this is in Jersey. Hoboken, I think. I would send you, but I don't got a single fucking car for you.'

'Remind me of her name. I mean I knew, but I forgot, so you wouldn't be divulging any secrets.'

'Pull the other one, honey. Don't worry. I already told you, I'm going to give it to you whatever. Her name is Meryl,' he looked up. 'Like that actress, you remember that one, you know, blonde, that did that concentration camp thing.'

'Meryl Streep.'

'Yeah, her. Very classy.'

'Meryl. Right. I remember.' She took the piece of paper and stuffed it in her bag, then put out her hand. 'Thanks.'

'Meryl Briggs,' he said and shook Betsy's

hand. 'You're welcome. I met her once. She passed by here to bring a check that was late. Nice girl. A schwartze. Cute, though. Something else I could tell you.'

'Yes?'

'Ketsen, you know, I met him once or twice. I drove him a couple of times when I was still driving, you know?' Al said. 'Excuse my language, but I think he was a fucking putz bastard.'

'Why do you think that, Al?'

'He thought he was God's gift to women, you know the type? Not outwardly, but something freaky about him, something you couldn't put your finger on. He told one of my drivers he lost some friends on 9/11, but I don't think he gave a shit, you know? And he was always going down there to Ground Zero, fuck knows why. I don't know what the hell it was, I didn't like the prick one bit.'

* * *

Come on! Answer the phone!

Halfway out of Kovlovski's place, she was already on her cell, calling Meryl Briggs. *Come on!*

There was no answer. There was a phone outage in Jersey and one of the PATH trains was stuck in the tunnel.

From Kovlovski's, she walked back to Cornelia Street and when she got home the light on her answering machine was flashing. There were calls from David, Bel, Mark Carey.

She returned Carey's call first. His machine answered, his voice deep and resonant, a bishop intoning a funeral service, she thought, silky and patrician. She left a message, then called Bel who was out. David was at home in London. She could hear him blow smoke to one side of the phone and she sat, still in her coat on the arm of the sofa on Cornelia Street and rummaged in her pocket for a cigarette.

He had information, he said, about Ketsen. Robert, right? Bobby Ketsen. Go on, she said, and David told her he'd been on to a few people and had some information that wasn't particularly nice. Ketsen, he said, was a bit of a thief. He stole other people's work, David said, just helped himself, took the pictures, fiddled with them so they appeared slightly different. Sold them.

'Like knock-off designer frocks,' David added.

'That's all?'

'I thought I was rather Morse-like in all this.'

'You are. What kind of pictures?'

'Anything, really. Fashion. Disaster. Football. Famine. That help any?' he asked and went on chatting to her, asking how she was and if she needed money because there was work for her, the chicken people would always have her. 'Of course, it doesn't matter anymore, does it?' David said.

'Why's that?' Betsy said.

'You didn't imagine that I'd fail to find out that this Ketsen you're so interested in is dead, did you?'

* * *

KETSEN IMAGES. The stainless steel plaque was screwed into the wall of Ketsen's building. A handwritten sign on the gray metal siding noted that the intercom was broken. Please call, the sign said. There was a phone hanging from the wall. It was bust. A few feet away, a cop in uniform watched the building.

She had only remembered that day: in the market, Saturday, he had taken her photograph. *Say cheese*. It would be in his camera. Had the cops found it? Was it still at his place? *Say cheese, Betsy*.

Betsy waited and a minute later, a black woman with an umbrella showed up and got out some keys. Her face was tense and gray and she shivered.

'You coming in?' she said.

'Thanks.'

The woman held the door.

Betsy said, 'You live here?'

'You kidding me? I clean here is all. You visiting?'

'Yes. That's right.'

The cleaning woman unlocked a door on the ground floor and disappeared. Betsy climbed the stairs. The stairwell, painted gray, was lit by bare bulbs hanging from the ceiling. By the time she got to the third floor, the light flickered, shuddered off and on again and then off. She was in the dark.

Under her fingers, the walls were damp and raw, the surface like wet pebbles. Somewhere she heard a cat. Music. The jumpy sound of Rap.

On the third floor Betsy pushed open the heavy fire door and looked down the hall that was dark and, as far as she could make out, empty. Cautiously, feeling along the wall, she made her way towards Ketsen's door. It was draped with criss-crossed yellow police tape. It was a crime scene. Nothing here for her. Betsy backed away.

According to Al, Ketsen's secretary had called the car service to get the address where they dropped her. Ketsen must have stopped by the building on Cornelia Street after that, or sent someone, to check the names on the buzzer. And hers was there. Her name was next to Pauline's which she'd left up in case mail came for her aunt. Pauline's number was still in the book. Easy enough to match the address and the number if you made the effort. Ketsen made the effort and then someone killed him.

Behind her, she heard a noise. The sound of someone removing the chain from the door, pulling a bolt, then another lock. The door opposite Ketsen's opened, and she turned and then, back to the wall, tried to flatten herself against it. There was a sense of someone watching her. She squinted into the dark at the half-open door ten feet away across the corridor. Something emerging from it disturbed the molecules of air. Betsy had a tangible sense of fear, she could hold it between her hands, and she waited. Someone coming out. Someone watching. The space between filled up as he moved towards her and she pulled back to protect herself, but she was already flat against the wall. No place to go.

The door slammed. The air thinned out. Without waiting, she turned and ran to the stairs and down and outside, stumbling, terrified of meeting someone who claimed to recognize her face.

From her pocket she got her phone and called Mark Carey, who answered.

'Can I drop by?' she asked and he said, 'It's not a good time,' and in the background she heard laughter and music.

'I could have a chat with Detective Dolce in the morning, though,' he added, 'would you like that, Betsy?' She said yes, hung up and was sorry. She didn't want him talking to Frank Dolce. She tried calling back, but all she got at the end of Mark Carey's line was a machine. Betsy stood in the street where a light rain was falling, and saw in front of her, neon sign alight, the Tribe.

11

'Can I have another one?'

'Same again?'

She nodded, the bartender threw the vodka into an iced glass, and set it up on the bar.

'A pretty good place for a burger,' Ketsen had said to her when they got in from the airport Thursday. He ate burgers once. Someone cracked Ketsen's skull and slashed him with a kitchen knife. Was it a kitchen knife? she wondered.

Tuesday night. Time seemed skewed to her, it seemed to slip and slide. Slipping and sliding and you went down the rabbit hole, but maybe it was the vodka, cold in the glass, going down warm. She finished it, her second, and felt better.

Ordering a third seemed like a good idea but Betsy was a lousy drunk and she ate some peanuts out of the bowl on the bar instead and ordered a beer and cigarettes. The bartender pulled the cellophane off the pack and she took a cigarette and he lit it for her.

The building with the bar on the ground floor had been an egg warehouse first, then spices. Betsy, a little stewed now, imagined she could smell it, the way you smelled clove in Zanzibar. The floor had the original white tiles, the ceiling was made of punched tin and windows ran the length of the narrow space with wooden tables under them. In back were more tables and a vintage juke-box with colors that bubbled up in the neon tubes, yellow, green, blue, pink.

On a blackboard the day's specials were chalked — blue-fin tuna and rib-eye steak, good California reds by the glass and beers from micro-breweries like Moose Drool. At the bar, most of the guys were drinking Bud from the bottle and watching the Knicks on TV.

Looking around, Betsy saw the objects first, bottles, nuts, blackboard, then the people came into focus.

People arrived, tossed their coats and umbrellas on the window ledge behind the table. The basketball fans cheered and moaned and made cracks at the TV set. Someone put money in the juke-box and Billy Joel came on and sang 'New York State of Mind'.

This was Ketsen's place, his joint, his watering hole. He'd lived upstairs. He would have fit in, she thought. Everyone was young and good-looking including a handsome fireman at the bar who said he was still digging down at the hole and knocked back a couple of shots of Scotch. He was in his twenties with a weary face. A girl in biker boots with sunglasses stuck in her cleavage was coming on to him. He looked at her and then at Betsy and shrugged his shoulders as if to say, Can you get me out of this? Betsy smiled sympathetically and went back to her beer.

Men noticed her. You get older, they stop looking, her mother used to say. Betsy liked men. There was Tom, others, but she had never sensed in herself the allure, the thing that made them turn around in the street.

In the Tribe, a guy tried to buy her a drink, the bartender was attentive, men swarmed. Or maybe it was just the booze. Sipping her beer, she wandered to the juke-box, put money in, chose Tony Bennett doing 'Steppin' Out'.

More people piled in. She was talking to a fireman called Hal when the door opened and a woman came in, shook out her umbrella carelessly, preened, took off her raincoat and waited for someone else to shut the door. Everyone watched. It was like the curtain going up in a theater.

'Caroline, hey, have a drink,' a man called out and ran to close the door for her. She pulled off a black watch-cap and shook out long blonde hair so it spilled over her face. By now everyone, even the Knicks fans in front of the TV, was focused on her.

'Kiss kiss,' she said as she passed down the line of guys at the bar. 'Edo, honey, can I have a Cosmo?' she said to the man who had shut the door for her. She bumped into Betsy and said, 'Hi, I'm Caroline.'

Her face was arresting, the skin shiny and pink and she had little apple cheeks like a girl's. She wore a white ski jacket, tight soft caramel leather pants and a black turtleneck.

'Betsy,' Betsy said.

'Betsy,' Caroline said. 'Uh huh.' She leaned on the bar and scanned the room and added, 'Men. Come on, let's grab that table before it goes. Edo, you'll bring the drink. Sweetie? Won't you?'

Swept to the back of the room by Caroline, Betsy sat with her at a table where four men materialized and took the remaining chairs and one of them, in a red turtleneck, leaned over her and said to Caroline, 'What are you drinking?'

'Edo's getting drinks.'

'Poor Edo,' he said.

Caroline said, 'So, Betsy, what do you do?'

'I'm a photographer.'

'Cool.' Caroline was interested.

She was an actor, she said. She modeled some, but her real cash cow was commercials. Voice-overs. Caroline sipped her pink cocktail.

The Kinks were on the juke-box and Betsy said, 'Remember this? God, I loved this album.'

Caroline said, 'Before my time.'

'Oh.'

'And yours, girl. And yours. Right?' She turned to look at a couple dancing near the juke-box and said, 'Jesus wept.'

Two men and another woman pulled up chairs. There were ten of them at the table and they ordered food and the table got jammed up with beer bottles and homemade chips and spicy green salsa. The crowd at the table yakked and dished and smelled of sweat and good perfume and sexual expectation. Betsy was hungry. She ordered quesadillas, which arrived dripping with white cheese, and ate them with her hands.

The action revolved around Caroline who invited it, basked in it, played to the crowd. When she talked to you, man, woman, it didn't matter, she locked her eyes on yours and made you the center of her world. A coquette, Betsy thought, the faintly arcane word popping into her head. A geisha. Gives great eye-lock. Caroline switched to red wine that stained her lips; they looked like burst cherries.

Practically everyone who came into the place stopped to talk to Caroline. Men and women vied for her attention and angled to sit near her and laughed at her jokes and bought her drinks. She flirted and drank, but there was something detached about her, Betsy thought; Caroline was guarded.

The woman who killed Ketsen, the woman in the police sketch, was in her thirties. Same age as Caroline, she thought. Caroline was blonde, but what did that mean, anyhow? You could wear a wig. She was an actress.

The booze was finally getting to Betsy and the noise and music and the voices swirled around her and she went through the motions and talked and drank, but she felt dislocated.

'So how come we've never seen you around here before, Betsy?' Caroline said.

'Just passing through,' Betsy put her hand on Caroline's arm and confided. 'Actually,' she said, 'I came by because a friend of mine used to live upstairs.'

'Who's the friend?'

'Friend of a friend, really. Name's Bobby Ketsen.'

'Poor Bobby,' Caroline said. 'Poor bastard.'

'You knew he died?'

'Died? Was murdered. Horrible, but exciting. I was in Miami when it happened, can you believe, missed the whole thing.'

'You knew him?'

'Course we knew him. I even dated Bobby once. Everyone knew him,' Caroline raised her glass and said to the man on her right, 'Let's get a nice bottle of Krug, Timmy, doll, and we'll do a toast.'

Timmy procured the champagne and everyone toasted Bobby Ketsen.

'Good stuff,' Timmy said to Betsy and put his arm around her shoulders. 'So you want to know about Bobby?' he said and then everyone wanted to talk Bobby. We all loved him, of course, they said, except when he forgot to pay his share, or when he hit on some woman you were dating. He was down here all the time. Life of the party. Let's all drink to Bobby.

Betsy said, 'You didn't like him.'

Timmy raised his voice. 'What? Bobby was the life of the party and all the girls loved Bobby, and after the World Trade Center attack Bobby negotiated all the best volunteer jobs, I mean he was down at Ground Zero, serving meals and getting on TV in a hard hat with Harrison Ford. He worked like a son of a bitch and got the goods, you know? He must have fucked more women than anyone else and after 9/11 people got laid in every doorway.'

'Shouldn't speak ill of the dead or something,' Caroline said. 'Poor Bobby.' She held up her glass. 'Let's have some more of this lovely champagne.'

* * *

Later, on her way back from the bathroom where a girl half her age offered her a line of cocaine that she turned down, Betsy stopped at the bar for a Coke and ended up with a chocolate martini. On the house, the bartender said, so she stood and drank it, and from where she was she could see Caroline and the long shafts of light hair that fell over her face. Betsy watched. Mesmerized. Tipsy.

Caroline threw her hair around, flicked it with her fingers, smiled with her mouth open, showed her pink gums and white teeth. She arched her back, the ribbed pullover stretched, high round breasts, hard nipples, showed.

She knows I'm watching. Martini in hand, Betsy strolled back to the table. Up close, she saw it: the expression in Caroline's eyes was haunted. You can't fix the expression in the eyes. No matter how much you fixed your face or how good the surgeon who cut you was, you couldn't change the look in the eyes. Caroline looked caged. She had hidden her real self, she was petrified someone would catch her.

It wasn't just the face she'd fixed, or her body. It was her self that Caroline had dumped. She made herself younger. 'Before my time,' she'd insisted when Betsy referred to an old song. Before my time.

How easy to trap her, Betsy thought. But Caroline had dated Bobby Ketsen. She might be useful. Betsy sat next to her. How many Carolines were there? How many women slipped in for a little work and came out somebody else?

Really, she was drunk. In the bar in Tribeca, Betsy had a vision of a planet full of women not quite themselves, a world where no one was what she seemed and memory disappeared. Everyone did it. She had done it. It was as easy as changing the color of your hair.

* * *

'Remember me? Betsy, right? Betsy. From the Chinese.'

She was on her way out of the Tribe when she felt a hand on her arm and turned and saw it was the young cop from the restaurant she'd seen again at the police station earlier in the day. Instinctively she made for the door, then smiled at him, this boy leaning over her and grinning.

'Dumbo, right?' she said. 'You live in Brooklyn.'

'That's me,' he said.

'Should I call you Dumbo?'

'If you want. Why not?'

'The free-lance, right?'

'You got a great memory.'

'For an old broad, I have got a fabulous memory.' She wanted more vodka. 'You can buy me a drink, if you want,' she said and he ordered a martini for her.

'So,' she said. 'What kind of free-lance are you?'

'Sexy one,' he said and rolled his eyeballs for comic effect.

Someone changed the music and turned it up loud and Cuban stuff poured out. Dumbo had a sly smile on his face now and a cigarette hanging out of his mouth and he looked like the young Belmondo, she thought. He was taller than she remembered, lean but not skinny, and the soft, faded jeans were low and tight on his narrow hips.

The sleeves of his white shirt were rolled up over the big arms, the muscles gleaming like fruit in one of Betsy's photographs.

Ketsen had big arms, she remembered. The kid, this Dumbo, was gastroporn.

When Betsy got drunk, which was pretty rare, she found herself narrating her actions to herself; the drunker she got, the more she listened to her own voice, as if she existed on a separate track.

Swirling the vodka in the fresh drink, she was aware she was very drunk. She perched on a barstool and stretched out her legs and made her thighs as tight as she could under the jeans.

She put her hand on his upper arm and said, 'Nice,' she said. 'What's your real name?'

Dumbo's name was Thurmon, like Thurmon Munson who was once the Yankees captain, he told her. His friends called him Thurm or 'Captain', he said. A great baseball player, Munson, he said. Died in a plane crash. He sighed. 'Thurm' stuck on him like latex gloves on your dentist.

If she got inside Thurm's head, maybe she could figure out who Ketsen was, what he did, who he knew, who killed him. Thurm would tell her what the cops thought. Frank Dolce was too cautious. Part of the research, she said to herself.

She would work on Thurm instead of Caroline. Keep Caroline as backup, in the bank. She could always blackmail Caroline into telling her what she knew about Bobby Ketsen.

The truth was, she wanted to, oh say it, Betsy, for chrissake, you've been so prissy all your life about sex, so say it. OK, All right, I want to fuck him. I want to take Thurm home, and get down on my hands and knees and have him put it in me. I've got thighs of steel now, could crack a walnut between them, OK, soft fruit. I could crush soft fruit. Maybe apricots. A ripe peach.

OK, all right, but she wasn't sure after all if she could sleep with a guy named Thurm, though he was standing against her, breathing lightly on her neck, giving off heat, running one finger along her arm, then pushing her sweater sleeve up so he could touch the flesh.

He tickled the inside of her elbow, flicking his fingers lightly and she could hardly stay on the barstool. He was kissing her neck, no one else looking, everyone dancing or making out or watching the Knicks or eating cheeseburgers.

Thurm's presence was making her stupid. The more she drank, the more interested she was, and she looked up at him, at the baby face, the hair and eyes dark as Greek olives, the big mouth, even the slightly unformed chin that was a little soft, a little boyish. She looked up and saw he was consumed by looking at her, hot for her. His hands worked on her neck.

He swallowed down the rest of his drink. 'Let's dance.'

Then they were on the floor dancing, her and Thurm, and the sound system was playing something Latin again, louder now, a samba, salsa, cha-cha-cha, and Thurm's hand was on her ass which was not bad under his palm. All those squats the trainer made her do. A million squats and she had a pretty good ass for fifty-one. She flexed her muscles a little.

From what seemed like the distant past, she remembered this stuff, how it was when some guy picked you up and you went somewhere and fucked all night. Did your nerve endings age? She couldn't tell, but she could tell that Thurm was enjoying it since there was a lump in his jeans. So was she, enjoying it, she meant, and she broke away, reached over to the bar, polished off her drink, then put her arms back around him.

The music changed. 'A Whiter Shade of Pale' came on. She sang along. Thurm was all over her. Trip the light fantastic. Who needs acid?

'You know all the words to this?' he said.

She leaned harder against him. 'All the

words, Thurm. And I could teach you.'

He smiled into her neck, examined her ear with his tongue and said, 'I bet you could.'

His hands were down her back and into the waistband of her jeans, and inside the thong Vic gave her for a joke. He had big cool eager hands, and half of her was laughing, half liquid. With Tom, when they'd been together, in London, the sex was fine once they got going, but she was never panting for it. She had figured it was the hormones and she was scraping the bottom of the barrel. She had been wrong.

Anyhow, she thought to herself, rubbing against this kid, Thurm was better than hormone replacement. The kid's hand was between her legs. She pushed herself against him in time to the music. Over his shoulder, she glimpsed Caroline watching her. Betsy put her head back on Thurm's shoulder.

'You want to go some place and fuck our brains out?' He was talking in her ear and she wanted to giggle, but who wouldn't if a kid named Thurm who couldn't be more than twenty-two had his hands on your ass. Inside your jeans, your thong. Making you come.

'All we need is some Quaalude and a bottle of champagne,' she said.

'Whatever. Let's go. OK? You want to?'

'Yes,' she said. 'Yeah, I do.'

Maybe they were right. The Carolines had it right, after all. It was better like this, drunk and with a new face and a young guy who had his hands in your pants.

'Where do you live?'

12

They fell out of the cab, her and Thurm, onto Cornelia Street where Marie Tusi was wrestling a black plastic garbage bag into the street. She wore a ragged Persian lamb coat over flannel pajamas and red rubber boots. It was still drizzling and her hair was plastered to her head. A cigarette hung from her mouth and she wheezed and coughed while she worked.

'Goddamn asthma,' she said and set the bag down and leaned on it. Then she leaned over and whispered at Betsy, 'You're having a nice time, hon? I'm glad. That's good.'

'You want some help?' Thurm asked Marie.

'I'm fine, I couldn't sleep. I figured I'd get a start on the garbage,' she said. 'It takes me a lot of time, I got this lousy wrist I sprained. I got the plaster off today. Dev says I'm compulsive.' She snorted in the damp air like a horse whinnying. 'Keeps me going. I like to be in shape even at my age. And he's not going to do it for me, is he?'

'You're great,' Betsy said, slurring her words. 'You are just fabulous and I love you.'

'I love you, too, girl. Now you both go on

upstairs, OK, or you'll freeze to death. You want me to make you some hot chocolate?'

Betsy shook her head and tried not to laugh until they got upstairs where she exploded, laughed so hard her ribs hurt. The sight of Marie Tusi at five in the morning, the fur coat, her flannel pajama legs stuffed into the red rubber boots, the huge garbage bag, the offer of hot chocolate, it all seemed hilarious if you were drunk.

They reached the top of the stairs and Betsy unlocked her door. Then they were standing in her vestibule, at the bottom of the short flight of stairs that led up into the living room. Her stairs. His hands were already inside her jacket, under her sweater, pushing her against the wall. He held her hard against the wall and she couldn't move.

'Stop it. Let me at least lock the door,' she said.

'No.'

Sexually, Betsy was pretty innocent and she knew it. She had her share of men, and she liked sex, but she was shy. Sometimes sex made her giggle, which was probably unseemly.

The new face helped, but she worried about the rest of her. It nagged at her. Her body did not live up to her face, she thought, but who cared, or did she care what this kid thought?

She was already disengaged from herself, watching herself, reinventing herself. With Tom her fantasies were always about wild domestic sex like something from an Updike novel; with this boy she found herself in the middle of her own cheap paperback.

The kid, Thurm, pushed her sweater up and, laughing, the two of them fell so they were half kneeling, half lying over the stairs. She wanted this, her counterpart, the heroine in her dirty paperback would think; she wanted it all, wanted it to go wherever it might take her.

Thurm reached in his pocket with one hand, pulling his jacket off with the other.

'You know what I got for us?'

'What's that?' she reached for his belt.

He pulled a plastic bag out of his jeans. 'I got some very nice weed for us to smoke.'

'That's good.' Betsy bent over to unlace her yellow boots.

'Leave them.'

'What do you mean?'

'I want to fuck you with your boots on.'

He laughed and half dragged her up the stairs into the living room and let go and squatted on the floor to roll the joint. He pulled her down next to him.

'Leave the boots.'

You can't say that, she thought, but she kept a straight face. The dope tasted delicious to her; the pungent smell made her dizzy. She was messing with cops and dope, but the wall of booze between her and her brains was fireproof. Even if Thurm was on her tail, she could play the game, and he was certainly on her, she giggled to herself.

He was pulling off her sweater, then her T-shirt; his cold fingers on her flesh made her nipples tight; when he leaned over her to suck on one, she almost came. She pushed his head down harder so now he bit the nipple and grunted when she moaned, and somehow she pushed his jeans down. She reached for his cock.

He yanked off her bra and pants and she was naked except for the boots. She would have done anything he wanted now. He pushed her head down onto his cock so she had it all in her mouth. Like a big hard banana, she thought inevitably. Hard fruit. Hard. Unripe. Full of cold ridges. She licked the head and flicked her tongue around it and returned to her narration, even as she slid her mouth down his cock, relaxing her throat to take him deep, feeling him tense with a pulse of excitement. As she moved her lips along the length of him with a slow gathering rhythm, he gripped her hand.

'Fuck my ass with your finger while you do that,' he said. The words, in her book, according to her fictional heroine, were somewhere between a command and a plea, but she did what he wanted.

She slid her mouth free and soaked her forefinger in it and with one movement put her mouth on his cock again and drove her finger into his ass. He jolted his head back and, in her mouth, she could feel the waves of his orgasm gathering, feel his ass contracting around her finger and she felt utterly possessed by pleasure, in control of him.

This was what she had always wanted, her, the heroine of her dirty novel. The salty sperm shot into her mouth. She pulled away abruptly now and offered her new face, her new, fixed, young, drunk face, to the rush of sperm, so it splashed over her eyelids and cheeks and lips. It streaked her hair. He reached down and rubbed it on her nipples, then sagged back against the wall.

Somehow, they were in the bedroom now and he recovered fast and then he was on top of her, upside down, his tongue inside her. She took a deep breath and came fast. She had stopped giggling. He had a finger in her cunt and one in her ass and his cock inside and all she had was the filled-up feeling, hard and dirty, until she came in spasms that made her jackknife half up off the bed.

⋆ ⋆ ⋆

Her mouth felt like the floor of a rabbit hutch when she woke up. She pushed the shade aside and squinted. The city was draped in white fog and the glare was blinding. She turned over and pulled the blanket up over her. The boy in her bed was asleep in a tangled mess of sheets and in the daylight, he looked even younger. He would wake up and see her, he'd see her body, he'd know how old she was, the skin on her arms like chicken feet, the brown spots on her hands. She struggled out of bed, clutching the blanket.

'Don't go,' he said, yawning. 'Let's do it again.'

'Get up,' she said. 'How old are you?'

'Nineteen,' he said. 'Almost twenty. I'll be twenty tomorrow.'

'Jesus.'

'I'll be twenty tomorrow, like I said.'

'Happy birthday. Get up.'

'Thanks. When can I see you again?'

Betsy's head was ready to crack like a coconut; the vision of a machete that would split it swam into her head, which was swimming like the milky insides of the coconut; her eyes seemed to push forward out of her forehead, her tongue was furred like mold on fruit.

'Get up,' she said.

'It's too early.'

'You have to go.'

'There's nothing happening today,' he said. 'Look outside. Nothing. Nada. We could stay in the sack all day.' He leaned up on his elbow and looked at her and put out his hand and pulled her back into the bed.

'Come on, Betsy, it was so great. You have such a great cunt. So big and wet and delicious.' He dove under the covers, found her hand and put it on him. 'If you don't keep me around, I might haunt you.'

It wasn't a threat and he smiled and tickled her and laughed. She was unnerved. There was nothing threatening in the words. He was smiling and laughing, like a kid, but she was nervous and hungover.

'Please, Betsy,' he said. 'Let me. Otherwise, I might keep you hostage. I could lock you up and we could do dirty stuff. I can think of lots of things we can do. I might stay here forever.'

13

Bay Ridge was serene in the morning, the fog that had settled over the city in the night was lifting, the sun out. So serene that it made Frank loco, it reminded him of growing up here in Brooklyn, far enough from the city to make you yearn for it.

Frank Dolce grew up in Bay Ridge, but as soon as he got to Manhattan, just like he expected, he was hooked. He got himself into Fordham, got the degree, got on the force and got married and went to live on Long Island. He hated it. After four years of marriage and the divorce, he heard about the lofts on Cedar Street.

How much he'd loved that building, how hard he'd worked to fix it up, him and everyone else in it, like pioneers.

On 9/11 everything was smashed to pieces. He stopped himself thinking about it. He didn't like thinking about what he'd seen those days and nights when the rubble was still red hot and your boots melted if you stayed in one place too long and the body parts and the crying. His sister crying all the time because her fiancé who was a fireman was dead. His own place full of ash. So when he left his mother's in Bay Ridge Wednesday morning, he was already majorly pissed off.

He'd had another argument about money with his girlfriend — about to be ex — who was living with her parents. They'd shared the loft on Cedar Street for six years. When they had to move out, it wrecked things. He was, as usual, broke, and he'd finally met a woman he could fall for in a big way except she was a suspect in a case. Jesus. Jesus, Frank, you're an asshole, he said to himself.

He was forty-three and broke and now this. He ought to take himself off the case completely, he was pretty much a straight arrow, had always been, even when everyone else bent the rules a little. It didn't suit him, bending the rules, even if it was only some freebies with the whores in the place in Chelsea. A free drink at a few downtown bars, OK, he could do that, or maybe a meal. Otherwise, he didn't feel good with it.

It bothered him, knowing he should be off the case, but what would he tell the boss? He'd look like an idiot. Everyone figured him for a soft touch anyhow and now he had to deal with Jimmy Grant, the evil, stunted little Mick they stuck him with for a partner. Grant didn't give a shit about anything; all he wanted was to close the case.

This Thornhill woman, thinking about her kept him awake at night. He got a haircut. He lost five pounds.

She was a great-looking woman and she was smart as hell and talented and tall. Sense of humor, the way she took things in, the way she could laugh at herself for knowing she watched too many movies and took her cue about cops from them. Of course she did. Like everyone else in America. Even cops learned how to behave from watching TV and movies. He had told her that and it made her laugh.

The photographs she took, he loved. He noticed she had a stack of Sinatra CDs. She made good coffee. Unlike most of the women he had known, she was really nice and her kitchen smelled of good things — and there were the blue eyes. Shit, he thought again, climbing into his car. What a sucker I am, he thought and rubbed his chin. He had shaved extra close that morning and put on a new blue Italian shirt he'd bought at Century 21 before it got trashed and that he'd been saving for something special.

It was going to be another freaky warm day. All fall, most of the winter, the weather fucking mocked you, he thought. It was warm and sunny, but what could you do with it? Make a picnic on the ruins? Jesus!

Frank finally pulled up in front of Betsy Thornhill's building and figured he better tell her one thing. He better tell her how pissed off he was at her right now, though he checked in the rear-view to see he looked OK, then wondered, as he did most hours since he met her, if she actually did slash Ketsen, the victim down in Tribeca.

* * *

She was drinking Alka-Seltzer in the kitchen and feeling only marginally undead and it took her brain a while to connect with the fact someone was hitting the buzzer.

'Frank,' the voice said. 'Frank Dolce.'

Hurriedly she buttoned up the green sweater she was wearing over her sweatpants and buzzed him in, listened for the heavy footsteps, opened the door. The light blue shirt looked good on him, his eyes were no longer bloodshot — he must have put something in them — but he was furious. She had been an idiot to trust him.

'You had to screw him, didn't you?' Frank said.

'What?'

'What the fuck were you thinking, taking the kid home, messing around with him?'

'How do you know?'

‘Oh, please, Betsy. He wasn’t in the station house ten minutes before he was bragging to one of the other guys about this woman who picked him up at Tribe, that bar they all hang out in, and who took him home and what a hot babe with great blue eyes she was and how the two of you were up all night doing it? You want to hear some more details from last night? You want me to tell you how you got down on your hands and knees for him? He knew your name.’

‘Stop it.’

‘This is your idea of helping yourself, hanging at bars, picking up kids?’

‘How come it’s your business?’

The kid was an intern, Frank said. He was pre-law at NYU. His father was something in the city and he was spending a few weeks at the station house learning about law enforcement. Everyone figured the kid would be OK for a couple of weeks. But not from predatory women, Frank added.

‘He’s not a cop?’ Betsy said.

‘Is that what you thought? You were going to get him all fucking worked up over you and find out what’s going on?’ Frank said. ‘So you fucked him good, did you?’

‘What is it, Frank? You want me to tell you the rest of the details so you can get off on it?’

‘Just stay away from little boys,’ he said.

'I hear you. Are we finished now?'

'I don't know, are we?'

It occurred to her, from his aggrieved voice, that, from Frank's point of view, they were having a lover's quarrel.

They were in the kitchen now and Frank sat at the table, stiff as a board, hands folded. She offered coffee. Food. 'Eggs? Frank?'

'What kind of eggs?' he said.

She pulled open the icebox door.

'I could do you lox and eggs, if you want. Fried. What about a cheese omelet?'

'Cheese,' he said.

'How many eggs?'

'Three?'

'What kind of cheese do you want?'

'What do you have?'

'Swiss, Provolone, Cheddar.' She stuck her head further in the fridge. 'There's a piece of really stinky Gorgonzola. I got the Cheddar at Murray's, it's good.'

'Cheddar sounds fine.'

Betsy made the omelet and fresh coffee and Frank ate. An overripe pineapple sat on the breadbox.

'I once went to a pineapple plantation in Hawaii,' he said. 'It smelled just like that. The whole place smelled of pineapples. Sweet. Heavy. Just like that.' In his jacket pocket, he found a crumpled pack of cigarettes and pushed it across the table. 'You want one of these?'

Betsy took one and held it, not lighting it.

'I'm on your side. I really am,' Frank said. 'I know you're upset. But you're acting stupid.'

'How come you're on my side?'

'I know you're telling the truth.' He paused. 'I know because I know you're not lying about your real age, for instance. I know you're a really good photographer.'

'How do you know?'

'Hey, calm down, it's OK. You showed me your book. The first time I came by. Your picture is in it. Your other face. Also, it's not that hard to check your birth date with immigration, is it? You thought I was just some dumb fat cop who's too poor to shop in the right places.'

'I didn't think anything.'

He leaned back. Told her the omelet was great. Asked which American cop shows she saw in England and told her he'd been an advisor on *Law & Order* for a while and that Jerry Orbach was a really nice man.

'I love Jerry Orbach,' she said.

'Can I ask you something, Betsy? How come you wanted to change your face? You had a great face, I mean you still do, but you were fine. So how come?'

She stubbed her cigarette out in the ashtray on the table.

'I don't know. It seemed like fun. How old are you, Frank?'

'Forty-three,' he said. 'Old for my years.'

'You know who I am. You know I'm this old broad. You know I can't have been at Ketsen's because the woman who was there was a lot younger.'

It didn't help much, of course. It was the face she had, it didn't matter if it was hers or she'd had it fixed, it was a problem. Frank put his hand out as if to touch hers, but left a space between them and lowered his voice. There was a second witness, he said. Someone who had seen her go into Ketsen's apartment.

'It wasn't me,' Betsy said.

'Look, it was after the first witness came forward, so we can't know if they talked to each other. I wouldn't worry that much.'

She kept her mouth shut.

Frank said, 'Honestly, people always see things in hindsight, you know, someone says they saw someone and then somebody else comes forward.'

'You showed them the picture of me?'

'My partner showed them.'

'I never even met Ketsen before last Thursday at the airport.'

'I know that. You live a transparent life. That's why I believe you.'

What did he mean by transparent, she wondered. How much did he know about her?

Frank said, 'You can talk to me off the record if you want.'

'How come you want to help me like this?' Betsy said finally.

He moved his hand so that his fingers grazed hers. 'I like you.'

From the freezer, she got a bag of coffee beans and shoveled them into the grinder. She put the coffee in the pot and watched it until the steam came up, poured it and sat with Frank at the table. They drank the whole pot, not talking much.

'Frank? Did whoever killed Ketsen have to break into his place or did they have a key?'

'It looked like they had a key, or else he answered the door.'

'So he knew who it was. Will you let me into Ketsen's apartment, Frank?'

'Don't ask me that. I can't. Come on.'

'What would it take?'

'I can't,' he said plaintively. 'I just can't. Tell me what you think you're looking for and I'll find it.' He wandered to the window and looked out. 'Give me a couple days. OK?'

'Yes.'

'Promise?'

It was what Ketsen had said on the phone. 'Promise?'

'I promise,' she said and held out his jacket and noticed that the faint scent of perfume that had nestled in the worn leather when she'd hung it up two days earlier was gone. His hand was sweaty. Betsy leaned over and kissed him on the cheek.

'Thank you,' he said. 'Betsy?'

'What's that?'

'It's just really routine, but so no one else asks, would you let me take a look around your apartment?'

* * *

After Frank Dolce looked in her drawers and the closets and under the bed and behind the bag of frozen peas in the freezer, he left and Betsy reached for the phone, then put it back.

In London she had friends, plenty of them, and you were never off their radar, but they were three thousand miles away, her house was rented out to Germans and all she had was this apartment in New York with the blistered paint in the kitchen and a cop who tried to claim her friendship.

There was no way she could go home to London without looking guilty. In the kitchen she got fresh film out of the fridge and her camera out of the bag. Do what you do, Mark Carey had said. She couldn't work. In the living room, she put Sinatra on the CD player and turned it up loud and danced around the apartment and tried to loosen up. Shake the dread, move on.

She hated the waiting and the introspection. If it meant denial, so what? If it made you disengaged, OK, that was OK. She was aware of all this.

In herself Betsy sensed a chilliness like her mother's, deep down, close to the bone. It came from the detachment. For the most part, she was gregarious, of course, she could go to a cocktail party of strangers and come out with friends. The rest of it, the cold center, she admitted to no one except once to Max, her next-door neighbor in London, and only when she'd had too much vodka. They got drunk and slept together and she told him.

Now, one long arm crooked at an angle behind her head, Betsy lay back on the sofa and stared up at the ceiling and noticed the water stain for the first time. It resembled a bird. For a while she looked at it, then tried to call Mark Carey, and after him, Meryl Briggs. There was no answer.

A second witness had identified her going

into Ketsen's apartment. But there was nothing to worry about, Frank had said. Nothing much. In the kitchen where the radiator banged and hissed, she got a Diet Coke out of the fridge and looked in the mirror over the sink. The face was intact. It was good as ever. The rest of her life seemed ready to topple over like the pile of luggage on her cart at the airport. The face, though, was fine and smooth.

Outside, it was still balmy and she went to the window and looked at the street where people were coming out of the restaurants after lunch. Get out of here, she thought to herself, get moving, she said out loud.

She went into the bathroom, took a shower, stood under the trickle of warm water for a long time and then fell into bed. She hadn't slept much the night before with the kid, Thurm, in her bed.

In her dreams, it snowed. Tiny figures jumped off buildings and landed, unhurt, in mountains of snow. Beyond the windows of the little apartment, the whole city buried in snow felt monstrous, oppressive, stalking her, slowly, relentless, her sinking in it up to her knees, then her neck. She would disappear in it and no one would find her. It was like a huge white muffled deaf-mute, the city, its heart slowed to a barely palpable beat. Feeling as lonely as she ever remembered, she reached for the phone and couldn't think of the number. In her dream, the apartment seemed removed from the rest of the city as it sank in the blizzard. There was no one to call. Her world seemed to shrink.

* * *

It was dark when she woke up. She got out of bed and put some clothes on and went downstairs and around the corner to Bleecker Street. She bought a semolina loaf at Zito's and a copy of *Food & Wine* and the *Post* at the newsstand and put them under her arm.

The air that evening was almost soft. The street was thronged with people looking for a place to eat. At the Spanish bar near her building, Betsy climbed up on a stool and asked for a beer, then spread her newspaper out on the scarred oak surface, flipping the pages, looking for the movie section. Enough already, she thought to herself, enough craziness, let's go to the pictures and she smiled at the bartender, who recognized her because she'd been by before.

He brought her a cold Corona, looked at

her face and said, worriedly, 'Hey, what's the matter?'

Betsy didn't wait. Didn't answer. She tossed a ten on the bar and snatched her paper and ran out and across the street, banging into a man who swore at her. She couldn't stop. People turned and seemed to stare.

Her picture was in the paper. Her picture and her name, both of them, in the *Post*. The article described witnesses who claimed to have seen her. A dark-haired woman in a red coat. Somebody else said a redhead. The *New York Post* printed it all.

Gasping for breath at the top of the stairs, she jammed her key in the lock and tried to joke to herself. Her fifteen minutes of fame, here it was. She was on display now, available to everyone. The police picture stared up at her through the grimy newsprint. Next to it was a real photograph of Betsy with her new face.

How did the paper get it? Who took it? Who?

Panic took over because she didn't recognize the picture, because except for her passport photo and a few snaps she'd taken of herself, she couldn't remember anyone at all having photographed her since she got her face done.

Except for Ketsen. Bobby Ketsen had taken her picture in Union Square. Betsy peered at the newspaper. Ketsen had taken the picture out of doors in sunlight. This picture had been taken indoors. It couldn't be his, she thought. *Could it*?

14

Newspaper in her hand, Betsy sat on the edge of the shabby sofa in her apartment. There was still no answer at Meryl Briggs'. Over and over she dialed the number. It was Meryl who had identified her to the cops, Briggs was Ketsen's secretary, was with him Saturday night and found him dead on Sunday. Now it was Wednesday. *Answer the phone*. Betsy dropped the newspaper and saw that her hand was smudged black with ink.

It was not knowing who gave her picture to the *Post*, who took it, if the cops were going to arrest her, that was worst. Until the paper published the pictures, in spite of everything, she had been sure about the outcome, more or less. Anxious, OK, but able to laugh, the events still faintly unreal. Not now. It was there, black and white, on her living-room floor, and it was lousy for her, this sitting around and waiting, and she got up hurriedly and sat down and got up and poured a drink.

Time passed. Still no answer at Meryl Briggs'. Betsy got hold of Al Kovlovski at the limo office and he tracked down one of his part-time drivers and got Meryl's address for her.

The apartment felt suffocating, the heat was too high, her anxiety filled up the corners. In a rush to get out and get some air, she put on the red coat. As she left the building she saw Dev, Mari Tusi's husband, lumbering in her direction. He was a large old man and he smiled and raised his hand in greeting, mouth open, on the verge of telling her some more of his war stories, World War Two, the Pacific, then Japan afterwards to clean up. He had been in Hiroshima. He had seen people burned to the bone. For a moment she paused to listen and then made an excuse and hurried to the corner.

A taxi with a light appeared and she ran for it and got in. The driver's name was Mohammed Idris, and Betsy said, please, Mohammed, get me to the train, OK, for Hoboken. Sure, lady, he said. You OK?

From the station in Hoboken, she walked to the converted brownstone where Meryl Briggs lived. Climbed the stairs, hit the buzzer hard. No one answered and Betsy left and walked up the street to a deli, then back-tracked to the station and watched while passengers emerged. No reason to assume the girl was coming by train, but Betsy watched anyway for almost an hour, surveying faces, looking for Meryl Briggs, the girl who worked for Bobby Ketsen. It was a face, small, brown, oval, eager, she would remember.

'This is Betsy,' Ketsen had said to Meryl at his studio that afternoon when they got in from the airport. 'She picked me up.'

On their way home, the evening warm as spring, people with their coats unbuttoned sauntered and stopped in bars and sat out at cafés. Betsy got some coffee, wanting the caffeine. Standing outside the coffee shop and drinking it, she reached in her pocket for cigarettes and her attention was distracted by an ambulance, lights blazing, siren shrieking. Suddenly, two doors down, coming out of a drugstore, was Meryl Briggs. She wore black Capris and a cropped black denim jacket.

It was idiotic, but she was on automatic now, driven by panic, and Betsy tossed her coffee in a garbage can and followed the girl back to the brownstone. She climbed the steps. Betsy was behind her.

A woman coming out of the door with a fat baby in her arms said to the girl, 'Hey Meryl. Hold the door, will you?'

'Hey,' Meryl said and held the door for her, then went in herself. Betsy followed her.

Keys in her hand, Meryl went to a door on the ground floor and only then seemed to realize Betsy was behind her and she turned around and held her hands up as if expecting a blow.

'What do you want?' she said.

'I have to talk to you.' She was sweating.

Hurriedly, Meryl unlocked her apartment and tried to slip in, but Betsy put her hand on the door and said, 'Please. Please. I really need to talk to you.'

'What is it?'

'There's something I want to tell you about Bobby Ketsen. Something he told me,' Betsy lied. 'We met, remember? I was up at his place Thursday. My name is Betsy Thornhill.'

'I know who you are,' Meryl said and slammed the door.

* * *

In the dim hallway, Betsy turned to leave when the door suddenly opened. Meryl Briggs stood on the other side, the chain on, peering out at her.

'So what is it you, like, want to tell me?'

'Can I come in?'

In the light from the apartment, Betsy could see Meryl Briggs's face, tiny, even features, light brown skin, hair in a pony-tail. She was twenty-five, twenty-six and her soft little voice and the way she used 'like' to break up every phrase made her seem adolescent.

Betsy said, 'I know it must have been tough, you finding him like that. I'm sorry. I wanted to say that. I wanted to see if I could help. You identified me to the cops, right? You said you saw me going into the building.'

'You knew that?'

'Yes.'

'You knew from the cops?'

'Did you mention it to anyone else in the building, seeing the woman who looked like me.'

'I don't know. Maybe. Yeah. So what was it Bobby told you?'

'He told me I reminded him of someone else,' Betsy said. 'So it's all a mistake.'

'You're saying you didn't kill him.' Meryl's voice was shaky.

'I didn't kill him,' Betsy said. 'Listen, could I come in?'

Behind Betsy, a couple, giggling, came in from the street. Meryl took the chain off and opened her door.

'Yeah, OK, come in,' Meryl said. 'You want something to drink?'

'Whatever you're having.'

'I've been needing a drink the last week,' Meryl said leading her through the small apartment, carefully decorated by a girl with plans for a future.

The apartment had stripped wooden floors, white walls, a few cautiously chosen pieces of modern furniture, a red leather easy chair. Pillows from the Pottery Barn were neatly arranged along the back of the spare gray sofa. A framed poster of Audrey Hepburn in *Funny Face* hung on the wall above it.

'Great movie,' Betsy said.

'Yeah,' Meryl said and gestured at the chair. 'Sit down if you want. Look, I let you in because I saw your face in the paper earlier today and now I'm not so sure if it was you Saturday night, if you want to know. You didn't kill him?' Her face was childish, wanting to believe.

Betsy sat silently in the red chair.

'I don't really care, you know. The sucker had it coming, but if you didn't you didn't.'

Meryl disappeared into the kitchen and came back with a tray with cheap vodka and a carton of orange juice. She made drinks and Betsy took the glass, and felt worn down by the domestic ritual that seemed to go with every conversation. The domestication of a murder case, death by coffee, and juice and drinks and oatmeal cookies for the cops. The window in the living room looked over the Hudson, the Manhattan skyline sharp and glittering on the other side.

Meryl followed her gaze and gulped her drink and began talking about Bobby Ketsen. Once she started, she couldn't stop talking. She knew Betsy was coming, Al Kovlovski from the car company called to say Betsy was looking for her. Al hated Ketsen as much as Meryl did, you know, she said, drumming her thin fingers on the table. He was a fuck, Bobby was, Grade A fuck, which was why she was talking to Betsy because why should anyone get fucked over by the cops for him getting what he deserved, she said, spitting out the words as if they clogged her mouth.

'Why was he a fuck?' Betsy slipped off her coat and leaned forward. 'Tell me.'

'Maybe it doesn't mean diddly, you know?'

She got up and went into the bedroom and came back with a large manila envelope that she placed on the low table between them, but didn't open.

'You want another drink?' she asked.

What Betsy wanted was to stick around. She saw that Meryl, her voice wavering, her eyes filling up, needed some company. Tentatively, Betsy asked for a cup of coffee.

'Instant OK?' Meryl said.

'Instant's great.'

They finished the vodka, they drank some coffee. Knees pulled up under her on the sofa, Meryl talked compulsively. She needed a friend and Betsy was warm, attentive, friendly.

Ketsen had been a good boss, it seemed. He believed in affirmative action. Helped kids up in Harlem, took interns at his studio, talked about giving back. He could charm the birds, too, she said. Everyone at work liked him.

'So he was a saint,' Betsy said. 'What else?'

'He took my picture.' Meryl looked at the envelope on the table. The voice was sharp with anger. 'What turned him on was photographing women different from how they were. You understand?'

'Help me,' Betsy said.

'He said it was every woman's fantasy, you know, to look like someone else. He said photo-journalism was bullshit and this was art. He reinvented them, make-up, digital, whatever.'

Betsy listened hard. Don't stop, she thought. Keep talking.

'He told them it was a social experiment, see how looking different makes you feel different. It was some kind of head game. Then he put them on the web.'

'I looked at his website.'

'Yeah, his business site. He had a different one, for connoisseurs. Someone shut it down the day after he was murdered. Some of the women tried to get the pictures back but he made sure he had legal ownership.'

'It's hard to believe that Ketsen was some kind of Svengali.'

'He charmed you, right? I mean, how come a woman like you takes a ride from a total stranger unless he's, like, you know, pretty nice?'

Ketsen knew all the angles, as Meryl put it. He was educated, he traveled right, he looked good, he wasn't just some rich guy, he was self-made, he was a talker. Women loved him.

'How long did you work for Ketsen?'

'About four months. I was a part-time student at Parsons, I was dying to get into photography, Bobby gave me a job.' She peered at Betsy. 'You're sure Bobby never took your picture?'

'Why?'

'I was cleaning up some files for him and I feel like I remember seeing pictures of you.'

'It wasn't me. I swear to God it wasn't me.'

'I guess not.' Meryl wound a strand of hair around her finger over and over. 'I'm not like carrying any torch for Ketsen, you know. You tell me it wasn't you, I'm OK with that.'

She asked Meryl how Ketsen got her

address on Cornelia Street. It was her, Meryl said apologetically. Bobby had asked her to call the car service and get Betsy's address, he made her stop by and check her name on the buzzer, she saw Pauline's name and got the number. Bobby told her Betsy was a brilliant photographer and he wanted to work with her but it would take some doing, she was timid about her talent. Meryl knew it was horseshit, knew Bobby was after her because she was good-looking, but it was her job. She apologized again. She didn't have a choice. Right? Betsy?

Betsy nodded and said she understood.

'You probably want to know what I was doing at Bobby's in the middle of the night,' Meryl went on.

'Yes.'

Meryl leaned on her arms on the table and gulped her drink. Ketsen had her stay late at work most nights, she said. He paid her extra and she came in weekends too if he needed her. Sometimes by herself. She had keys. Saturday night, just back from London, he wanted to catch up. There was another trip the next week. Las Vegas, Meryl said, some kind of photo convention. He stayed at the Hard Rock Hotel, she added.

So they worked late and he ordered dinner

from Nobu, which was around the corner and where they knew him. Meryl picked it up and brought it back and they ate. Then she called Al's car service.

She looked at Betsy. 'There's phone records of Ketsen using his phone after I left, and I made a call from my cell phone in the car coming home, in case you were still wondering.'

'Go on.'

Al told Meryl there'd be a car waiting for her at 2 a.m., so she left Bobby cleaning up from supper, drinking a glass of white wine. He was pretty high when she left, the wine, the weed.

The elevator was bust, like it mostly was, and she walked down and waited in the vestibule. It made her nervous being on the street so late, so she waited until the car came. Watching for the car through the glass pane in the door, she saw a woman across the street just hanging out, which seemed weird at two in the morning. She was wearing a red coat. Then the car came and Meryl went out and got in it and saw, at the same time, the woman jog across to Ketsen's building.

'She had a key?' Betsy asked.

Meryl shook her head. The woman buzzed, she said. It was easy to see because of the plaque Ketsen had up on the wall next to his bell. People were always ringing the wrong door, so he'd put it up.

It bothered her, this woman ringing so late, and she told the driver to wait while she watched. The woman buzzed again. In the streetlight, she could see her clearly.

'She had on sunglasses, but she took them off when she looked for his buzzer. She buzzed and the door gave.'

'So he probably knew her if he buzzed her in.'

Meryl nodded.

'And she looked like me?'

'From what I could see, yeah, she looked a lot like you, tall, same kind of hair.' Meryl glanced at Betsy's coat that was hanging over the chair. 'Her coat was red, too, but sort of shiny. I guess the cops told you, there was someone else, a guy who lives on the same floor as Ketsen was going out to walk his dog right after I left, and he told me he saw you going into Ketsen's apartment. I mean her. Not you. Whoever.'

'You talked to him?'

'The dog walker? Not that night. I must have gone by the time he got to the street. We were kind of friendly and he called me yesterday and said he remembered seeing someone except he was really stoned that night, and didn't tell the cops right away, but they were still bugging him, did I see anyone? I told him.'

'You described the woman you saw?'

'Yeah. He went to the cops and they probably showed him the picture. I'm sorry. I just got scared.'

'I understand,' Betsy said. 'Did the police talk to the driver who picked you up that night?'

'Probably,' Meryl said. 'Maybe. I'm sorry if I screwed up.'

'Can you get me into Ketsen's place?'

Meryl looked at her watch.

Give me the keys, Betsy wanted to say. Give me the keys to Ketsen's place. Meryl was already jittery, moving around the room now, straightening cushions, dropping an empty glass, like a flustered bird. She disappeared into the kitchen, returned with a platter of muffins and looked at it.

'I made so many of these damn things, could I give you some to take home? I can't really cook, but it's my mom's birthday tomorrow and I wanted do something, and they just kept coming,' she said.

Betsy asked if she could use the bathroom and Meryl said sure, she'd bag the muffins meanwhile.

* * *

Tears were streaming down Meryl's face as Betsy came back to the living room and she leaned over and put her hand on the girl's arm and said, 'What is it, sweetheart? What's wrong?'

'I slept with him,' Meryl said.

'What?'

'I did it that Saturday night. We ate, and he said, oh, Meryl, honey, please come to bed, I miss you, you're the one. So I did, I didn't tell anyone, how could I? And then I came back on Sunday and he was dead.' She took the manila envelope off the table and held it tight against her chest and fumbled with the clasp and wiped her eyes. 'You want to see the pictures?'

'I'd like that a lot.'

She tossed the envelope at Betsy.

'Yeah, OK, you can look at the fucking pictures if you want. Go on.'

Betsy extracted a sheaf of color prints and turned them over one at a time. In the skillfully printed photographs, Meryl Briggs was dressed up in a navy blue suit and a prim white blouse, shoes with kitten heels and a velvet headband, a preppy uptown girl from the 1950s.

The pictures were adhesive, Betsy couldn't

take her eyes off them. It was the make-up that kept you looking, the blonde wig and the make-up.

'So you understand?' Meryl said. 'I bought into all that sociological bullshit he talked, you know? By the time he was finished, I half believed him. After all, he said, all he wanted was to see what I looked like, that it was an experiment, seeing how being a different color makes you feel different. And there was something else.'

Betsy looked up.

'My mom,' Meryl said, weeping. 'He knew she was my role model, he knew I wanted to be like her.'

'I see.'

'My mom is white,' she said. 'So he did it. He convinced me. Bobby made me believe all he ever wanted to do was show me how I looked as a white girl.'

15

Meryl Briggs murdered Bobby Ketsen. Betsy was convinced of this by the time she got home from Jersey. In her apartment, the answering machine was jammed with messages. As soon as she got in the door, she saw the light blinking.

She tossed the bag of muffins on the kitchen table. In the living room, the newspaper was on the floor where she'd left it. Her picture stared up at her. The photograph in the *Post* had been on her mind all the time she was in Hoboken with Meryl Briggs, and on the way home something had occurred to her so before she got her coat off, she lit up a cigarette and sat at the desk and opened her computer and went on line.

She typed in Russell Newman's name. Waited, impatient, struggling out of her coat, looking out the window, smoking and waiting for the site to come up.

With one cigarette already burning in the yellow saucer she used for an ashtray, she lit another one and waited some more and then the screen filled up. When she saw the image take shape and recognized it for what it was, she figured, for the first time in her life, she might pass out.

Feet pressed hard against the floor, bile burst into Betsy's throat, her eyes blurred, then focused.

It was her face on the screen. Russell Newman's name, his credentials as a cosmetic surgeon, the address of his office in London and photographs of her. Before-and-after pictures.

Her face. Her face was everywhere.

Betsy reached for the newspaper that lay on the floor, picked it up, held it next to the computer. The same picture.

It was Russell Newman who took the photograph of her after the surgery, the picture that showed up in the newspaper. It was what she had remembered coming back from New Jersey.

May I keep this, Betsy? May I keep your picture?

It was at her final appointment that he had asked for it.

A dozen people knew about the surgery, friends and acquaintances. Easy enough to get the picture off Newman's site and give it to the newspapers, or sell it, if you knew where to look. Out of vanity, Newman himself could have given it to the tabloids. She recalled the hats. He was a vain man. He had stolen her face. He thought he owned it.

The phone rang. It was Thurm, the kid from the bar.

'I can't talk,' Betsy said briefly.

'Can't I come over?'

She said, 'You must be kidding,' and hung up the phone.

For a while, paralyzed, she sat in front of her face on the computer screen, then switched it off and slammed down the top. Her instinct was to call Newman, but it was the middle of the night in London and he'd deny any involvement.

Did she ever give permission for the pictures? Was it in the fine print on the form she had signed so casually when she authorized the surgery? Was it legal? Did she sign? She couldn't remember.

'You, I can give, ten, even fifteen,' he'd said to her in his office. 'Think of it. Fifteen years.'

* * *

It had begun before that, though, in London in August when, the sun shining, she stopped for coffee off the Portobello Road on her way home.

'May I?' He gestured to the chair where she was sitting in the late summer sun and smoking and drinking coffee.

It was the day she walked out of the meeting at the TV company where she sat on the flesh-colored sofa. In the street, she felt unexpectedly free of the whole silly business and ambled along and bought bananas in the market and checked the show times at the Electric Cinema and went to see Rosie at the bookshop where her book was in the window.

Fruit was selling nicely, Rosie said. Brisk sales. It took the sting out of the meeting and she thought, to hell with TV and people who wanted someone younger and she went to the café next to the bookshop and flopped into a chair on the sidewalk and held her face up to the sun.

A few minutes later, he was standing on the pavement, small, dapper and smiling. He wore a cream summer suit and a Panama hat.

'Would you mind terribly?'

He raised his hand as if to tip the hat but instead put it in front of his eyes to shade them from the sun and waited.

The other chairs were occupied and Betsy looked at him and said, 'Sure. Of course. Please.' She smoothed her linen skirt and jacket and crossed her legs and was glad she was wearing the strappy sandals and not some espadrilles with broken backs.

He put his Hermes briefcase — from the years she worked fashion, she could read the labels if she paid attention — on the ground, and when the waiter came out, ordered an espresso.

He waved at the clear August sky and said, 'Nice.'

'It's been so gorgeous all month.'

The small talk was fine with Betsy, she didn't mind, she was enjoying the sun on her face.

She put a fresh cigarette in her mouth and he flicked a heavy gold Dunhill lighter.

'You're American?' he said. 'I like the accent. The South?'

Brits always said it, she thought. The South, they asked if they wanted to flatter you.

'New York.'

He smiled. 'Better still.'

The waiter brought his coffee and he drank it and they smoked. He had a slightly odd inflection when he spoke, not foreign, but seductive. He was short but sexy. But she had Tom. She was meeting Tom in an hour.

'Of course,' the man said and hit his forehead with the flat of his hand, a self-consciously theatrical gesture. 'I know who you are.'

'You do?'

'Yes. Look!'

With a magician's flourish, he snatched a

book out of his briefcase and put it on the table. It was a copy of *Fruit*.

That was why he was here, he said. He'd been to the bookshop next door to the café to get a copy of her book for a friend. He'd already bought two and loved it. He loved the pictures, the way she made fruit seem a metaphor for everything. It was funny, he said, terribly witty.

'You wrote the text, as well, didn't you?' he asked.

'Yes.'

She beamed back like an eager puppy when he asked her to sign it, and he removed a gold Mont Blanc pen from the inside pocket of his jacket.

It felt opulent in her hand and she wrote in the book and he thanked her. She was flattered. She was a sucker for anyone who liked her work.

'Thank you,' he said and they talked a while about food and restaurants and where to get the best vacherin in season and the coincidence of their sharing a table. Betsy thought how civilized it was.

After a few minutes, the man in the hat, finishing his coffee, replaced the cup on the saucer, put some money on the table, stood up and put out his hand out. She shook it and the skin was soft and gave off the faint rich scent of expensive cream. Grapefruit, the scent. He thanked her again for the book and gave her his card, and with a tiny nod, a little bow almost, waved lightly and walked away. He turned into Kensington Park Road and disappeared.

At home later, after dinner, she took her jacket off and found the card. A flash of excitement went through her when she read his name.

Russell Newman. Mr Russell Newman. The guy was a plastic surgeon and the card was beautifully engraved. It was in the cards, she thought, first Vicky doing her face, then Tom saying she'd been a dish once, and the TV people wanting someone younger, now this. In the cards.

Pinching the saggy skin around her neck, she ran into her office and slammed the door and called Vicky.

'You believe in the devil?' Betsy said. 'That you make a deal?'

Vicky laughed.

'I don't believe in anything except food, sex and rock and roll, which shows you what a born again hippie I am. You're the one with the demons in the closet, sweetie. You're the one who believes in some God,' Vic said.

'But what about synchronicity? What about fate? That kind of stuff?'

'Are you telling me you met some guy you want to fuck?' Vicky said. 'You want to cheat on Tom? Is that it? You know I'm OK with that.'

'It's not that,' Betsy said. 'Never mind.'

'Darling, you know how I feel. If it feels good, do it. Whatever gets you through the night.'

* * *

At the little desk in her dead aunt's apartment in New York, she thought back to the appointment with Newman at his office and how she had liked the way he had a worn but beautiful leather sofa and roses the color of apricots with a spicy smell and a Hockney drawing on the wall. It seduced her, the way the rooms looked, the agreeable, motherly receptionist, Newman himself.

She had checked him out. Talking to her friends, she discovered half the women she knew secretly yearned for some work, the other half had it done already, some at home, some on holidays in Brazil or California or Cape Town. What's his name, Betsy? Russell Newman? One of the best.

In his office, Newman sat not behind a desk, but alongside her, both of them in comfortable armchairs. He asked if she wanted to see what could be done and she said OK, and with a digital camera and his computer he showed her herself younger.

Did he see in her a woman who could be persuaded? Was it Betsy who was too eager?

An appointment was available right away, something that never happened, he said, it was normally a six-month wait, but someone had canceled. It appealed to her, making the decision fast and there was some extra cash in her account; she said to Newman: OK, when?

Three weeks, he said.

Before the surgery, every night she dreamed he stuck a knife in the fleshy white part of her eyeball. A mistake, the surgeon said afterwards. Sorry. An accident. The liquid in her eyeball ran down her face.

Deep down she felt it was a Faustian deal and things would go wrong and she'd end up ghoulish or dead. What was it she always said about facelifts when she was little? 'Is that where they cut you up and sew you back together and you come out looking like somebody else?'

Just before they put her under when Newman was in his surgical gown and wearing the embroidered cap, he said, 'It's OK, Betsy. I'm here. Squeeze my hand. It's Russell.'

When it was all done, after the pain and the

swelling and the way her cheeks went numb, Newman was delighted. He said it was to do with the shape of her face, that she looked so good. Thrilling, isn't it? Thrilling, they all said.

This happens, he said. Pretty much what I anticipated, of course, but sometimes you get especially lucky, I do what I do, it's just sometimes God gives you the extra tools,' he said and asked if he could take her picture. Let's have some of that lovely coffee again soon, he added and left for another appointment wearing a different hat, an autumn felt.

At first, she was coy with her friends. It was a kind of mistake, she said, the shape of my face, the texture of my skin, how I healed. It was a kind of accident. No one believed her, but no one cared much either. A few friends were judgmental. Most of them just wanted some. Most of her friends said, Who did you?

'You look fabulous,' Vicky said.

'I can give you ten, even fifteen years,' Newman had said. And he did.

* * *

Someone was banging on the door.

'It's Marie, honey. From downstairs. I brought you something.'

She opened the door and found Marie with a plate in her hand.

'It's late,' Betsy said.

'I know but I saw your light and I know you're having some troubles, hon. Can I help?'

Marie must have seen the story in the newspaper. Marie was the kind of woman who read her *New York Post* cover to cover.

Betsy shook her head. 'I'll be fine.'

Negotiating her way into the living room, Marie said, 'I know you have things on your mind. I'm very empathetic that way. I'm an intuitive person, so, you need me, you let me know.' She held out the plate. 'I remember you liked my short-ribs, though you also loved the pot roast. Right? I got some memory,' she added.

'It's really nice of you.' Betsy was grateful, though she wished Marie would go.

'I'm usually home, you know? I run the business from my little computer, and I can get real good deals on air tickets, if you need anything,' Marie said and started coughing.

Noises erupted out of Marie, the big face caved in, she held onto the desk.

Betsy said, 'Are you OK?'

'I'm fine. Don't mind me.'

'Get some rest.'

'Hon, you are sweet to care. I better get

home, you know what Dev's like. But, Betsy?'

'Yes?'

'I meant to tell you, we had a couple break-ins over the last year or so. Double-lock when you go out, right? Put the chain on when you're home. OK?'

'Thanks.'

'You're welcome. I'm always here for you.'

Marie passed the plate she held to Betsy who set it down on the table. When Marie hugged her, she could feel her bones.

'I'm going to eat that for dinner,' Betsy waved at the food Marie had brought. 'I'll bring your plate back.'

Betsy closed the door. Her face was on the website, there was the item in the *Post*, Marie knew. Marie had come looking for gossip. Marie sat in the window and talked to everyone in the street. People would know. They would put out the garbage and walk the dog and they'd know about her.

The sense of dread had grown, it seemed to have a free-standing quality as if it was something you could touch. It could suck up your oxygen. Betsy took Marie's short-ribs into the kitchen and put them in the garbage.

It was Meryl Briggs who killed Ketsen, then told the cops she saw a woman like Betsy enter the building. Meryl told Ketsen's neighbor, the dog walker, who confirmed the description with the cops. It was Meryl, but who would believe it? Even made up as a white woman, Meryl didn't resemble Betsy. No one would make that mistake, not even at night.

By now, she was fixated on Ketsen's studio, sure it was where she'd find the camera with the picture he took of her at the market. Sure there was evidence in it about Meryl Briggs. Had to be. Meryl had been nuts about Bobby Ketsen.

In the bedroom, Betsy caught her reflection in the mirror over the dresser and wanted to smash the glass. It was as if everything and everyone was unknowable, an Adobe Photoshop version of life where nothing was stable. She sat on the bed and thought: what did I do? How did I get here?

This was no cautionary tale she was living, no fall from grace, no parable about some aging asshole who gets her face fixed and has to pay up for it. Joking, she'd told Vicky that she had thought of Russell Newman as the devil who wore hats to disguise his horns. On a stand in his office he had fedoras and the Panama and a baseball cap. There was no devil, not even a cartoon demon or Al Pacino in the movie — what was it called? There was no God. There was no fall.

Millions of women got their faces done.

They did their bodies. Young girls, too. They got bigger boobs. Smaller boobs. Tighter buns. Everyone was in this game and there was no pay-back, no moral dimension, just bad luck and a horrible mistake. Somebody looked like her. She looked like someone younger, someone who killed a guy she met by accident at an airport, a guy who was a creep, a thief.

Before she had her face done, there were the soft jowls and the lines on her forehead. Afterwards, everything was smooth and she had loved her reflection. The pleasure she'd felt was gone now, dulled by the feeling she had done something wrong. Her face was on the web and in the papers and in the mirror.

She had been comfortable with herself before she did it. Knew who she was. Things stayed the same. There were no dead bodies, no cops or solitary nights in an apartment in New York that she could not escape.

If she could put the lines back on her face, she would do it. Would press the rewind button. Betsy imagined clawing off her face so when she got up in the morning and looked in the mirror, she would be her real self.

PART TWO

16

Witnesses came out of the woodwork after her picture turned up in the *Post*: two people remembered them on the street, her and Ketsen, a year earlier when she was actually in London; a woman said for sure the two of them were eating oysters and practically making out in a booth at Balthazar around the same time, or maybe after, maybe it was half a lobster, but definitely shellfish and definitely Balthazar.

Betsy knew that two witnesses had identified her to the cops, the dog walker in Ketsen's building and Meryl Briggs. Meryl who was in love with Ketsen and slept with him the night he died. No matter what she'd said in the kitchen in Hoboken, Meryl would never tell the cops she had been wrong about Betsy Thornhill.

Hard to put a lid on once the buzz began, not just in New York but in London: the *Daily Mail* got hold of the story, milked it big time; everyone in London knew, calls came non-stop: Vicky, Max, David, other friends, reporters. Tom called and wanted to help and she was tempted, but she said, I'm all right for now. Vic's cousin, a criminal lawyer, gave advice that Vic relayed twice a day.

'Don't let them put you in an ID parade,' Vic yelled into the phone Thursday. 'I've got hold of Hilary Hard who is the absolutely best criminal lawyer in London and says not to let them. A line-up, the cops call it there.'

Betsy looked at the calendar. Thursday. It was a week since she'd arrived in New York. A week. A lifetime.

'Be confident,' Vicky said on the phone. 'Aggressive if you have to. You didn't do anything. Right? You hear me?'

'Yes, Vic. Sure.' But Betsy wasn't listening. She was halfway out the door.

* * *

Words spilled out her mouth as soon as she saw Mark Carey.

'I know who did it.'

He was coming out of his house in a battered camel-hair coat with the collar turned up; in spite of the frigid weather, he was hatless.

'Hello, Betsy,' he said. 'How are you?'

Mark closed his front door, stood back from it, looked up, waved at someone on the second floor she couldn't see.

'My associate is up there,' he said. 'Nice

young woman. I saw your picture in the *Post*. I was going to call you.'

'When?'

'When I had a moment free,' he said. 'But now you're here, which is much better.'

Impatient, she said, 'You told me to think and I did that, and I know who killed Ketsen.'

'Good.'

'I probably need help.'

'Then that's why you're here,' he said. 'Why don't we go for a walk?'

'It's freezing.' Betsy stuffed her hands in her pockets.

'It's nice. It feels like winter ought to feel.'

'What's that got to do with who killed Bobby Ketsen?' Suddenly, irrationally, the thought of the woman lawyer in Mark's house made her petulant.

'Nothing,' Mark said. 'Nothing at all, it hasn't a thing to do with you, just me. Come on, let's walk. And we'll talk about you.'

'I don't feel much like walking.'

'Don't sulk.' He put his arm lightly over her shoulders. 'Come on. Talk to me. Who do you think killed Ketsen?'

'His secretary. Meryl Briggs.'

'What makes you think that?' He let go of her shoulders and got a pack of cigarettes out of his coat pocket.

'I went to see her last night,' Betsy said. 'I know I wasn't supposed to, but I couldn't sit still, you see that?'

'I see.'

'He humiliated her.'

'How's that?'

'She's a black woman, young, and he took a picture of her in a white face. He made her look white.'

'Do you think she could disguise herself as a white woman and then someone else would get picked up. You, for instance.'

'She's twenty-five years old.'

'You could pass. If she passed for white, you could pass for twenty-five. You could both pass.' He laughed, said, 'Bad choice of words. I'm an ass sometimes. She saw you with Ketsen the day you came in from the airport and could describe you to the police — it was a perfect alibi, is that it?'

'Yes. She told Ketsen's neighbor. He backed her up.'

'The newspaper runs the pictures of you and she hits pay dirt. Interesting. Neat.'

'Don't patronize me.'

'Tell me your theory.'

'Ketsen's apartment wasn't broken into, right?' Betsy said. 'It had to be somebody who had keys. You're with me?'

'Completely.'

'Someone who hated him. She had a motive.'

'What did you say her name was?' Mark asked.

'Meryl Briggs.'

'What motive?'

'She was in love with him and he messed her around,' Betsy said.

Mark cocked his head attentively, said, 'Why do you imagine that Meryl told you all that?'

'She needed a friend.'

'You made yourself her friend. Very good. I'm impressed.' Mark's voice was not sarcastic; he tossed his unsmoked cigarette into the gutter and pushed his hair back from his face. 'Making friends, it's one of your talents?'

'I thought it was yours,' she said.

They walked, not touching, along McDougall Street. In front of Villa Mosconi, again near the law school, men stopped and greeted Carey; he talked to them patiently about cases; the contact lit him up.

A whiff of stale Marinara sauce came from the door of one of the Italian restaurants. Spaghetti sauce, pot, dirty feet, sandal leather, vegetarian cheese from a sandwich you carried in your woolly Peruvian bag, girlish sweat, unshaved armpits. Smells that instantly conjured up the early seventies for her. Betsy could get the smells back but not the girl.

The city had seemed glamorous, then, seedy, alluring, anonymous, a big city alive with ambition, thrilling and lonely, where you could slip through the cracks and lose yourself. Now it felt claustrophobic, a hurt, watchful, small town that penned you in. Everywhere she walked with Mark through the Village, people on the street seemed to stare at her.

'Mark?'

'What's that?'

'I'm scared. I'm not sure I can even remember things right anymore.'

'What about the cops?' he asked. 'Any pressure yet?'

'I don't know. I let them do my fingerprints. Was that stupid?'

'Let's go to the park,' he said.

'What for?'

'I like the park.'

* * *

There was a shrine at the bottom of the metal fence around the Washington Square Arch were candles in glass jars and wilted flowers in cellophane cones and pictures of a group of firemen and a flyer with a face on it. Missing person. Still missing.

As if remembering a speech, Mark said, 'The city convalescent. A patient anaesthetized. You ever read T. S. Eliot?'

'Please. Listen to me.'

Mark looked around him and pointed at the fountain in the middle of the park and they sat on the rim and watched a gang of school kids throw a baseball and some elderly black guys head for the chess tables and a girl with a stud in her tongue play the guitar. 'All my troubles, Lord, soon be over,' she warbled.

'We can talk now,' Mark said.

'Why?'

'It's better to talk out in the open,' he said. 'I like the park.'

'Am I in that much trouble?'

'Maybe,' he said.

She was going nuts. There was nothing anyone could do for her. She was a sitting duck on the edge of the dry fountain in Washington Square Park, everyone circling around: Vicky and her cousin giving advice long distance, Marie Tusi and the food, the detective she cooked eggs for. There was the fact that she was falling in love with Mark Carey. Not in love — infatuated. Someone to lean on was all, she told herself. Who needs an old man? A vain guy? Who needs this?

This was unfamiliar territory for her. There had been Joe, of course, Franny's father, and other boys. A few men in London she almost married, but not quite. People she liked. People she slept with. Tom. She had been in love twice, she thought, but never dependent. She'd never felt she wanted someone to take care of her, and she actually shook herself, like a dog drying off, unaware she was doing it.

'Are you all right?' he asked.

'I'm fine,' she said.

'Your theory about this Briggs woman is a little pat for my taste.'

'She slept with him.'

'You said, but so what? Did you believe her?'

'Why wouldn't I?'

'Did you stop to wonder what her game was or why this woman who could easily be a suspect herself would talk to you? Anything else you forgot to tell me about her?'

'I told you, she needed a friend.'

'Think about that, Betsy. I mean, so what? What else?' His face was curious. He waited attentively for her answer. He took note of what she said. He paid attention.

'She gave me a bag of muffins.'

He laughed briefly.

'I had another talk with Detective Dolce, off the record, and he needs this case, he wants it, so does his partner who is a total shit and doesn't care who goes down so long as he gets someone,' Mark said. 'It was Meryl Briggs who was the witness, by the way.'

'He told you?'

'It doesn't matter who told me,' Mark said. 'We can play Dolce, though. He likes you more than he should — you know that, don't you? He wants the case and he wants you and I could sort this out while he fights with himself.'

'How?'

'Let's start with your picture. How did the papers get hold of it?'

She told him about Newman and the website with her photograph.

'Son of a bitch,' he said. 'I assume you never gave him permission to post your pictures like that.'

Betsy was silent.

'You don't know, do you? Then when we're done here, we'll take him to the cleaners, if you want. How's that?'

'I'd like to wipe the floor with him and ruin Newman's miserable business.'

From the fountain where she sat next to Mark, she watched the kids playing ball. A boy in a black sweatshirt dropped it and it rolled towards Mark who leaned down and picked it up and tossed it back gracefully like a man whose muscles still remember the game he once played.

'You take a ride, the guy gets dead, your name is on his desk, the cops show up,' Mark said.

'Yes.'

'Someone hammered the victim and then cut him with a knife.'

She nodded.

'Japanese, with a long thin blade, the kind you use for sashimi. I know, it's ridiculous, but it was, and an old-fashioned one, World War Two vintage. The hammer looks as if it had a triangular head of some kind.'

'How do you know?' she said.

He smiled. 'There are always people who can get information if you share with them. There were threatening messages on Ketsen's answering machine.'

'What kind of threat?'

'Stop taking pictures or we'll come after you.'

'It wasn't me. You believe that. Don't you?'

'There's no match on the voice yet,' he said.

He looked at his watch. 'I have to go. Do you want me as your attorney officially? It's your call.'

It would make Frank Dolce angry. Put a wall up between her and Frank, make her look guilty. She liked Frank. The rough face, the heavy body, the sappy desire to please, his nervous come-ons, the way he ate the food she fixed for him.

Climbing down off the fountain, Mark held out his hand. She felt like one of his causes.

He said, 'Do you want me, then?'

* * *

They walked out of the park and Mark hailed a cab and she got in. They sat behind the plastic barricade that was riddled with fossilized lumps of chewing gum.

He didn't believe her about Meryl Briggs. He didn't believe her about anything. It was why Mark was interested: he liked hard cases. It got him air time.

'You're shivering.' He held out an arm. 'Come here.'

'Don't.'

'I'm sorry. Why not have me?'

'What do you mean?' she said.

'To help you. Let me get on this officially and sort this out for you. I can do that.'

'You're too expensive,' she said.

'Not for friends. I can be a very cheap date. I can be practically free. You think Detective

Frank Dolce will feel less inclined to help you if I'm on board and you'll look guilty?'

'Yes.'

'Are you guilty?' he said. 'Don't answer.'

'Don't be ridiculous.' She felt her old self re-inhabit her body. 'This is nuts.'

'Don't count on Dolce because he likes you, though I can understand his point of view.'

'Don't flirt with me.'

'Why not? I like you.'

'You like everyone.'

* * *

The cab pulled up at a storefront on Seventh Avenue near 14th Street. Mark paid and climbed out; she followed.

Bel's clinic. There was a plain sign on the front door, a metal gate over the window, a buzzer. Inside, Bel sat at the far end of the room, talking to a skinny black kid, who, when he saw them, fled, banging into Betsy as he hurried out.

Her black medical bag on the table in front of her, Bel took off the white coat she wore, slumped in her chair, hands in her lap, legs at awkward angles. She looked tired. Old.

'How are you, dear one?' Mark reached down to hug her.

Envious, Betsy watched them chuckle over some shared joke. He looked at his watch, gestured at Betsy who stood near the door and said to Bel, 'I brought Betsy here because I think she needs looking after, you know. Take care of her. You have the papers for me?'

From her desk drawer, Bel pulled a file in a blue cover and gave it to Mark. 'Don't worry,' he said. 'We'll sue the ass off the city for what they did to those kids when the cops pulled them in.'

'Thank you,' Bel said. 'By the time I saw them, they were black and blue and bleeding.'

'I'll be in touch,' Mark said and nodded towards Betsy. 'Don't let her out of the house too much.'

Before he left, he got hold of her arm and whispered into her ear so she could feel his breath on her skin.

'Do me a favor, Betsy,' he said. 'Don't sleep with Detective Dolce.'

'Fuck you,' she said under her breath and turned away from him.

'I ought to get home,' Betsy said to Bel after Mark left.

'Sit down, cara. Take your jacket off. Your mother called.'

'Oh, God. I tried her three times,' Betsy said. 'I couldn't get through. I figured she was on some church retreat.'

Bel pointed to a copy of the *New York Post* she took from her bag. 'Why didn't you tell me? This is why the cops came to see you?'

'Yes,' Betsy said. 'What did my mother say?'

'Out of left field, the saintly Eva who doesn't talk to me from one bloody year to the next, is on the phone telling me God judges by your actions, tell Mary Elizabeth to get her ass to church. She didn't quite put it that way. She sounds old. Blind as a bat, on her knees in that church twice a day, what's she always praying for?'

'My soul,' Betsy said.

'Call her.'

'She saw the newspaper?'

'She saw the paper,' Bel said. 'Her neighbor next door Mrs Press saw the story, the priest saw the story, everyone on Long Island saw it. *Newsday* ran the picture, a local TV reporter was out at Eva's house.'

'I'll call.' Betsy got up.

Bel said, 'Can you pull the blinds for me? I'm weary tonight.' She stretched out her feet. 'My dogs are killing me. I wonder why we used to call them dogs.'

'Come home with me,' Betsy said.

'Let's just sit for a minute.'

Betsy went to the door, turned the locks.

The street outside was crowded, people passed, she watched from behind the door. She pulled down the shade and went back to Bel.

'You never read the *Post*,' Betsy said. 'Who told you?'

Marie Tusi had been at Bel's with the paper first thing that morning it came out, just showed up with a pot of fresh coffee and two croissants as an offering and stood, unmoving, outside Bel's, the *New York Post* under her arm, smoking, wheezing, in tears.

She was upset for Betsy, Marie told Bel. She howled at the injustice, but Bel kept her standing in the doorway, refused to gossip. Finally, Marie backed off and clattered down the stairs, the bag of food still in her hand.

'Don't let her get in your business,' Bel said. 'She wants you to use her cousin who's a lawyer. He also works for Mafia creeps. You need a lawyer, you use Mark.'

'I don't think Mark Carey can be bothered with me.' Betsy laughed briefly. 'I'm a mess.'

'You like him that much? Kiddo, I saw your face when he was here. Give me one of those smokes,' she said.

Betsy gave her the pack. 'Is he a nice man, Bel?'

'Don't get involved, cara. Nice is not

necessarily the word I'd use. Sit down. You make me nervous getting up and down like a yo-yo. Please.'

'I'm not getting involved,' Betsy said. 'He's married, anyway.'

'That never stopped Mark. I've known him since the Sixties, he was always on the front line. He liked me in the old days because I was a real card-carrying hellraiser; I had even been in the Party. I knew everyone. God, all those meetings and fund-raisers and demonstrations. I always said we have to do the business, it's a bore, but good will come of it. We fought. Segregation. Vietnam, sexism, homophobia, corporate sellouts, much good that did, look at us now, the economy fucked, the city broken, a President who says 'nuk-u-lar'. Mark was always there. Still is. He clawed me out of plenty of trouble. He has that marvelous house on St Luke's Place, his parents' place that he inherited. We had some good parties.'

'What's the wife like?' Betsy said.

'Boring,' Bel said. 'Beautiful. No politics, no real interests, except her own work, and very very vain.'

'What else?'

'Voracious sexually, I would have said. She always looked like she wanted to fuck every man in the room. Women, too. I only met her a couple times. Everybody had a thing for Mark Carey. He was the best-looking man in New York, he loved everyone, especially if they needed him. He'll win your case if you need him, but you won't get anything else from him. Betsy? You listening to me?'

'Yes.'

'Just don't go to the cops and don't listen to Marie Tusi,' Bel said. 'So you had a nice boyfriend in London and you dumped him? You need someone, darling.'

'What is this little old Jewish lady bullshit?'

'It's my cover, baby,' Bel said. 'You have to negotiate with all the assholes in this city, you want to be a little old Jewish lady. I kvetch and beg and they give me money to keep this place open. The kids I see down here got AIDS and other stuff and no one wants to talk to them or get them the meds they need. I tell the city if they shut me down, I'll go to the press. I tell everyone about it. It gives me social control.'

'You're never alone in New York, are you?'

'Of course not. We all got our networks, I always tell Sissy who wants me to live in a home, assisted living they call it, I tell her fuck off, don't I? She says, what happens if you get sick, or you need something, and I say, in New York, you're never alone. Not exactly fuck off because Sissy would faint. I have to go stay with her again. Give me a kiss.'

Betsy kissed Bel's cheek and the skin felt powdery and dry and ancient.

Bel pushed the newspaper towards her. 'You want to talk about this thing?'

'Not now. Thanks.'

She helped Bel tidy up the clinic. She could feel Bel aging; she could see it in the way she walked and how, at the end of a day, she sagged when she sat down. One of these days, Bel would die and it would be unbearable.

'Cheer up,' Bel said. 'Let's get a drink at that Café Loop and then we'll go home.'

'You were friends with my father, right? I wish I could remember more about him.'

'He was funny and silly and, even when he was a cop, he was a righteous man. He was good to everyone, especially his sister. Everyone said, 'Pauline's older brother is a lovely guy.' '

Bel packed her black bag, the two of them went out, Betsy locked up for her.

'Can I ask you something?' she said.

'Anything.'

'Did you ever sleep with my father?'

'Oh, baby, no, of course not. Is that what you thought?' Bel laughed and pulled her gray coat tight around her, buttoned it to the collar, took Betsy's arm, started across Seventh Avenue.

'It was only ever women for me,' Bel said. 'I thought you knew that. I only ever liked women.'

A car screeched to a halt as Bel made her stately way across the street without looking at the light.

Betsy clutched her arm. 'You and Pauline?'

'She was the love of my life,' Bel said. 'I was sure you of all people knew. But you never did care much for knowing other people's secrets, did you? You never liked looking too close at things. Come on, I could use that drink.'

17

Desperate, she went to church, carrying a bag of mozzarella. She had left Bel at her apartment. Called her mother, had a short, tense conversation, said she'd be out to see her soon, went out to get film, stopped at Joe's Dairy on Sullivan Street for smoked mozzarella.

At Joe's, the woman behind the counter who bagged the cheese and took Betsy's money worked alongside her daughter who wrapped up Provolone, chatting to her mother companionably.

The brown paper bag in her hand, Betsy started across to Pino, the butcher, noticed St Anthony's was next door and climbed the steps to the ugly, solid old church with the white plaster Madonna covered in soot out in the yard that faced Houston Street.

Except as a tourist, and then not if she could help it, it was decades since she'd been in a church. Betsy sat in a pew in the back and avoided the priest who glanced at her. All she could think to pray for was bad weather. She couldn't trust God on the big stuff; maybe he could manage a blizzard. A big storm would put other stories on the back page. There would be less space for a downtown murder if it snowed hard. In the back of St Anthony's, in the gloom, smelling the leatherette covers on the prayer books and the cheese in the bag on her lap, she begged God to let it snow.

It didn't snow. It stayed cold and bright and the sun shone relentlessly as she walked aimlessly to Broadway. People were out shopping after work or going home or buying bags of sugar-coated nuts that perfumed the air.

Betsy moved through the jammed streets and pulled her knit cap on and over her ears. She had the feeling again that everywhere she went people saw her. They stared at her from under wool hats, inside hoods on their down coats, behind sunglasses. She seemed to recognize some of them: people she had once known or thought she knew, faces that popped from the crowd. My God, it's Kitty Kazaras.

Kitty was idling in front of a shoe store on the corner of Spring and Broadway, wearing the leather mini-skirt she always wore, a silver down jacket and calf-high boots. Big ass, small waist, dark eyes and hair. Kitty lingered by the store window, smiling dreamily, always a hick kid in the big city.

For a while they had shared the apartment on Cornelia Street. Kitty's family was Greek and when she married — an Italian boy she met on vacation — Betsy was a bridesmaid; she wore a pink mini-dress. Kitty?

'Kitty?'

Her contemplation broken, the girl looked at Betsy, put on sunglasses and jogged away down Spring Street towards the subway.

Betsy held back from crying in frustration and wanted to run after the girl and say, Hey, Kitty, it's me. Nothing's changed. But the girl was twenty and, like her, Kitty was a middle-aged woman. Betsy was losing her sense of age and place; emotional cataracts seemed to have blurred her feelings for time and place. She was coming unglued.

A few minutes later, a small woman in a large fur accosted her outside Dean & DeLuca and Betsy drew a blank until she heard the voice, husky, but relentless.

'I don't believe it. Finally! I've been desperate to find you. Desperate. I've called everyone. It's Delia. Delia Vaio. Betsy, for heaven's sake, it's me, Dee.'

Betsy pulled back. It was another mistake. Turning to go, she felt the woman grip her arm and looked down into the familiar face. A ferret, she thought. No, a frog. Dee always looked like a frog in a wig.

In the crowded street, Dee locked her arms briefly around Betsy, stood back, looked up; Dee was very short.

'Nice work,' she said. 'The face.'

She looked back at Dee: big round eyes, large lids, plump mouth, streaky blonde hair.

Betsy said, 'You haven't changed.'

'I saw you in the *Post* and I thought, God, it looks like a younger Betsy Thornhill, and it was you. Come on, I've got a car and I want to hear the whole thing, it sounds like a nightmare.' Dee was breathless.

Like a mink-covered tugboat, she guided Betsy towards the curb where a driver lounged next to a black Lincoln.

'I can't,' Betsy said. 'I'm busy.'

'Don't be silly, I want to talk and I can't spend my whole life tracking you down and I have to be at the theater early. Come on, get in.'

In college, Dee had been small, dumpy, secretly driven. She talked with a Jersey accent and around Barnard there were rumors her father was an upper-level Mafia guy, though Betsy didn't believe it.

Dee's ambitions were never girlish. She set out to make a mark, first with a wacko brand of feminism. If she ever had a daughter, Dee proclaimed junior year, she would want to have her child's breasts removed so she wouldn't suffer the indignity of being a female. Senior year, Dee discovered acting. She had some talent and by the time they graduated, she had somehow transformed herself into a small but glamorous woman who already knew important theater people. She never had the daughter, but she became a star, worked in the theater in New York, got some big movies later on. Once in a while Betsy saw pictures of Delia in magazines.

In the car, Dee reclined against the leather seat, studying Betsy's face. Betsy wanted out. Dee, like all bullies, knew how to push until you were too tired to resist and you caved in and did what she wanted. As far as Dee was concerned, as a potential suspect in a murder case, Betsy had a name. Her picture in the papers. A celebrity. Delia Vaio was interested; she could retail the friendship with Betsy to her friends.

The car pulled up at a theater off Sheridan Square, Dee got out, shepherded Betsy to the stage door.

'I'm going to take off, Dee,' Betsy said. 'Nice seeing you.'

'Don't you dare. We can talk in my dressing room. I don't need much time to get ready, it's just a benefit thing, a reading.'

'What for?'

'For 9/11, for the firemen. Lovely those

firemen, real heroes — and handsome. I have a friend that calls it firemen chic.' Dee removed her fur coat with a brisk gesture. 'You'll meet some of them later.'

Under the fur coat, Dee wore tight Prada pants, a cropped sweater, a thick gold chain around her neck. She looked at Betsy, saw the faded jeans she'd been wearing three days running, raised her eyebrows.

In the shabby basement dressing room with bars on the window, Dee rummaged for wine in a fridge; perched on the edge of a day-bed, Betsy sat on a chair.

Dee held up a bottle of white wine. 'You want some?'

'Sure,' Betsy said.

'What's that thing you've been clutching like the Holy Grail?'

Betsy looked at the brown paper bag. 'Mozzarella.'

The lights over her dressing table made Dee look pink and peeled as a shrimp; her skin was shiny. She poured the wine into a couple of glasses.

'You could do with some work on your ears,' Dee said, handing Betsy a glass.

'My ears?'

'We've always known your ears grow when you get older, but it turns out it's not your ears but your earlobes. And they've got a brilliant new procedure. No scars.'

'I think I've had enough done.'

'It's never enough.' Dee's fervor was evangelical. 'Who did you?'

Betsy gulped some of the wine. 'Who did what, Dee?'

'You're not paying attention. You always did that, even in college, you just stopped listening because you were bored and you drifted away.'

'I'm not bored.'

'Then who did your face? I don't know why some women are so furtive about it.'

'Russell Newman,' Betsy said.

Dee nodded, satisfied. 'I thought so. Only two or three people in London could do that quality of work. Newman's ace, if you ask me. You know what they say about Russell, the devil's in the detail, he's so incredible. I once did some Botox with him when I was working in London and he was awesome. I was doing that play at the Aldwych, you remember? No, you wouldn't, you didn't come, did you? I tried to get in touch and you never showed. You know what else they say?' She leaned forward, a conspirator.

'What do they say, Dee?' Betsy looked at the door.

Dee giggled. 'They say he's done a couple of terrorists that needed new faces, he did it to prove he could, he has such a humongous ego. Think of the skill.'

'It's probably bullshit,' Betsy said.

'Good story, though. Tell me all about the murder.'

'I can't talk about it.'

'Come on,' Dee said. 'I could do something marvelous with a story like that. Why don't you sell it to me, you know, like for money?'

'Sell you what?'

'Your story,' Dee said. 'We're the same age, we've both had our faces done, mine, of course, for professional reasons. There's not a single actress out there or anyone on TV who hasn't had work, though everyone lies like crazy or they say they're ambivalent or guilty or whatever, I don't know why. I never lied. I plan to look good until they stick me in a box.'

'You've got a new religion, Dee. They should pay you.'

'They do and why the fuck not? I write a column, I'm syndicated.'

Betsy finished her drink and said, 'Good for you. I really have to go.'

Oblivious to the sarcasm, Dee kept talking.

'I mean, everyone wants it,' she said. 'It's like sex. Tell me you don't feel a lot hornier since you got the work done. It makes you feel alive. Do you know practically the only growth business in the whole city is cosmetic surgery? People think, shit, if I'm going to die, I'm going out looking good.'

'I believe you.'

'People have been doing it for a hundred years. If you don't do your face, the photographers do it with digital. Even the eighteen-year-old babes you see in magazines get something fixed.'

'Fine.'

'How come you're so fucking furious?' Dee asked. 'I don't mean the people who are addicted to plastic surgery. I read somewhere someone wanted to look like Johnny Carson and kept having work done; I even know at least a few women who tried to look like me.' She snorted with laughter. 'Come on. I'll get you good money. We'll make a movie. Get you more than the goddamn stock market these days.'

Betsy got up and went towards the door. 'Nice to see you, it was great and all.'

'I want you to stay. There's people coming for a drink. I won't talk about your case, OK? You ever hear from Kitty Kazaras? Any of the others? Weren't we earnest little girls, all that politics and poetry and shit.'

'I guess,' Betsy said.

'I can see you're downed by all this. Stick with me, we'll have some fun. I'm going to get this new thing that makes your lips really plump up, better than collagen. I'll treat you.'

'No thanks.'

'What? You're superstitious? Yeah, so was I at first and you should have heard my mother. I told her it's a sin to go around with a neck like a chicken. Everyone judges you by how good you look. They don't mean good either. They mean young.'

Betsy laughed. 'What did your mother say?'

'I bribed her. I gave her money for new tits. There's the phone.'

Was she surprised when Mark Carey came through the door to Dee's dressing room?

Other people had arrived, two firemen and an actor in a corduroy suit, then Mark. He picked Dee up off the floor and kissed her on the mouth.

He said, 'I'm just passing, Dee. I just came to wish you well.'

He shook hands with the firemen. More people filtered into the small room. Mark gestured to Betsy and cornered her against the barred window.

'I'm glad I ran into you,' he said. 'I have to go out of town.'

'I see. Well, bon voyage.'

'Do you want to stay or should we get out of here and I can take you home. I have a car.'

'Let's go home,' she said and while Delia was busy with her guests, they slipped out of the dressing room and through the underground hall-way that smelled of damp and up to the street.

'Can I come up for a moment?' Mark said when they got to her building.

A maroon car turned the corner and pulled up on the opposite side of the street, far enough down the block so she couldn't see who was in it. Betsy wondered if it was Frank Dolce or his partner.

'Come on.' She pulled at Mark's hand and they went in and up the stairs to her apartment where she shut the door, left the light off and went to the window.

All she saw was Mark's car, the engine idling, the driver hanging out of the window, smoking.

'I would never have put you and Dee together,' Mark said. 'I wanted to see you before I left. Bel's worried about you.'

'I'm fine.'

'You should know something,' he said.

'What?'

'I don't think Meryl Briggs killed Ketsen,' he told her. 'There's evidence he was alive after she left.'

She felt numb. 'What do I do?'

'Nothing. Nothing's going to happen to

you, either,' he said. 'I won't let it.'

He kept his coat on. She left the light off. It was involuntary what she felt; idiotic, but involuntary. She disliked his voice, the arrogance, the camel-hair coat, but in the dark living room, she wanted him to kiss her. She wanted to say: stay with me. In the half shadow, she could see his face; she saw he knew how she felt.

The buzzer sounded.

'Company?' Mark said.

'Probably the wrong apartment,' she said. 'Leave it. When will you be back?'

'Sunday,' he said and glanced towards the door. 'Someone's pretty insistent, you sure you don't want to answer?'

'No,' she said, not wanting any interruption. 'I'll call you Sunday.'

'I'll call you before that. Betsy?'

'Yeah?'

'You'll be fine,' Mark said and flipped his hair over his collar. 'I'm always at the end of the phone. And Bel knows how to find me. It will be all right.'

'Not for me.'

'It will. Do you want to give me a quick drink before I go?'

Still in his coat, he sat on the sofa. She got the vodka and poured it into two glasses and they sat, not talking. Mark finished his drink and put the glass on the table and got up. The buzzer rang twice more.

'I must go,' he said and she opened the door for him and listened to him on the stairs. Before she could get to the window, she heard the car rev and pull away.

Betsy tried to photograph the mozzarella and she couldn't concentrate, put her camera down on the kitchen window sill, noticed the plastic bag Meryl Briggs had given her. It was a dark blue plastic Gap bag with a cotton drawstring. She pulled it open. Began unpacking muffins.

The muffins were big and stuffed with berries, some of them crumbled and came apart in her hands, stained them blue.

At the bottom of the bag was something heavy and Betsy turned it upside-down. A small bag landed hard on the linoleum floor; she squatted and picked it up. In it, wrapped in tin foil, was a set of keys.

The keys to Ketsen's place. The extra set of keys Meryl mentioned the night before at her place in Hoboken. No accident, not the way they were carefully tucked in with the muffins. If Meryl had believed Betsy enough to give her the keys, she was probably innocent. Unless . . . unless she intended that Betsy implicate herself, slide deeper in the shit she was already struggling with. She held the keys in one hand as if weighing them.

If Frank Dolce wouldn't let her into Ketsen's place, she'd use the keys. She sat up late and watched TV and went to sleep and slept badly because a call from London woke her at four in the morning. It was the *Daily Mail*. She slammed the phone down so hard the plastic mouthpiece chipped.

In bed, Betsy lay rigid, tense, sweating. The nightmares leaked into the morning, and she couldn't make out where she was. A slit of light came from around the shades, she realized it was New York, and listened for sounds from the building. Marie on the ground floor, Bel a flight up, the mother and daughter, away now, on three, then her. A building full of women, Betsy thought.

For the next hour or two, she lay in bed and leaned, half asleep, against the silence that was so thick it felt solid. It was Friday.

That morning, Betsy was aware, as she had been two days running, that a car was parked in front of her building. It was only in the mornings that she heard it. The previous morning and again now, around six, the engine turned over. She could hear someone connected to the car shout directions to the driver. In the silent dark morning, the distinctive voices reached her, no words, but voices. Cops. Watching her. Always there on the periphery of her life, two of them, maybe more.

Surveillance, they called it. She felt suspended in an emulsion of anxiety, as if the anxiety were plastic with stretchy sides she could punch and push at but never rip open. By the time she climbed out of bed, she was thinking again about Frank and how to make him let her into Ketsen's place. It would be legal if he opened the door; she wanted his OK.

I have to see it, she thought. I have to know. Her heart pounded. The keys were on the bedside table.

18

Frank tapped on the window of the coffee shop near his station house and mouthed her name.

'Betsy?'

She was already inside. Bent over the *Times*, a cup of coffee on the table in front of her, her hair in her eyes. Frank tapped on the window again and she turned her head and smiled and the blue eyes lit up. To Frank, she looked great. The smile made her beautiful and he smiled back and thought, Oh, God, I want this.

'Hi, Frank.' Betsy looked up as he entered, smoothed the collar of her white shirt, made room for him at the table. She had on a short black skirt and black boots.

'Hey.' He sat down opposite her. 'You said you needed to see me.'

'This is as straight as I know how to ask — I have to get into Ketsen's place.'

'It's a sealed crime scene, Betsy, leave it be.'

He waved at the waitress behind the counter and looked at the pyramid of cereal boxes.

'You said you'd help me.'

'If I let you in, I wouldn't be helping you,' Frank said. 'I'd put you in real jeopardy.'

'OK,' she replied.

She turned her head towards the window. Concentrated on the scratched glass and the sidewalk beyond, where a girl stood with a dog the size of a rat at the end of a yellow leash.

'Don't do like that,' Frank said.

'Like what?'

'Turn your head away like that.'

'You should go back to your wife, Frank, or get a girlfriend. Maybe you have one already.' She thought about the smell of perfume on his jacket the first time he came to Cornelia Street.

He looked hurt; he drank some coffee.

She leaned on her arms, face close to his.

'What would it take for you to let me in?' she asked and felt for Ketsen's keys in her pocket, hard and metallic under her fingers.

He flushed. 'What do you mean, what would it take?'

'You know what I mean.'

'Let's get out of here and I'll buy you an early lunch.'

'I don't want lunch,' she said.

'I can't let you in there.'

Betsy hesitated and put her hand out and

tugged his sleeve. You could come home with me afterwards, Frank, spend some time together, she wanted to say and couldn't.

He took a pack of cigarettes out of his pocket and toyed with the cellophane, folding it, balling it up, smoothing it out. The crackling noise irritated her.

'I wish we could get this over with,' she said. 'I wish . . . never mind, it doesn't matter, does it? Nothing will make any difference.' She looked at the counter. 'Could I get some juice or something? I'm thirsty.'

There were a couple of guys at the counter, drinking coffee, but no one looked up when Frank ordered orange juice and brought it back to the table. Betsy drank it in two gulps.

'You really want to get all this shit over with?' he said.

'Yes.'

'There is something that could help a lot. I don't know, just an idea.'

'Tell me.'

'We could put you in a line-up,' Frank said. 'You know and I know you didn't do anything, you weren't at Ketsen's except that Thursday afternoon when you got in from the airport. It's all some kind of mistake. Why not let us bring in the witnesses and you come on by and we get this thing done.' He touched her hand. 'Then maybe we could go to dinner and all. Maybe I could even let you get a look at Ketsen's place.'

Don't do an ID parade, Vicky had yelled down the phone, but she was three thousand miles away in a world that had ceased to exist for Betsy.

'Can I think about that?'

'No pressure.'

'I'm not hiding anything. I was a jerk trying to find out what went on by myself, I admit that. I even went to see Ketsen's secretary. I'm telling you because I want you to trust me.'

'Thank you.'

She said, 'What did you think of the secretary? Meryl Briggs?'

'I don't know,' Frank said. 'I didn't talk to her much. Jimmy interviewed her. She seemed OK. Jimmy didn't think she was involved.'

'I'm not going to ask you again if she was the witness.'

'Thanks. For not asking.'

'Did you know about her and Ketsen?'

'That she slept with Ketsen before he died? Yeah, we knew,' Frank said. 'There was evidence on him that he'd had sex not long before he died and she told us it was her.'

It flattened her, the discovery that he knew the one thing that had convinced her

Meryl Briggs was guilty.

'Why would she tell you that?' Betsy asked him.

'Because she didn't do it? Because she knew he was alive when she left him and she talked to him on the phone from the car as she was going home. She knew there'd be phone records.'

'I see.'

'So it doesn't add up, even if she slept with him,' Frank said. 'Tell you the truth, I'm sort of nowhere on this. I hope you're not going to let that asshole, Mark Carey, take your case. He came by to see me and I thought he was a real smooth-ass operator. You're a really nice woman and I don't think you need to be in bed with a guy like Carey, so to speak. That's my opinion. He's very slick.' He hesitated. 'Was he with you last night?'

'What do you mean?'

'I buzzed you,' Frank said. 'You didn't answer and I had this idea he was there.'

'You were spying on me?'

'I wanted to see if you were OK, I saw the limo, I asked the driver who it was, he told me Carey went upstairs with you,' Frank said. 'It's none of my business.'

'You really think if I did the line-up thing it would really help you out?'

He grinned. 'Be great on your résumé.'

'You'd forgive me?'

'What for?'

'Tuesday night.'

'I already forgave you,' he said.

'When could you arrange it?' Betsy said. 'I'd like to get it over with.'

'Later today probably, if you want. Then I think you'd be out of the woods.'

'I hate the countryside,' she said. 'So I'd like that.'

'What?'

'Being out of the woods.'

* * *

The smell was cigarette butts and dried sweat and fake Chanel you could buy on Canal Street, and when she saw the other women in the line-up, Betsy knew it was bad and wanted to run away. Five, counting her, and the others all resembling hookers. Maybe it was tough getting the others on short notice, like a last-minute dinner party where you had to take what you could get.

The girl next to her had dyed black hair that looked like an animal had dropped on her head. Her blue eyes were dead like a junkie's. A cop in uniform passed around striped knitted caps.

With the others, Betsy shuffled to the

middle of the narrow room and knew she was screwed. Her picture was in the papers again that morning.

There had been an item on local TV the night before. She was identified as a successful photographer who lived in London, a middle-class white woman with a book to her credit, so she was screwed. People used what they knew: they saw the woman who fitted the description that was already in the papers.

Don't do a line-up, Vicky had said, but Frank wanted it and told her it would fix things. One of the women in the line-up cracked gum with a pop like a pistol. Betsy stared straight ahead.

Was Meryl Briggs on the other side of the one-way glass? Her, she'd say, pointing at Betsy. It was her. She would identify Betsy and be off the hook herself. Meryl gave her the keys so she'd dig herself in deeper.

The system works, Betsy said to herself. But the voice in her head was feeble and unreliable. She was a middle-aged photographer with the wrong face and she was going to jail and her hands were cold as a corpse. At her father's wake, she had reached in the coffin and touched his hand; she remembered the feel of the skin.

The voice — she thought it was Jimmy's

— came over the PA system. Three times, the voice ordered her forward. Let me out, Betsy thought. *Let me out of here!*

⋆ ⋆ ⋆

In a room at the police station where he let her sit on a hard chair and drink a cup of coffee after the line-up, Frank looked mournful.

'I'm really sorry,' he said.

'Sorry why?'

'It was inconclusive. No one seemed sure. It didn't work like I hoped, it doesn't rule anything out.'

She stayed quiet.

'Do you want a lawyer?' Frank said.

'Was one of the witnesses Meryl Briggs?'

The door opened and Jimmy Grant came in and sat on the table and leaned down so his face was close to hers and she could smell his breath and see the grease on his hair.

'Listen, Ms Thornhill, I know you did it, you know you did, too, so why not help us out? Help yourself out. Tell us what really happened. Maybe Ketsen roughed you up, something like that? You came back at him? We could make that stick easy.'

'I told you. I told Frank.'

Jimmy looked at her with contempt, then

turned and went out of the room.

Frank's cheek twitched uncontrollably and he excused himself and left her sitting in the empty room with the empty coffee carton. She wondered if Frank forgot to close the door by mistake or on purpose.

* * *

Jimmy Grant had not always hated his life. Growing up in the Bronx with his mother around to tell him how handsome he was, even if he knew otherwise, and the guys on the street to hang with, it was OK.

When the fireman thing didn't work out because he couldn't do the physical, he slid into the police academy in a year they were desperate for recruits, squeaked by and ended up a detective. He wasn't stupid. He was pretty cunning. He got to know the right people, even if they put him with a dick like Frank Dolce for a partner.

Frank was an asshole, if you asked Jimmy. He was cautious about legal shit and now he was hung up on this Thornhill woman. Jimmy knew they could make a good case for her slashing the Ketsen guy. It was a female crime, the drunk victim, the little hammer, the thin foreign knife. He told Frank this.

'She's not lying,' Frank said. 'OK, she's an

unreliable witness, she's in denial . . . But what's the motive? She didn't fucking do it and she sure as shit didn't plan it.'

'She's guilty as fuck, Frank, so just, please, do me a favor and put away the bullshit you heard from some shrink. You got the hots for her. You got hurt feelings because she took up with that lawyer fuck? She's still guilty, man.'

'There's no motive,' Frank said.

'Maybe she was one of the women Ketsen took pictures of. You saw the stuff. It was fucking weird, making them all look different from what they was.'

'There weren't any pictures of Thornhill. If she killed him, where's the pictures?'

'How the fuck do I know? Maybe he destroyed them. Maybe she got them and squirreled them away.'

'Which makes it everything's based on the computer image of Betsy from a couple of dubious witnesses, that's what you're saying?'

''Betsy'?' Jimmy sneered.

'I just wish to fuck the *Post* didn't run her pictures to start with.'

'Yeah? Me, I think it's great,' Jimmy said. 'More people going to show up and tell us she did it. Make our case for us.'

Frank shook Grant by his bony shoulder, squeezed hard, wanted to shake him until blood flowed from every lousy orifice.

'You're a stupid dumb fuck, you know that, Jimmy? You're a creep, sometimes. You gave her picture to the paper, didn't you?'

Jimmy scratched his eyebrow. 'Don't get mixed up with her.'

'I'm not mixed up with her,' Frank said.

'Then what?'

'I'm playing her.'

19

Playing her? Did she hear right? Imagine it? Frank playing her? Like a violin, wasn't that what they said in old movies? *Playing her?*

Somehow, not stopping to talk to Frank or Jimmy, she got out of the police station and ran home. Even inside the craziness and terror, she heard him say it or thought she did and wanted to laugh. Frank wasn't going to help. Around nine that same night, she took a shower, put on jeans, a sweater, her ski jacket, and jogged downstairs, where she knocked on Bel's door. She went in and had a glass of wine so Bel would remember seeing her that evening. Friday night? I was at Bel's, she'd say. My old friend, Dr Bel Plotkin..

For a while she sat on the window seat in Bel's apartment and looked at the souvenirs that were carefully arranged on the mantel-piece along with photographs and a bunch of daffodils in a Mason jar. Bel offered food, Betsy refused. They made conversation, Betsy was preoccupied, Bel told her to get some sleep. She kissed Bel and left.

On the ground floor, Marie's door opened, Marie stuck her head out, like a cuckoo responding to the time. Gray hair loose to her shoulders, she was in big jeans with an elastic waistband and a thick flannel shirt.

Poor Marie, Betsy thought. In spite of Bel's resentment, she liked Marie. Inside the sagging face, under the thinning bones, she could see remnants of a vital woman who had been a state swimming champ as a girl. Betsy leaned towards her and kissed her cheek and hugged the skinny frame.

'Yeah, hi, Marie,' she said.

Marie beamed at her, just lit up like a bulb coming on.

'Come in for a sec, girl, OK? Come on in,' she said. 'Dev's still at the church. Tell you the truth, I could use some company. It's kind of lonely, him being gone so much and just sitting in that chair when he's home. I saw this double Barcalounger,' she added. 'Two people can sit in it, so I was thinking, maybe we could sit together. What do you think? Let me show you the catalogue.'

'I can't right now. Thanks for the short-ribs, they were fabulous, and maybe later I can drop by, OK?'

'Please.'

She kissed Marie again, felt the crust of her dry skin, smelled the lilies of the valley perfume she wore. Betsy left. Started walking south.

The streets were a blur. She walked through the Friday night crowds on Bleecker and Seventh, past pork stores, gay bars, Thai restaurants, tattoo parlors, video shops, the Mexican restaurant where underage high school kids slurped giant Margaritas on the sidewalk and Samba Sushi where Brazilian music poured into the street. She walked without stopping.

In Ketsen's studio she would find evidence that it was Meryl Briggs who had killed him. It would finally end. She pushed everything else out of her mind, the photograph, the newspapers, just walked.

* * *

Across the street from Ketsen's building, she stopped. Through the windows of the Tribe, she saw the throng of bodies, the neon of the juke-box, the bronze glint of beer bottles, the box of colored lights that was the TV over the bar. She wondered if Caroline was there, drinking her pink cocktails, tossing her blonde hair, smiling through burst-cherry lips, pretending she was young.

For a few minutes, Betsy stood against the wall of the building opposite Ketsen's, her hand in her pocket, fingers closed over the keys. Except for the Tribe, the street was quiet. The wind was icy. Winter had, briefly, settled in.

Her arm ached as she reached behind her and pulled up the hood of her jacket. She looked for the cop she had seen before. No one there.

Keys in her hand now, she ran across the street, reached the door, tried it, jiggled the key, crouched to examine the lock.

The voice came from behind her.

'Hello, Betsy,' Frank said quietly.

She turned, saw his expression; he wasn't surprised, only sad.

'You didn't trust me,' she said. 'Did you?'

'I was right, wasn't I? Not to trust you?'

'I trusted you. I did the line-up. I told you what I knew,' she said.

'What are you doing here?' Frank's voice was wiped clean of emotion.

'I thought something in his place might make sense to me. I couldn't just sit still.' Her voice was flat. 'I wish this was over.'

'Betsy?'

'Yeah?'

Frank looked at her. 'I'll take you up.'

'Where's the cop who was on duty?' she said.

'I told him I'd take over for an hour.'

From his pocket he got keys and unlocked

the door, then held it for her.

'You must have known the tenants would change the locks,' he said. 'Didn't you?'

'I didn't think.'

* * *

She was in.

As soon as she entered the studio, in the time it took Frank to switch on the lights, she knew there was probably nothing for her. It hit her, standing in the dark, the only light coming from cars that passed in the street, that it had been a stupid obsession, an idea to keep her going, fuel the possibility she was in control. The cops would have been through the place a dozen times; whatever it was that would give her a glimpse into Ketsen's world would be unavailable. The dread she had been feeling in her sweaty nightmares that left her wide awake at five in the morning was all there was.

From the street came the noise of people going in and coming out of the Tribe. Across the hall was the thump of music, the bass turned up so loud you could feel the floor vibrate. Friday night. The compulsion to get here became meaningless. It was just a place. She was in, and so what?

Frank flipped a light switch. Betsy automatically looked for the photographs on the wall, the lobster and peapods and onion. The glass on the photograph of the onion was smashed. Across the surface of the beautiful picture someone had drawn a crude version of a woman's face with crayons. Her face. A message for her. Then her eyes focused; there was no face, no message, just angry random scrawls.

'Where do you want to start?' Frank said.

'I don't know.' She felt defeated.

'There's nothing here. Didn't you know we'd look at everything?'

'I don't know anything anymore.'

In Frank's face, she saw the disappointment: coming to Ketsen's made her seem guilty to him, and unlovable.

He said, 'Go on, look around.'

'Thank you.'

Frank lit a cigarette and watched as she made her way around the studio and told her not to touch certain surfaces. In the office, the darkroom, the living space, she peered into closets that held only Ketsen's clothes and the office drawers that contained neat rows of stationery and photographic supplies. The darkroom was pristine, empty.

Ten minutes went by, neither of them said a word. Unsure if he had intended to do it or it was impulse, Frank reached in his back pocket, took out a photograph, tossed it to her.

'Is that what you were looking for?' he said.

It was the photograph of herself at the Union Square Greenmarket. The picture Ketsen had taken. *Say cheese*.

She said, 'How long have you had this?'

'Ketsen had a storage locker in the basement of the building next door. We only found it yesterday,' he said. 'Is that why you were so anxious to get in here?'

'Partly. Yes. He took it before I knew what was happening,' she said. 'Do you believe me?'

'Sure,' Frank said. 'But you had to know we'd take anything that could be important.'

'How would I know?'

He rubbed his cigarette out on the sole of his shoe and put the butt in his jacket pocket.

'How would I know, Frank? From watching TV? From watching *Law & Order*? Tell me how I would know.'

He shrugged. 'I don't know. You wanted this. You got it.'

* * *

She rode back to Cornelia Street in his car. If he guessed how she got the keys, Frank didn't mention it. He drove without talking and let her out at the curb in front of her house. He should have quit the case in the beginning. It was compromised. He blew it the minute he met her.

'Goodnight, Frank,' she said finally as she climbed out of the car and looked up at the building and saw the light was still on in Bel's apartment.

Weary now, legs heavy, she trudged up the stairs and heard muffled music. 'Goodnight, Irene' came through Bel's door.

Pete Seeger sang through the door. Bel's old Weavers album. For a moment, out of breath, Betsy paused on the landing and listened.

What was it that made her stop? What made her knock on the door? Afterwards, she couldn't remember the exact moment when she knew there was something important on Bel's mantelpiece where there were daffodils in a glass jar.

'It's me, Bel. Betsy.'

The door opened. Her hair in a thin bun, the strands of white hair escaping, Bel was in an old blue wool bathrobe.

She was sorry, she said to Bel. Sorry to get her up, but Bel offered her a nightcap and turned down the volume on the stereo. Betsy refused and said she'd left her scarf at Bel's earlier. Bel proposed tea; Betsy said, yes, fine, thanks.

'I'll make tea with cherry jam like I used to,' Bel said.

The smooth wood mantelpiece was crammed with photographs, some neatly framed in silver, others propped up against a mahogany clock and the jar with the daffodils.

The photos had lured her back to Bel's: Bel, as a young woman in a summer dress with a bicycle in Red Square; Mark Carey in bell bottoms, hair to his shoulders; Bel and Pauline on vacation in Venice, standing in front of the Salute; her own father, young and grinning in his cop's uniform, but making a peace sign with his hand, Bel and Pauline on either side. There were pictures of her and her ma when she was little. Other photographs. Oh God, Betsy thought, staring at them.

Behind her, Betsy heard Bel in the kitchen. Quickly she reached up to the mantel, took three of the snapshots, slipped them in her jacket pocket.

She put her head through the kitchen door. 'Bel, I think I'll skip the tea. I'm desperate for some sleep.'

Bel looked out. 'Well, then, go on up, cara. You look bushed. Betsy?'

'Hmm?'

'Your scarf is around your neck.'

* * *

By watching TV, she forced herself to stay awake until two in the morning when she dialed Russell Newman's office. It would be seven in London. He went into surgery early. He picked up the phone.

'Who is it?' he said. 'Betsy Thornhill? Right. How can I help?'

'You put my face on your website.'

'Well, why not? You looked wonderful.'

'Come off it.'

'It was agreed.' His tone hardened. The voice was smooth and cold as a surgical knife. 'You've forgotten. We discussed it,' he said. 'Is that why you're ringing me at seven in the morning?'

'Yes.'

'How can I help?'

'Turn on your computer.'

'What?'

'Turn it on. Download my face. You know where it is, don't you?' she said.

'All right,' he said irritably.

'Tell me something,' Betsy said. 'You have patients with daughters, don't you? Don't you?' Her voice was shrill.

'Of course,' he said. 'Can't this wait?'

'No!'

'Fine.'

'Just tell me.'

'As a matter of fact, I'm doing a paper and there's a conference on age reversal I've got coming up. Frequently if they're close in age, I present both women, mother and daughter. In fact, I often suggest women bring pictures of their daughters if there's a family resemblance. It's a good way to see how one will look after surgery.' The subject interested him, he warmed to it, knew his stuff, lectured on it easily even at seven in the morning.

'Go on,' she said.

He was impatient. 'There's not much more. I can send you some examples. It's in the literature. I've done two monographs. I'll send them to you, if you like. But, yes, if a woman has a daughter, it's really quite common for them to look rather like one another after I've worked on the mother.'

'Why didn't you tell me?'

'I'm not sure I remember you saying that you had a daughter. You do, don't you? Betsy? Must go now.'

20

The family face. The weird thing, and she had seen it first in Bel's apartment, was that now, after the surgery, she looked like her mother when her mother was young and she was a little girl.

In her apartment, after she talked to Newman, Betsy went into the kitchen and took the mirror off the wall over the kitchen sink and put it on the table. She sat down. Next to the mirror, on the surface of the scarred pine table, she dealt out the photographs she'd swiped from Bel's. One was a black-and-white snapshot taken at the Jersey shore, and in it, this resemblance was the first thing she noticed.

The photograph was faded but she could imagine the green grass, how it looked, how it smelled that summer when it rained all the time. Her mother, a beautiful woman, her brown hair in a smooth French twist, ankle-strap wedgies on her feet, wore a strapless sundress, flowered cotton, washed so often it felt like silk when you rubbed against her, though she was never a woman who liked you rubbing against her much. The top of the dress was smocked and elasticized; no one wore bras in those hot summers before air-conditioning.

Beside her, also in a dress with a smocked top and rick-rack on the collar, was Betsy, aged four. Her hair was in a knot on top of her head. Big eyes looked out from under a tidy hedge of platinum bangs, though when she got older her hair turned dark. In her fat little hands she held the teddy bear that had no eyes; the eyes had pins on the backs and little kids sometimes pulled them out and swallowed them by mistake.

Betsy turned the picture over. The date was on the back: August 15, 1954. Her fourth birthday.

Again she looked at the pictures and at her face in the mirror and steel bands knit together around her head and everything felt hot and damp and crowded. She put the other pictures she had taken from Bel's next to the snapshot of herself and her mother. They were of Franny. Franny as a baby. Franny all grown up, a reporter, standing on some dusty road in a foreign country. Franny, her daughter. The three women, the same face.

Betsy's skin turned hot enough to burn her, then a chill rippled down her arms and formed as cold pit in the middle of her being and she couldn't shake it no matter how many sweaters she put on. She thought about her mother, how she'd barely called, how she resisted the old woman's calls. Didn't ask herself why. She thought about Franny.

We all have it, her mother always said with disdain. You came with it, you had to fight it. It was your face, she was convinced, that would make you bad; good looks were evidence of sin. Even while despising it, Eva used her own beauty. The family face.

* * *

Betsy graduated college when she was nineteen, went to London that June, met Joe her second night there and got pregnant, was twenty when she had Franny. Betsy wanted to call her Zoë, but her mother put her foot down and said Zoë was no kind of Christian name. On Long Island, in the dark house in Rockville Center, Betsy sat on the gold silk settee in the front room where it was hot and still and humid.

Eva wore a dress and stockings and white pumps and she, three months pregnant and sick as a dog all the time, clutched a glass of ice water. She didn't show yet, but Ma knew. She heard her throwing up every morning, but she would have known anyhow.

Betsy averted her eyes, then remained silent for ten minutes while the clock on the mantel ticked them out and Ma crossed herself for the third time and said, 'What will you call it, then?'

She tried corrupting her mother with a smile. 'Michael for Pop if it's a boy. Zoë if it's a girl.'

At least her grandchild would have a decent name, Eva insisted, so they settled on Michael Francis for a boy, and Mary Frances Michelle for a girl. From the beginning Betsy called her Franny.

The baby was beautiful. An ugly grandchild would have been a sign of some kind of warped grace for Eva Thornhill, who arrived at the hospital with a gold cross in a little box for the grandchild and nothing for Betsy.

Leaning over the baby, she said, 'She has it. We all have it,' and pursed her lips up tight as an asshole. Eva was a beautiful woman but sour.

Betsy took Franny to London and Joe took off after a while. He left her the ramshackle house he had inherited because he didn't believe in the material life, he said. He always sent money if he had any. He sent little gifts, prayer flags from Tibet, a Black Panther beret, a Mao jacket. He was a sweet, skinny guy who played bass guitar and wanted to save the world; his kid took after him.

They got along fine, her and Franny, and they talked on the phone, even when Franny was working in East Timor or Afghanistan, where she went for the BBC — just walked in with her tape recorder or sometimes a little DV camera and got her stories. Betsy was proud of this. Thirty-one years old and the kid was smart and brave, though sometimes, when she was unhappy, she called Betsy up late at night and picked a fight.

But kids did that. Even at thirty. She had the intellectual equipment and she was fearless about her job, but she wore a chip on her shoulder and blamed her mother.

One night in London, a big yellow moon hanging in the back garden, Betsy was in the kitchen with the door open when Franny called. Betsy listened to her agonize about some guy she'd met in Burma. Myanmar, Franny called it.

'Betsy, you there?' She called her mother Betsy and Betsy hated it.

'Yes, I am. You sound far away, sweetie. I miss you.'

'You haven't heard a thing I've said.'

'I have. Mike. You like him. He's an astrologer.'

'Mick, and he's an astronomer.'

'Right. Mick. From Canada.'

'Australia.'

'Same thing, right?' Betsy laughed. 'Hey, I'm sorry, I was watching this incredible moon that's just hanging off the trees in the garden.'

'You always do that. Never mind,' Franny said and got off the phone.

From time to time Betsy asked about Mick from Australia but Franny clammed up. Still, they talked plenty and kids were kids, even at thirty, she said to her friends and they laughed indulgently. Franny came home most Christmases and let Betsy buy her things. Before she left for New York, she sent Franny a fat check.

* * *

The three pictures she'd taken off Bel's mantel, one of herself and her mother, the others of Franny, lay on the table. Betsy never carried family pictures with her. For her, photographs were professional, she always said, though she kept a few on her dresser in London. She hadn't talked to Franny since she'd been in New York. She hadn't *thought* about her.

Betsy's picture was in the papers, she was a murder suspect, but she didn't call her daughter. It had never occurred to her.

Franny was thirty-one years old. She led an independent life. Betsy didn't interfere. It was *her* life. Betsy's friends were still involved with their children, even the grown-up kids who spent holidays with them and came home for dinners and to get their laundry done. Other women went on doing laundry for their children.

I'm a cold woman, Betsy thought. Really cold. A femme fatale. I could kill with this coldness. Anyone else would have called her daughter by now and said, 'I'm here, darling, I'm in New York.' Betsy was speeding now. If she hadn't fixed her face, it wouldn't have happened. There was no connection, except in her mind. Betsy thought: I'm losing my mind. Or something else: she had always known. She had known all the time. Who else looked so much like her?

Again she looked at the pictures. Franny as a baby. Franny as a young woman. The extraordinary hair that had stayed blonde as gold dust when she grew up was dyed brown and cut short and blunt. As soon as she started working in the Middle East, Franny dyed her hair dark. She got herself up so she looked older than she was, it made her less visible, she said, the age, the dark hair. Betsy remembered this now. It was easier, Franny told her. Easier if you didn't have platinum hair like some Barbie doll.

As a child, she'd been beautiful in a way Betsy never was. More like the old lady, like Eva, her grandmother. She had the fine skin and wide-set blue eyes and long bones and her mother's Roman nose and a little mole near her upper lip, the irregular thing that made her so ravishing that it was hard not to stare. Hard for Betsy to resist taking her picture. Just one more, Franny, sweetheart, she always said. When she was sixteen, Franny got the mole removed.

By the time she was eighteen and in college in New York, she'd made herself over. She wore ugly, baggy clothing and her eyebrows were overgrown and met near the middle of her face. Her posture declared her unavailability; she was permanently bent from the books she carried on her back, and the world seemed to make her angry. Except for old people. Franny was lovely around old people. She had a sixth sense with them.

Photograph in her hand, Betsy hurried to the living room and picked up the phone and called Franny's mobile and got a busy signal. *Where are you? Franny?* Again she tried and got a robotic voice that said the call had been diverted. Diverted where? Where was she? *Franny?*

Franny could hide. She could fold herself

into small spaces. On planes, she remained perfectly still, hunched over in her seat, ear-phones on, book open. She never used the toilet on a plane even as a child; it was the only thing that alarmed her, the toilets on airplanes.

Once, when she was eight, she ran away and no one knew where she'd gone until Max's daughter, Rima, found her hiding in their house in an airing cupboard no one used anymore. Franny could always slip into the smallest space in the basement or a closet and conceal herself like a cat, curled up with a book and a bag of Licorice Allsorts.

Franny had lived in the apartment on Cornelia Street when she was in college and, methodically now, Betsy now searched the apartment. She went through the closets and turned over the mattress. It was almost a decade since Franny left the place and there was nothing, of course, and anyhow, Franny never left a mark. She lived like a nun. She carried her belongings with her.

Where was she? Franny?

At the house Franny shared in Brixton, one of her room-mates answered and said Franny wasn't around. Any messages from her, Betsy asked him, and then a girl with a sour voice came on and told Betsy it was none of her fucking business who called Franny at

Franny's own place.

For an hour, crouched on the sofa, Betsy dialed the phone obsessively. She called Franny's mobile again. Friends. A producer at the BBC, who said she'd seen her last week in London.

Fretful, panicky, Betsy roamed the apartment, poured herself a shot of vodka into a coffee mug because the mug was on the kitchen counter. Then she poured it down the sink. She opened her computer and sent Franny e-mails and the e-mails came back, address unknown.

Over and over in the photographs on the table she read what she already knew. Smoking, and drinking the vodka straight from the bottle now, she tried to comfort herself. She shuffled the pictures over and over, looking at them as if they were Tarot cards: her mother, Franny, the police picture of herself. It wasn't her, the picture the cops had brought. It was a picture of Franny.

She got up and went to the window and ran her hands flat over the glass and looked down. Four floors to the sidewalk.

No way out, she thought and watched the street. She was outside the limits of her intelligence, banging her head on its ceiling. She thought about calling Frank, confessing: I did it; I killed him.

A picture of the knife and Ketsen dead floated into her head and made her feel sick. He had been hammered and slashed. Someone took a knife with a long thin blade and slashed him as if with a sword. She gagged and went into the bathroom. The wind blew off the river so hard the panes in the bedroom rattled and a crack formed in the upper right-hand corner.

⋆ ⋆ ⋆

The moon slid out from behind a cloud and lit up the river and as she looked out over it, it was bright as silver and eerie as a moonscape on the desert or an Ansel Adams picture. New Jersey, on the other side, seemed a foreign planet in the strange light, and the rotted stubs of an old pier, like burned out cigar butts, showed above the water that lapped at them.

She jogged along the deserted path for a few minutes then stopped and stared down into the water again. For a while, as she leaned on the railing, smoking, blowing the smoke out in frozen puffs, she wondered how deep the water was, how long it would take until you went numb, how fast you'd sink.

Everything was sharp now. It was all clear.

The outlines were defined. All the panic was gone.

What was it that had forced itself into her mind? The photos on Bel's mantelpiece? The remembering that when she was in college and even afterwards, Franny always traveled the same airline as Ketsen, the same time of day? That Ketsen taught at NYU where Franny was a student once? That she worked at the school in Harlem where he helped out? Or the cheese store on Sullivan Street where the mother and daughter looked so alike. Dead ringers. Or the photographs missing from her house in London.

It was Franny who had extra keys to the London house. She kept them and sometimes spent a night in her old room.

If she asked Frank, Frank would check. He would check and he'd find Franny's prints at Ketsen's place. All schoolteachers were fingerprinted in New York, Frank had said. She would have been fingerprinted when she worked at the school in Harlem and there would be a match. Once you gave them your prints, you gave up scraps from your body, you entered yourself into the digital universe. Nothing belonged to you afterwards, your name, your fingerprints, your face.

Betsy had kept it hidden from herself. 'You remind me of someone,' Ketsen had said it. It was Franny he meant. She had reminded him of Franny.

It made Betsy sad that her first instinct was to save herself. It was the unsayable thing. She stood along the railing and looked down helplessly at the river and felt tears freeze on her face. She didn't know your tears could freeze. She took the picture of Franny out of her pocket and held it in one hand, the cigarette in the other, then tossed the cigarette over the railing and saw it land on the water. In the bright light, she saw it perfectly.

In the picture, she saw her daughter who was, blonde hair dyed now, her own double. Who was this girl, her own kid, who would do this? Unless it was an accident. It might have been an accident, she said out loud and didn't believe it.

My first instinct was not to save my daughter, Betsy thought. *My instinct was not to stand in front of her*.

She was not completely willing to give herself up to save her child, not utterly and instinctively the way she always imagined she would, the way people said any woman would. This upset Betsy so much she held on tight to the railing of the fence near the river. It was a brutal surprise to her and she stood and listened to the wind and tried to shake the sense that she had a bad heart.

Instead, she would try to save them both. If it was an accident and she got Fran to admit it, she could save her. Save them both. That was the point.

You always figured yourself for the kind of person who would be better. You assumed you would, if you saw your child in the street, a car careening at her, you'd hurl yourself in front of it. That's what people did. Didn't they? They said they did. You'd do that. You did that kind of thing automatically. It was like breathing.

A tall thin man in a blue coat that billowed out behind him walked a pair of big lilac poodles down the path by the river, and Betsy watched until they disappeared. Then, her arms across her chest, she rocked back and forth and comforted herself for her lousy shortcomings.

The moon shifted back behind the clouds, the water turned dull, Betsy looked down. If she climbed over the railing and into the water and vanished, she would never have to tell anyone that it was Franny, her daughter, who killed Bobby Ketsen.

PART THREE

21

The hot sun hit her like a fist and made her reel. Betsy came out of the airport early Sunday afternoon into the desert and her mind drifted back to New York where she had stood looking, two nights earlier, at the icy river. Friday night, the city was black and white and silent. In Las Vegas, it stunned her, the heat and color and noise.

In the terminal, as she got off the plane, was the relentless jangle of slots and then outside, the endless blue desert sky, the sun tossed up into it like a big yellow fruit, the red shimmer of mountains that clung to the horizon.

A freak heat wave fried the West. The western half of the country seemed to have sucked up all the heat and left the East freezing. The air in Las Vegas was bone dry and somehow dead, she thought. Like old chicken bones, picked clean.

She shed her coat, but even the thin blue sweater she wore felt heavy as she got in line for a taxi. Bobby Ketsen had been due in Las Vegas today, or was it tomorrow? She wasn't sure which, it didn't matter, but Meryl Briggs had said he was coming.

Was Franny coming with him? How were they connected? What made her daughter, Franny, the girl with the beautiful face, stun him with a hammer then slit his throat with a sashimi knife the way you slice raw fish?

Franny had disappeared. No message Betsy left anywhere on earth — hotels in Islamabad, Afghanistan, Jerusalem, a series of mobile phones, the BBC — was picked up, no query answered. Nothing. Franny's father, Joe Darling, lived in the desert near Las Vegas, it was all Betsy in her chaotic panic could think of. She'd lost touch with Joe years ago. Unlisted number, information said.

In the back of Betsy's head was the memory of a conversation with Franny the year before: Joe was in Vegas, she'd said from the sofa in London where, Christmas week, she was stretched out reading a translation of the Koran.

'Joe who?' Betsy asked.

'My father,' Franny said. 'Remember him?'

* * *

It had started on Saturday when she found a guy from one of the London tabloids on Cornelia Street, milking Marie Tusi for information. He had bad breath, a receding hairline, acne, as if the stuff he wrote showed on his skin. It was a great story, he enthused to Betsy, her doing her face, then a suspect in a murder case. He waved a copy of his paper at her, the headline visible: WHAT HAPPENS IF YOU HAD THE FACE YOU ALWAYS WANTED?

He was authorized to offer money, he said. She fled upstairs, ignored the phone, let the answering machine pick up.

The idea of Vegas and Joe took shape that day and she counted the money that remained from the stash Pauline left her and there was plenty. She called and got a ticket for the early flight out Sunday. Get away. Escape the papers, TV shows, Delia Vaio, her mother's calls. Marie's gossip. Frank Dolce's longing, disappointed looks.

Hemmed in, jammed up, it gagged her, the feeling she was surrounded by them all, but isolated, couldn't talk to anyone, not even Mark Carey, not even Bel. How could she tell Bel that Franny killed Bobby Ketsen?

By Saturday night in New York she felt like a prisoner; the apartment was a cell and, down below, people clamoring to get at her. What was it that Frank Dolce had said about her transparent life? It was plenty transparent now.

The trip began to look like salvation.

Before it was light on Sunday morning, she packed a small carry-on and slipped out of the house, looking both ways up and down the street, searching for the police car she felt sure had been there every morning. The street was empty. At the corner, she grabbed the lone cab that passed and went to the airport, where she killed time at the terminal inspecting souvenirs.

Her flight was called, she stepped on the escalator and looked up. At the top was Jimmy Grant in a black down jacket staring at her.

The steps shifted under her feet, she held the rail, looked up again and saw him still looking down. When she got to the top he had gone, like an apparition.

The 7 a.m. Continental flight out of Newark was half empty and Betsy curled up in a window seat, head against the side of the plane. Magazine in her lap, she kept her eyes closed, and her sunglasses on.

A passage of clear air turbulence jolted Betsy out of her half-sleep and she pulled on the seat belt.

Breakfast came in a blistered silver bag. The woman in the aisle seat ripped the bag open, a stream of steam shot up, and she bit into the egg sandwich that oozed fake orange cheese. Her appetite gone, Betsy took a plastic cup of coffee. Her throat constricted every time she thought about Franny and Ketsen. Franny was always near the surface, never out of her consciousness.

Without warning, the plane hit two deep pockets, then settled; Betsy looked down at flat farmland and neat squares of winter fields bisected by lines of snow and longed to live in one of those remote empty places. The Rockies appeared, jagged peaks, ocher slopes, red craters.

She wasn't afraid of flying. Turbulence didn't bother her, she could fall asleep before take-off. What scared her was not finding Franny.

When did they talk? She couldn't remember when she had talked to Fran except for a few ritual phone calls over the holidays, the exchange of some presents and the cards. Franny was in Islamabad then, on her way to Kabul. Or Kashmir. Or Gaza.

Where was she now? If Betsy could find her, if she could find out why Fran killed Ketsen, she could save them both. Save herself. She was already in it up to her shoulders and sinking; the trip to Meryl Briggs in Hoboken, the line-up, her visit to Ketsen's apartment put her in deeper. Frank Dolce had called her the night before. She didn't call back.

As soon as the plane landed, her instinct was to turn around and go home to New York. She was acting crazy. She knew it, could see it, she kept moving forward.

⋆ ⋆ ⋆

In the vast glass aquarium in the hotel lobby, stranded in a tank in the desert, exquisite tropical fish swam languidly: shocking pink, aquamarine with gilded fins, albino, the color bled away.

Betsy checked in and took the elevator to the twenty-ninth floor. She unlocked her door. The huge room had a bed on a platform and a patterned — squiggles like grass snakes crawling on it — green carpet and a glass wall that looked out over Las Vegas.

Face pressed against the window, she saw the neon and endless desert sky that curved over the instant city below. From up here, the other hotels and casinos looked as if they were made out of cardboard and a harsh desert wind could blow them away. The landscape was fake cities: New York, Paris, Venice, ancient Rome. A single gust would wipe it all off the earth and toss the pieces across the sand like garbage spilled from a broken plastic bag. Unlike the World Trade Center, there would be no implosion, no industrial-scale violence necessary; just wind.

For the first time in days, she instinctively reached for her camera and it felt good in her hands, solid, real. She missed work. Somehow, she would extricate herself from this nightmare, wake herself up, get some work — David said he could get her plenty of chicken shoots — and the craziness would end. Through the lens, she surveyed the city below her, the whole world faked up on the baking desert, the seared white sky, the hallucinatory mountains on the horizon.

It was sex. Sex was the reason Ketsen went after Franny. He pursued her, a flight from London to New York, at NYU, the school in Harlem. He wanted her and she rebuffed him, something went wrong. Franny was a determined girl, a stiff proposition if you got out of line. Hurt, Franny could kill.

Betsy put her camera on the bed, wondering if Ketsen had followed Franny, offered her a lift? Did he say, Have dinner with me, Franny, please. Did he beg?

The scene came back to her in detail, Ketsen, the airport, first Heathrow, then JFK where he took possession of her, flirting in the car, attentive, interested. *You just looked like someone I once knew*. The sentence that caught her attention. She had reminded him of someone.

She crossed the room and sat on the bed and picked up the phone and tried to get a number for Joe. A sympathetic operator believed her when she said there was an illness in the family, kept her waiting, chattering urgently to someone in the background. She gave Betsy a phone number and address that Betsy scribbled on the back of her air ticket. She was relieved; in London it wouldn't happen, they didn't keep ex-directory numbers.

Hurriedly, she dialed; there was only a machine: 'Hi, this is Joe, leave a message.' In the background, George Harrison played 'While My Guitar Gently Weeps'.

Betsy left a message. She wanted a drink.

From the mini-bar, she took a vodka miniature. A can of juice — someone had opened it, drunk some, put it back — tipped out and dripped orange liquid onto her shoes. She drank straight from the miniature bottle, finished it, started a second and switched on the TV. Martha Stewart was potting a lemon tree.

Somewhere her cell phone was ringing. Betsy ran across the room, got her bag, extracted the phone; it had stopped. No message. It shook her out of her stupor, and she changed into a thin blue cotton skirt and blue espadrilles and a sleeveless white shirt.

Turned off the TV. Tied her orange sweater around her shoulders, picked up her bag, went out into the heat that was like a blast furnace to look for her kid.

22

Las Vegas offered itself up for a little bit of sin, fun and money and sex and booze, but it wasn't sexy. Standing in the lobby of the Hard Rock Hotel, Betsy talked to one of the girls on duty who responded like a good little apparatchik in a state stitched together with rules as rigid as any socialist country. State of mind.

He stays at the Hard Rock Hotel, Meryl had said. Betsy asked about Ketsen's reservation. The girl on the other side of the front desk looked in her computer and made a phone call and couldn't help her. The manager was on his break. He would be back in fifteen minutes. Meanwhile, the girl, her name was Wynona — it was on her name-tag — was sorry. It was against house rules for her to give out information on the guests. Sorry, ma'am. Out here in America they called you ma'am.

Betsy couldn't make out if the girl was stonewalling, if somehow she knew about the murder and the New York cops had been in touch. Wynona was tan and smiling and vacuous and wore thick pink blush on her dewy cheeks. She looked about nineteen.

At a slot machine that featured Jimi Hendrix, Betsy sat and watched the crowd in the lobby whose walls were infested with the outfits of dead rock musicians.

Loitering nearby in front of video poker machines were a pair of men in blue Oxford button-downs and two women in tan summer suits; strays from some convention, they wore name-tags and the eager, flustered look of corporate kids in search of sin. A quartet of hopeful sinners. Same age as Franny.

Did Ketsen hurt her? Make her angry? Franny could wrinkle her face with a particular icy disdain, eyes frozen, mouth shriveled like a nut. If you were bad and messed with one of her causes, Franny could punish you.

The frigid air in the casino gave Betsy gooseflesh, she pulled on her sweater, rubbed her arms for comfort. A man in overalls dragged an industrial vacuum cleaner into the slot pit and started cleaning the carpets. A wild-goose chase, Las Vegas, she thought; she leaned against the machine. Fruit machines, her father called them. Fruit. Like her book.

Much more likely than sex was the idea that drifted into her head. She got a pack out of her bag and held a cigarette and rested against the smooth cold metal of the machine. No smoking, the sign said, so she just held the cigarette and thought that Franny had seen Ketsen as a bad man, a man who made a black woman white, a thief, a *gonif* was the word Max would use. How bad was he? Bad enough to make Frances Thornhill slash him and leave him bleeding and dead? Was he dead before she left? Did she check, crouch down, put her fingers on his neck to try his pulse, feel his still warm flesh? Franny had small, blunt, capable hands.

'Ms Thornhill?'

The manager who materialized at Betsy's side wore a black suit and had a mouthful of large teeth that were white as milk. Could he help? Was there something he could do for her? he asked, showing his glistening pink gums and wonderful teeth.

She was from a magazine, she said, and interested in doing a shoot in the hotel. She worked on his vanity, told him she could use him in her pictures. He said she'd have to talk to people in Public Relations. He let on that, in his spare time, he was a top-of-the-line Elvis impersonator, not just one of hundreds who worked Vegas, no wedding chapel fly-by-night Elvis; he was a post-modern Presley who made good money playing conventions. Sure he sang the songs, but his specialty was Elvis' food; sometimes he brought an electric fryer on stage and made deep-fried banana sandwiches and gave the audience samples. Burger and the King, right? He offered to meet her with his gear on; she accepted.

'What's your name?' she asked.

'Elvis Aaron, Ma'am,' he said.

'I mean your real name.'

'My real name is Elvis. My parents got hitched right here in Vegas in the old Elvis chapel.'

An hour later, on his lunch break, Elvis Aaron met her in the Pink Taco Restaurant where they shared blue cocktails and warm tamales and Elvis Aaron spread a clean napkin over his gold lamé jacket because he was in costume so she could see.

Gold lamé, satin tuxedo pants, tooled white cowboy boots that were too big, hair in a pompadour, sideburns; he was a handsome boy.

'I hope I could be real good for your magazine,' he said.

'I'm sure you could.'

By the time they'd had a couple more drinks, her own private Elvis was warming up to the idea that she could make him famous on a national, possibly international scale. On the table where he cleared a space, he spread his publicity photographs, pulled his chair close to hers, emitted the scent of grassy cologne.

OK, he whispered to her. A room had been reserved at the hotel for Ketsen who was due in tomorrow with a friend. What friend, she asked, but he didn't know her name. Ketsen always came with a friend, everyone in the place knew because Ketsen was a favorite, a big tipper, real nice to the kids who worked there.

Every few months he showed with the girl. A chick. A real babe. Everyone noticed her, the blue-black hair, the light blue eyes.

'Would you recognize her?' Betsy asked.

'Maybe.'

'Have another drink.'

They ordered more to drink. Betsy pushed away her plate, put the photograph of Franny flat on the table between them. He stared hard at it, trying hard to give the right answer.

'Yeah, maybe,' he said. 'Except the one that was here with him was really sort of beautiful. Wait a minute.' He got up and stumbled in the too-big boots out of the restaurant.

When he returned, he had the girl from the desk in tow. Wynona loosened her suit jacket and showed off her pink tank top and the caramel-colored breasts — they were a lousy match for her pink face — that were so high and tight they resembled sports equipment.

'That's her,' Wynona said, peering at the picture of Franny. 'You can only just about make it out though, because the babe with that Ketsen guy was sensational, and this one's sort of a dog, if you'll excuse me saying so. But I can see it's her from the eyes. She must have been here with him three, four, times. I remember him because he always tipped everyone great, and she was hot when I saw her.'

Wynona examined the picture again, looked at Betsy, scrunched her face to show she was thinking.

'Hey, I get it,' she said. 'You guys are sisters, right? Is that right? Man, you could be her double. When she's looking good, of course, you know what I mean.' She tapped her long orange fingernail on the photograph. 'Excuse me for asking, but what is she in this picture?'

Betsy said, 'What do you mean what is she?'

'I mean is she fixed up all dreary like this for a reason? Is this some kind of disguise?'

* * *

Her head hurt from rum and sugar, the air tasted of heat and gas fumes, it was as if, outside the hotel, she had fallen into an oven. Betsy's feet hit the hard black tarmac as she jogged along a narrow strip of road, feeling, again, someone behind her. A stalker. A cop. As soon as Elvis and Wynona had begun asking too many questions, Betsy bolted from the hotel, started running.

Sweat poured down her face, her shirt clung to her back, buildings skittered by her at the periphery of her vision like some psychedelic apparition in the harsh sunlight. The desert was like a mirage at the edge of the world.

Not looking back, she ran until she saw a taxi, flagged it down, fell into it. The freezing air inside dried her sweat; it felt like beads of ice trickling down her back.

'Where you want?' the driver asked.

'I'm looking for the photographic convention — you know where that is?'

'I try few hotels,' he said. 'I take you and wait if you want, OK?'

The taxi driver was from Mostar. Making a new life in Vegas. On the dashboard was a copy of *Genius*, a book about Richard Feynman. The driver was studying physics at the university here. Loved the place, he said with the fervor of a convert. You could be anything in America, and Las Vegas was America. He was saving already for a house, bring his family over. Anything possible.

Past building sites and strip-malls and skinny palms, he took what he claimed was a short-cut to the Strip.

Look, he said, at the desert. Every day, city eats more of desert, he said with excitement. More houses. Schools. Casinos. Work. He loved Las Vegas. He looked in the rear-view at Betsy.

'You OK?'

He pulled into a hotel driveway and beckoned over a Venetian gondolier who was having a smoke. The guy leaned down and the driver conferred with him then drove a few hundred yards further and stopped.

'Over there,' the driver pointed to the other side of the Strip. 'I wait for you?'

'No,' she said. 'Don't bother.'

⋆ ⋆ ⋆

'Luck, be a lady tonight,' Sinatra sang. The hotel where the taxi had dropped her was the wrong place. She got directions, set out, walked down a piece of sidewalk covered in green carpet. Through outdoor speakers, Sinatra sang, the air smelled of cherry disinfectant which was used to scrub vomit off the sidewalks, the fountains at the Bellagio danced to the music.

Water shimmied in huge arcs, swerved and ducked in choreography as snappy as the tune which played on a loop in her head the rest of the day, over and over, luck be a lady.

She walked, the aural assault kept coming — music, fountains, voices resonating out of more hidden speakers into the desert air, the cacophony of come-ons making her feel as if she'd dropped acid: $9.99 buffets, yard-long purple Margaritas, topless babes, free shots at slots, impersonators with three hundred voices, Sammy Davis, George Raft, Bogart, Mike Myers, and Sinatra, and the water whooshing up in the fountains and the shuffle of the crowds moving back and forth. *Luck, be a lady*.

A multiplex appeared. It was weeks since she'd been to the pictures and, for a second, she thought about escape into the dark theater. Spend the day, see two, three, four movies, eat popcorn by the bucket, drink tubs of Diet Coke. Forget everything.

Instead, she cut away into one of the hotels. It was dark and cold, the noise ferocious, the incessant clatter of coins in the slots like some Las Vegas rap you couldn't avoid — you felt yourself strutting, keeping time.

As she walked past, she took a quarter out of her pocket and slid it into a machine that had Betty Boop on the front. The second coin, she hit. The lights flashed, pictures of fruit popped into the windows, cherries, limes, lemons, coins jingled into the tray, Betsy reached down for them.

A woman at the next machine leaned over, eyed her winnings, shrugged, went back to her own bucket of coins. Perched on a stool, legs splayed, the bucket grasped in one hand, she worked three machines at the same time, feeding them money while she smoked a little brown Tiparillo and intermittently scratched her neck.

Betsy won sixty-four quarters and gathered them up from the tray, dropped them into a wax bucket, felt the silvery coins slide through her fingers. For ten minutes, she fed them back, sitting in front of the machine, blankly, mesmerized, pushing the coins in. She had never gambled in her life, she could feel the obsession creeping up, slammed her last coin in the machine and fled for the front desk where she asked about the convention.

'Second floor, miss,' he said. 'Take the escalator.'

* * *

Jumbotrons suspended from all the walls flashed photographs a hundred feet high as the music changed — Britney Spears, Enya, Kenny G, Andrea Bocelli the blind tenor.

Checking her phone for messages again, waiting for Joe to answer her, she looked around the photo show. If he didn't call by evening, she'd go looking for him, but he lived miles from town out on the desert, so she cruised the cavernous convention hall for half an hour.

Products were displayed in stalls, on tables, in booths, in rooms hung with shimmery curtains. There were cameras, film, software, digital equipment, editing gear. There was stuff that would enable you to make your own epic from your dining room, travel to the moon, see your wife as the star of a porn movie. Everywhere in the huge hall were throngs of tech freaks and antique camera buffs and wannabe professionals who worked for freebie magazines.

She searched the crowd, looking for Franny. She talked to the reps and they talked back at her new face. It felt tight. It was like wearing a mask. She felt as if she was hiding behind it and they were talking to it, but not to her.

What was she looking for, and who? Bobby Ketsen was dead. Franny had disappeared.

Joe didn't answer his phone. Phone in hand, she dialed Mark Carey, then hung up. Nothing he could do for her from here. She needed him; he was busy, married.

At one end of the hall, a parade of beauty queens was in progress: girls from a hundred small towns, sixteen, seventeen, eighteen years old, strutted the catwalk, all dolled up in evening dresses and bathing suits. You could take their pictures with some of the new cameras, try out the equipment. It was a corporate peep-show.

Little kids ran around the catwalk, taunted the girls, called out catty remarks, stuck out their tongues. Distracted, the girls teetered on high heels. A chubby brunette in a skintight fishtail raspberry-pink nylon evening dress stumbled, stopped dead, bent over, removed a shoe and fixed the toilet paper stuffed inside. Like Elvis, her shoes were too big.

Next to the beauty show was a red and white circus tent. Outside, a barker in a straw boater and a striped blazer stood at the entrance and waved a cane and smiled and shouted: Come on in. See yourself as Madonna, a New York City firefighter, President George W. Bush. Don't miss the chance. Free ice cream when you get inside. Free popcorn. Fun for everyone.

Betsy entered the tent. It was dimly lit, no

windows. Strings of colored lights and silver disco balls hung from the ceiling. The air conditioning tasted metallic, smelled chemical, felt heavy on your skin.

Funhouse mirrors stood everywhere inside the tent and the crowds wandered by, posing and laughing, looking at themselves — fat, thin, elongated, tiny as midgets. A man in a mint-green leisure suit pushed a wheelchair, the woman in it clutched a brown paper sack full of coins for the slots. Her reflection came back at her from one of the freak-show mirrors. She burst into tears, tried to push herself out of the chair and started to scream. Hurriedly, the man shoved her away and out of the tent. Three teenagers in big shorts laughed at them.

Acrobats on stilts strode above the crowd, clowns in yellow clown suits and big floppy clown shoes teased the younger kids who giggled and bawled. A girl in a gold bikini rode a unicycle. Boys and girls in candy-striped shirts handed out miniature ice cream cones and tiny boxes of popcorn and little puffs of cotton candy; the spun sugar was pink and blue and yellow and Betsy ate some; it was like eating sweetened air.

She sidled up to people and eavesdropped and wondered if Franny could be here somewhere in the crowd, but there were only the throngs of strangers and lights that made colored dots in front of her eyes.

In the center of the tent, marked out by circus rings, were six large computer set-ups. This was the main attraction. Behind each computer sat a salesperson with a name-tag and a toothy smile. Betsy took a seat opposite a salesperson named Colby. Colby, she said. Like the cheese?

Like the cheese, he said, and grinned.

So show me how this works, Colby. I'm a photographer. I'm interested. It's my trade.

This is great stuff, he said, even better than Adobe Photoshop, my opinion, of course, better than anything we've seen so far, this can transform a picture, change the place, the people, the way they look. If you were a bride, for instance, you could use it to see how you might look in different outfits. Listen, he said, you never really have to leave home if you don't want to or can't. If you were a pro, like she obviously was, he said, this was also better than Polaroids. You could check out your picture, your light, your setting.

How much time would that save, said Colby with a big smile full of his excellent white choppers. Maybe everyone in Las Vegas had great teeth, Betsy thought, and listened to the sales pitch.

Law enforcement, too, Colby added. Many

police departments had already switched from sketch artists to computer morphing.

'I know,' Betsy said.

She wasn't law enforcement, was she? Colby wanted to know.

He stroked his computer and hit some keys, offered to put her in the picture, as he put it.

Show me, she said, suspended suddenly in some creepy déjà vu. The last time she'd sat in front of an imaging set-up like this had been with Russell Newman at his office. He showed you yourself after the surgery, showed you yourself wrinkle-free, wrinkle-proof, younger.

'Can I have a print-out?' Betsy had asked.

'No,' he said. 'I don't do that.'

It was clear now why he had refused. If the face wasn't what he promised, a patient might sue.

'Say cheese,' said Colby and took a picture of Betsy with a miniaturized digital camera.

Great camera, he said, so easy, so small you can wear it around your neck, hide it in your smallest pocket, have it with you all the time. He fed her picture into the computer. Her face popped up on the screen. Her skin was white and papery and there were rings under her eyes.

He fiddled with the program. He dropped

Betsy into London, then onto a South Sea Island. He put her in a bikini. He showed her her own baby picture.

'How about older?' he said. 'I could show you how you'll look.'

Avid to entice, Colby played with the mouse. Her image came up on the screen: Betsy at fifty. To Colby, fifty was old; he could barely imagine anything beyond.

On the screen the grooves from her nose to her mouth deepened. The upper lip was sprayed with fine lines, jowls softer, brow furrowed, nose thicker. In the circus tent with the colored lights and eager young salespeople in striped jackets, she felt she had been sucked out of herself and replaced again by somebody she once was. Putting out her hand, she touched her digital face on the screen.

'Oh, please, you shouldn't touch it.'

Can you print it for me, she said to Colby.

Sure, he said. I can print that. You look better the way you are, if you don't mind my saying, though you look good here, too, of course, he said, then put his hand over his mouth. Excuse me. I'm sorry. That wasn't real polite.

He printed the picture of her and offered her a second copy free, as an apology, or a reward.

You like our little bag of tricks?

Yes, she said. Yes. I would consider using your tricks.

In your work? he asked.

Definitely, she said, yes, sure I'd do that, she said, and could feel her body disconnect from her brain as she took the print-outs and said good-bye to Colby.

On her way out of the tent, clutching the print-outs with her other face, she passed the bendy amusement park mirrors and saw her reflection and in it, depending how she stood, in her blue skirt and orange sweater, she looked fat, tall, thin, tiny, but always young.

* * *

Sprawled on the huge bed in her hotel room on the twenty-ninth floor, she tried to figure things out: Ketsen, Franny, why Fran killed him, how she learned to use a knife. Violence made Betsy physically sick; even Tom and Jerry cartoons upset her. In her whole life, she had never hit anyone, never slapped or spanked her child, never, not once.

She picked up the phone and called Joe again. No answer.

The TV played mute in the background. She dozed; when her cell rang, she rolled over across the bed and got hold of it.

Frank Dolce was on the line; the pleading in his voice made her uneasy.

He said, 'Where are you?'

'Nowhere,' she said, knowing he assumed she was in New York.

'We should talk. I'm coming over.'

'Can it wait? I feel lousy today.'

'What's wrong?'

'Headache,' she lied. 'Migraine.'

'I'm sorry. Stay indoors, Betsy. The cold's bad for a migraine and it's fucking freezing out today.'

She glanced out of the window at the blasted Nevada landscape, listened to Frank and heard the worry in his voice.

'Sure, Frank. I promise.'

'You'll call tomorrow?'

'Yes,' she said and switched off the phone and pulled a map out of her bag.

23

In the rear-view mirror of the rented metallic green Taurus, as she drove out of town, the map on the seat beside her, she watched the city recede. With the lights full on, Las Vegas looked like something from a sci-fi flick, an unearthly planet that glittered behind her and stayed bright in her mirror no matter how far away she drove.

Off the Strip, the traffic thinned out. Betsy reached the outskirts of the city where there were ramshackle buildings and cracked streets; homeless men were scattered in doorways like brush off the desert. Drunks and hookers, shabby clothes, faces sucked inward, wandered the crummy edges of the town. The way the side mirror of the car was tilted, they seemed to drift just behind her, along the edge of the car. At a red light, a sad-eyed squeegee kid attacked her windshield; rolling down the window, Betsy hurriedly pushed five bucks at him.

Joe's address scrawled on the edge of the map, she glanced at it, drove to the interstate, picked up speed.

Joe Darling, Franny's father. She tried to

remember the boy she'd met at a club in London a hundred years ago, tall, slight, blond, impetuous, but earnest. It was a gig in a basement off Oxford Street, a cellar jammed with kids smoking dope, dancing, protesting injustice, fists in the air, though she couldn't remember what the injustice was. Still, a Black Panther in a beret called her 'Sister', which impressed Joe who took her home for the night. She fell for him because he played guitar and for his name. Joe Darling seemed a name out of *Peter Pan* to her. More than thirty years ago in London.

Betsy switched on her brights and swerved a little while she got her bearings. It was years since she'd driven on the right side of the road. London seemed as far away as a remote star in a distant galaxy. Trucks passed her, the eighteen-wheel rigs, big as dinosaurs, coming up behind out of the dark then pulling ahead. She watched for the exit signs, but she was tired and her eyes seemed heavy; she put the air conditioning on high, found an oldies station on the radio and turned it up loud. Buddy Holly singing 'Peggy Sue' into the night.

At night, most of America was empty, even the cities. You went to a hotel in Dallas or Denver, you looked out of your window because you were restless and couldn't sleep and there was nothing below, no one in the streets except for a snowplow on the late shift or a garbage truck at dawn. Except for Las Vegas. And New York. New York, where you were never alone, was always crowded, there was always someone on the street, drunks staggering by, cops, the homeless, teenagers looking for doorways to smooch in.

A casino with a blue neon dog on top appeared on the far side of the road. The neon tail wagged the dog. The road was empty now and after a while the prefab houses dribbled out into the sand and the half-built instant suburbs turned back into desert.

Without any warning, an animal skittered across the road in front of her. She tried to swerve out of the way, skidded, held the car into the skid. She felt a bump and something splattered and she knew it was dead, whatever it was.

She changed the radio station, hunting for news, for a voice, but all she got was a Christian cowboy praising Jesus for his big win at the rodeo. She turned it off. Her hands sweated on the steering wheel and she squinted out into the night, looking for the exit signs. She was lost. There was no one around. No gas station. No signs. Nothing.

At the next exit, Betsy turned off the

interstate, drove onto a service road, pulled up on the shoulder, put a light on in the car and unfolded her map. Lighting a cigarette, she opened the door, got out, stretched her arms over her head. Her shoulders felt cramped. A noise distracted her.

Above her, it appeared: the tiny aircraft buzzed the night sky like a wasp, flashing its lights, swooping down low, dipping its wings left and right, then spiraling back into the clouds.

'Tourists,' she said half out loud to reassure herself.

The plane came back. There were no tourists on the desert at night, she thought. They were cops. Tailing her. Looking for her. Did Frank Dolce know where she was? Did he have someone on her tail?

She tossed the burning cigarette butt onto the road, stumbled back into the car, slammed the door, turned the key, stepped on the gas and pulled back onto the road. The plane stayed with her. Trying to lose him, she drove too fast, bumping down the narrow road; like a hungry insect, the plane kept on her tail.

Go away, she thought as the plane pursued her and she put her foot flat on the gas.

At the next crossroads, she turned the car around and drove in the other direction, back towards the interstate, but the plane flashed its lights some more. Was she hallucinating?

In the mirror, she saw the sweat that glistened on her forehead. Her lips tingled and she felt light-headed. Her hands slid over the wheel, she saw the needle pass 80, then 90, shiver at 100. She was out of control. She would crash the car and it would be over and the nightmare would end. Press harder, she thought. Push down on the pedal. 110. Then she saw a gas station.

The turn-off was steep, the half-paved road narrow and dark. Holding tight to the wheel, Betsy plunged down the hill to the ramshackle gas station where she made out a boarded-up building, a couple of pumps and lights from a pick-up truck. She bumped down the rough road. Gravel sprayed up against her windshield and through it she saw the figure of a man.

He was leaning against the truck, smoking in the dark. The tip of his cigarette glowed and overhead the plane blinked its lights. Betsy tried to turn but the space was too narrow and the grade was too steep and she was stuck. There was no sound except the plane.

* * *

Joe Darling had sent Jack up with the plane to see if he could spot her. He kept his headlights on. You could get bloody lost out here. Betsy had left him a message, said she was coming out and he didn't want her lost. Didn't want her showing up at the house, either. It would make Pam unhinged, this woman showing up out of his past, even though, when he sold a piece of land, he got Pam the house she always wanted, including the sub-zero fridge thing. What the hell did Betsy want after all this time? It excited him, though, her coming here.

All those years ago, Joe had been out-of-his-gourd mad about Betsy and he only left her and Franny because he was young and stupid and stoned. Betsy was the sweetest girl you could imagine, but he was really young and very English and didn't know anything about anything. He leaned against his truck and kicked gravel with his custom-made boots.

He was fifty-four and still skinny. Joe ran his hand over the stubble on his chin, and caught his reflection in the side mirror of the truck. His face was lined and the skin leathery from years in the sun. He tucked his denim shirt into his worn jeans. From the near distance came the sound of a car. A few seconds later the green car bounced down the road into the gas station and Joe went over and tapped on the window.

'Betsy?'

She peered into the dark. 'Who is it?'

'Turn the window down,' he shouted through the glass. 'It's me, Joe.'

She opened the door and said, 'You scared me.'

'What the hell are you doing here?'

'Looking for you. I got lost.' She climbed out of the car and Joe kissed her on the cheek.

'I meant in Vegas.' He laughed. 'And you didn't get lost. I live a mile up that road. You were heading right for me. Someone gave you good directions, man.' He leaned against his truck and waved his hand. 'You all right? You look white as a ghost.'

'The plane.' She pointed at the sky. 'What is it?'

'It's mine,' he said.

'Yours?'

'Yeah. Takes the tourists up, show them stuff they never see, the desert, wildlife, shit like that.'

'At night?'

'Guy who flies for me likes to fool around at night.'

'He wasn't following me?'

'I told him keep an eye out for a car that

looks lost, you know? A woman driving. You said you were coming. You can get lost out here, there's snakes, wild animals.' He chortled. 'Jack saw you drive off the main road and called me and I came down here in case it was you. What's the matter with you? Oh, that, you mean he was coming on to you, flapping his wings, that kind of shit? He loves doing that shit. Asshole uses up the fuel I fucking pay for.'

Joe pulled a cell phone out of his pocket, flipped it open, dialed a number and mumbled into it. The plane came down so low, they could see the pilot wave. Then he pulled back up and disappeared.

He said, 'You want something to drink? You seem real edgy.'

She nodded.

'Come on then. Get in the truck.' He peered at her. 'Jesus, you look great, you know that? You look fucking wonderful. Get in the truck and we'll drink something.'

Betsy climbed up into the front seat and Joe got in beside her. He reached into a cooler on the back seat and pulled out a can of beer and she turned to take it and saw the rifle.

'You have a gun?'

'This is America, sweetheart. Sure I have a gun. It's like owning a toaster, man. I have a lot of guns.' He reached over her and opened the glove compartment where there was a black pistol. 'Everyone has a gun. There are real jerks out here.' He looked at her and laughed and put his hand on her arm. 'It's for shooting animals is all, Betsy. Deer, whatever. Things wander into your house out here at night. Relax. You still based in London?'

Gulping the beer, she held the empty can between her hands, looked out at the shuttered gas station, then at Joe.

'I'm in New York for a while. My aunt died. She left me the apartment on Cornelia Street,' she said and saw Joe wasn't surprised.

'Very nice,' he said. 'You getting that place. Listen, you came all the fuck the way out here to see me after all these years? Should I be flattered?'

Next to Joe in the front of his truck, she looked sideways at him. Maybe what you felt at nineteen didn't count. In the thin, sunburned face that was laced with wrinkles, she could just make out the boy she had loved. The blond hair was mostly white and thin, there was something vacant about the beautiful gray eyes even when he smiled. The long almost girlish eyelashes remained. The empty stare made her uneasy. Years of drugs, she figured. Booze. Sun. The desert.

He pulled a couple more cans of beer from

the back seat and offered her one. She shook her head. Something about Joe made her cautious. Go easy, she told herself. Make conversation.

'How's your mother, Joe?'

'Dead.'

'I'm sorry.'

'Yeah, thanks,' he said. 'What about yours? She was some piece of work, your old lady. The couple of times I met her she looked at me like I'm the devil or something, and I just thought, fuck, lady, I wish you'd get down on your knees for me. She was a dish, a babe, she was only, what? Forty-five when I met her. I bet she had a few innings with some guys back then.'

'My mother? She was in perpetual mourning for my father. I would have known.'

'You were never that interested. I was always fascinated by the way you and your old lady chattered all the time and never said anything. I was going to use your family for a psych class. She's still going strong? How the hell long is it since I saw you?'

'A long time.'

'Fifteen years,' he said. 'Five since we talked.'

'You counted?'

'I kept score,' Joe said. 'How many times I

called, how many times you never called back. This is just nostalgia, Betsy? You're here on business? I wouldn't figure you for some kind of gambling freak.'

'I'm not. You don't sound English anymore.'

'I've been in America on and off thirty years. I hardly ever went back to England, you know, man? Who needs it? It just fucking rained all the time and people cared how you talked. It wasn't for me. Never was. Everyone changes. Except you.'

'Joe?'

'Yeah?'

Betsy turned, put her hand on his arm, looked at him, smiled.

'I need to talk to you,' she said. 'Can we go to your place?'

He thought about Pam and shook his head.

'I don't think that's such a good idea,' he said. 'I've got someone there that wouldn't like me bringing another woman around, especially someone she never exactly heard of, and she's a little weird, she thinks all English guys are spies, you know, like she's married to a double agent or something.'

'You're married?'

'My third. They like getting married in America. We can ride around if you want or go for a drink or coffee, whatever. That OK?'

'Fine.'

'Come on, you can follow me in your car. There's a Denny's about ten miles back and I feel like pancakes. I won't bite you,' Joe said. 'Unless you ask me nice.'

* * *

Opposite her in a booth at Denny's, Joe ordered three fried eggs, pancakes and double bacon, very crispy. When the food came, he appraised the bacon which looked incinerated, then drenched everything in maple syrup.

'I love Denny's,' he said and put his hand out to touch her wrist. 'It's good to see you.'

Betsy ordered coffee and said, 'When Franny graduated I think I called you,' she said. 'Didn't I?'

'Not that it's not nice seeing you, like I said, but what are you doing here?'

'I'm looking for Franny. I can't reach her and I'm worried.'

'You thought I might know something?'

'Yes. I don't know, she mentioned you once,' Betsy said. 'I just thought you might know.'

'You thought she might even be in Vegas?'

'Yeah.'

'She isn't coming,' Joe said.

'What do you mean?'

'You were right, she was thinking of maybe coming out this weekend, but she isn't coming.'

'Why not?'

'She's busy. She has a job.'

'How do you know?'

'We keep in touch.' Joe gobbled his pancakes.

Betsy said, 'She stays with you?'

'Depends.'

'She knows your wife?'

'Sure. She was always looking for a surrogate mother.' He chewed some more. 'That's pretty brutal, huh?'

'Yes.'

'Sorry, babe,' he said; he looked sorry.

'You didn't come to her graduation.'

'She didn't want us both there,' he said. 'Too much angst, she told me, too much shit out of the past.'

'She never told me. About you and her.'

'She wanted to keep it for herself.'

'So it all started when?'

Joe played with his fork, plucked the tines, drummed with it on the table. He told her it began when Franny went to college in New York. She called him and said would he visit her. He went. He felt he could be a bolt hole for her. No one knew they were related, they didn't have the same last name or know the same people. She could just be. With him, she could be herself.

He stabbed the last piece of pancake with his fork and used it to wipe up the smear of maple syrup on the thick white plate.

Betsy drank the coffee too fast, burned her tongue, swallowed the bitter scalding liquid, cleared her throat and looked around Denny's where no one was young. No one had sporty tits like the girls at the Hard Rock. At the next booth to her right was a quartet, two men, two women, all with sagging jowls, loose bellies, wattled necks, the two men sunk in a torpor with only enough energy to work through the piles of food. The women, the wives, talked to each other, but the men only sat and ate.

Joe said, 'So you're looking for our kid?'

'Yes.'

'She said she might come out for the big digital photo show this week. This guy she liked was coming.'

'What guy?'

'You'll have to ask her yourself. That's privileged, you know, father-daughter stuff.'

'She's my child, Joe.'

'Mine, too.'

'What the hell are you doing in a place like this? Las Vegas, I mean.'

‘I thought you’d never ask.’

Wiping his mouth on a napkin, Joe said he had first come to the Vegas area because Fran was working with some Indians in Nevada. He was living in New Mexico, in Madrid. It got commercialized, he said and Fran asked him to come to Nevada and they met up and he rented a little place way out on the desert. He sold prayer flags and Indian bracelets and Fran stayed with him.

‘It was nice,’ he said. ‘Sweet.’

Eventually, he settled in Nevada because Franny thought she might drop out of school and live there with him. It didn’t work out — she got the travel bug, turned herself into a reporter. Joe stayed on anyway and Las Vegas grew and he found himself in the way of a new casino. There was a lot of money in it.

‘You sold out?’

Joe laughed and said, ‘More ways than one, honey.’

He bought a ranch on the desert and started a tourist operation. He flew them over the desert and the red rocks, showed them real Indian crafts at out of the way settlements, they bought plenty. He taught music and art at the local college. Met Pam. Built the house she wanted. Sometimes, when he was fed up, he got a ticket and traveled a while.

Betsy put her hands around the coffee cup to warm them. Franny had a life and a connection with her father that Betsy wasn't part of and she felt cheated and left out. Joe knew their daughter better than she did.

'Tell me about her boyfriend,' Betsy said. 'Bobby Ketsen, right?'

'You knew?'

'Yes.'

'She said you didn't know anything.'

'Was he a creep?'

'No, he was fantastic, man,' Joe said. 'About her age. He was incredibly nice, and nice to her, and she was relaxed and all spruced up. All dolled up like that, she looked like you used to, you know? She was great.' He slurped up the remainder of his coffee. 'I think they were thinking marriage.'

'That's a fantasy. Come on. She never told me anything about it.'

Joe reached in his back pocket and got some glasses out and put them on, then looked at her. 'What did you do to your face?'

The smell of maple syrup made her queasy. Joe was restless, fidgeting with pats of butter, taking off the foil, balling it up and tossing it across the table.

Betsy looked at him. 'There was never any animosity between us. You and me. Was there?'

'Yeah, there was. She said you didn't like me much. Didn't approve. Of her either.'

'What?'

'She said you were always riding her — get a haircut, get a boyfriend. She said you thought she was probably gay and it drove you nuts.'

'Is she?' Betsy said.

'Is she what?'

'Gay, Joe. What we were just saying.'

'I just told you she had a guy. If she was gay also, how would I know? And why would I care? Maybe she's bi, maybe not. I just care that she's happy.' He scraped some bits of yellow egg off the plate.

'Where is she?'

'Why?' He pulled some crumpled bills out of his pocket and paid the waitress.

Leaving the restaurant, Joe started across the empty lot towards his truck and she followed him and it was hot in the parking lot and she pulled off her sweater.

'You watch the news ever, Joe? You read the papers?'

'Nah, hardly ever. What do I need all that pain for, man, right?'

He didn't know. She wouldn't tell him.

Desperate to keep him talking, Betsy said, 'Listen, come back into town and I'll buy you a drink. My treat.'

'Yeah, maybe later. I have something I have to pick up. Which hotel?'

She told him and added, 'What time are you coming?'

'Whenever,' he said, got back in his truck and put his head out of the window.

Joe smiled. 'You know, I was in London a few years ago, and I was going to call up and say, hey, Bets, let's get together, man, after all these years, let's meet up and tell each other some lies.'

In the parking-lot lights, his face was white and shiny and full of glee. For her failure to return his calls, he had been waiting to get even. The middle-aged Joe Darling seemed suddenly cunning and had a mean streak and kept guns.

'You've changed,' she said.

'Like I said, we've all changed except you. You just keep looking like you always did. You could be Franny's sister, except for you probably had your faced fixed, right? Spooky,' he said, grinning.

'Where is she, Joe?'

'Tell me why you're suddenly so interested in finding your kid, and I'll tell you where she is.'

24

Unless she gave Joe something, he would never help her. There was no way he would believe her lies. At the hotel she stood in the shower of her fake marble bathroom and let the hot water stream over her, then turned it ice cold to wake herself up. A few minutes later, wrapped in a towel, she heard a knock at the door. A muffled voice called out, 'Room service.'

'I didn't order anything,' Betsy yelled back.

'We have a gift for you.'

'I don't want it.'

'It's from management.'

'Just leave it, will you?'

'I need a signature,' the voice said and she figured it was a fruit basket from the hotel. 'Please, lady, I'll get in trouble, just sign this, OK?'

She hitched up the towel and pulled on a shirt and buttoned it hastily, then opened the door a crack.

It was Joe. He put his hand on the door.

'I want to talk to you,' he said.

'About Franny?'

'Yeah.'

'Come in.'

From a chair, Betsy took a terry cloth robe, pulled it on and tied the belt tight.

'You look good, man,' he said and lurched in her direction. 'You look hot. I mean you look like you used to, practically. You wouldn't like to do it with me for old times' sake?'

'Are you nuts? What is it? How come you're so angry at me? You left me in the first place,' she said. 'I woke up one morning and you were standing there with your duffel bag and you said you were going to join the revolution.'

'You always treated me like a dog,' he said.

Joe was nervous. He sat down on the edge of her bed and played with his hands.

'What are you talking about? You were the second guy I ever slept with. I was nineteen years old.'

'Yeah, well, so what? I was like a pet for you. I was scenery, honey. You didn't even notice.

'I never thought of you like that,' she said and it was true. She never thought of him as a pet. Joe Darling. She always thought of him as Peter Pan.

'What do you want, Betsy?'

'I want Franny.' The backs of her eyes were hot as tears welled up. 'Please.'

Abruptly, he got up and paced the room and stared out of the window. He turned back towards her.

'You want to smoke some weed?' he said.

'No thanks.'

'Come on.' He got a plastic bag out of his jeans and took a joint from it and lit up and passed it to her.

'I don't want it.'

'I want you to.'

She took the joint and puffed it lightly and said, 'Let's go for a drink, OK?'

'You get dressed and then maybe we can get the drink. Maybe I do know how to get in touch with Frances. You got anything in that mini bar? She likes to be called Frances. She hates Franny.'

'You call her Franny. Take whatever you want.'

'It's different with her and me. I want some champagne,' he said.

'The key's in the lock,' she said and picked up her shirt and started for the bathroom.

'No.'

'What do you mean, no?'

'Let me watch.'

'Joe, for chrissake.'

'I mean it,' he said. 'I want to see if the rest of you is as good as your face. You always had great tits, nice and high and round with those big pink nipples, I remember. I want to watch.'

He got the champagne out of the mini bar, popped it open, found a pill in his pocket and swallowed it with the wine.

'What's that?'

'Quaalude and bubbly. You remember, right? Hey, I know where she is,' he said and lay back against the pillows on the bed.

'Tell me.'

'Get dressed.'

'This is really silly,' she said as lightly as she could manage. She leaned over and kissed him on the forehead. 'Come on, Joe.'

'I'm serious, man. Let me watch you. Then we'll go for a drink and maybe I'll tell you where Franny is. Maybe, maybe not, but probably, OK? That's the deal.'

She reached for her jeans.

'Take the towel off first. And the shirt.'

Joe went to the window and began pulling the curtains shut.

She said, 'We're on the twenty-ninth floor.'

He ignored her and shut the curtains and then lay back on the bed, arms folded under his head.

'You didn't used to mind,' he said. 'So do me a show.'

'This is blackmail.'

'Come on, man, we all have a price.'

It was only Joe, she told herself, lying on the bed, his face expectant as a guy at a porn show. He made her nervous.

Her back to him, she took off the bathrobe and the shirt and found her bra and started dressing as fast as she could, but the clothes bunched up in her hands.

'Slow the fuck down,' he said. 'What's the hurry? Turn around, OK? Show me the tits.'

'No!'

Joe sat up. 'What do you mean?'

Carrying her clothes, she went into the bathroom, slammed the door, changed, not knowing if she was furious at him or herself. It bothered her that her body, unlike her face, would look old to Joe. Joe would remember how she had once looked.

Emerging from the bathroom, she said, 'Get out of here.'

'Betsy?' His voice was soft; she didn't answer.

Joe stood up and walked towards her; she pushed him, he stumbled over a chair leg and landed on the floor. He laughed.

'I deserved that,' he said. 'Come on, sit down. Let's start over.'

'Just go.'

He got to his feet and put a hand on her shoulder. 'I'm really sorry. Tell me what you want, OK? Honey?'

She looked at him. 'Bobby Ketsen is dead.'

Joe was silent.

'Someone murdered him,' she said.

'Poor Franny, Jesus, poor kid.' He leaned against the door. 'My God. You think she was involved. That's why you're here. Isn't it?'

'No,' she said too loud, too quickly. 'I only wanted to be the one to tell her,' she added, looked at Joe, saw it.

'You knew. Did you? You knew all along.'

He hesitated for a split second.

'Of course I knew,' Joe said. 'You think I wouldn't know something like that about my daughter? I was just waiting to find out what you wanted from me.' He pushed the wispy strands of hair back on his head. 'You're pathetic. I know you. I know what you're thinking, you think she was involved in some way, don't you — you fucking believe your own kid would get mixed up in shit like that.'

'How did you know about Ketsen?' Betsy asked.

'None of your business how I knew,' he said.

Betsy walked towards the window, Joe held her arm.

'So you believe she did it,' he said. 'Who's going to believe you, man? You never were a reliable witness. You even told yourself lies. If she needs someone, she'll call me. So long, Betsy. Bye-bye.'

* * *

All the way back to New York she slept fitfully. Too wrecked to stay in her room, after Joe left, Betsy had gone to the Vegas airport and waited in the terminal, guzzling Diet Coke until the first flight out in the morning.

She was angry with herself that she'd confided in Joe, unsure if he really had known about Ketsen anyway. Already he would be calling Franny: Stay away. Keep clear of your mother. She's a crackpot and you should stay away, OK? He'd tell her this and Franny would listen because she had a relationship with Joe, was friends with him, trusted him. He would tell her and she would disappear completely.

In Newark, Mark Carey was waiting. He wore the camel-hair coat and old brown corduroy pants and ancient desert boots. The tan had faded, he was sallow, the eyes seemed worn and dry and he was unshaved.

'I got your message,' he said.

'Thank you for coming.'

'You want one of these?' He held out a pack of cigarettes.

'Thanks.'

'I worry about you.'

'I'm sorry.'

'It will kill Bel if anything happens to you.'

'What will happen to me?'

'Nothing if I can help it. But you don't make it easy, running off to Las Vegas in the middle of this.'

She had called Mark and asked him to meet her but she felt like a jerk now. There was nowhere to hide from the craziness that hung around the edges of her being and made her run to Las Vegas.

'Say I needed the sun,' she said. 'Say I was light deprived.'

'If you want my help if would be better if you told me what's going on.' Mark put his arms around her and looked over her shoulder as if he expected someone.

'What is it?' she said. 'Are you OK? You look lousy,' she added without thinking.

'Yeah,' he said. 'Defending terrorists who killed people you love is bad for you, you know? I feel old.' He took her hand and they walked out of the terminal. 'Come on, I'll take you home. I've got a car and driver.'

'To your place?'

'To yours,' he said.

'I don't want to go home yet.'

* * *

The room was yellow and had a window that looked out on the back yard and the bed was made up with white sheets and a patchwork quilt. On the wall was a photograph of a young man and three little boys on a beach. Other people she didn't know about, had never asked.

She glanced at it and then at Mark. 'You?'

'Yes.'

'Your kids?'

'Yes.'

'Where are they?'

'All grown up now,' he said. 'I'll introduce you some time.'

She put her bag on the floor and sat on the bed and Mark sat next to her. Sunlight came in through the window. From somewhere in the house came the smell of roasting meat, lamb and garlic and rosemary.

'Did you kill him, Betsy?'

He pulled it out of the air, where it had hung, unspoken.

'What?'

'Did you kill Bobby Ketsen?'

'No!'

'I'm not going to pretend. You're in a bit of trouble and you have to help me.'

'I didn't kill him,' she said.

'Do you know who did? I think you do. I think you know and you're protecting someone.'

Betsy leaned against the wall and the plaster was cool on her skin. Her face was hot, burned, from the Las Vegas sun. Her eyes half shut, she counted colored squares on the patchwork quilt.

'Betsy?'

'I'm sorry.'

'Talk to me.'

'I don't know. Why wouldn't I say if I did? Why wouldn't I just go to the cops and say, look, I know who did this?'

'The part I don't get is you going to Vegas.'

'It was a wild-goose chase. It came to nothing. I just couldn't sit still and wait for the cops.'

'The line-up was a bad idea.'

'I know, I know, I fucking *know*, OK?'

Half to himself, Mark said, 'I wish I knew what kind of information the cops actually have. Did Detective Dolce share anything with you? Share, I think, is the correct word nowadays, isn't it?'

She shook her head.

'Then maybe I'll see if I can have another chat with him later.' He looked at his watch. 'I have to go. I have to be in court in half an hour. Try to get a few hours' sleep.'

'Thanks. Thank you.'

'You'll be all right, won't you?'

'Yes.' She rubbed her eyes. 'Yes, I'll be all right now.'

'Good. There's someone I want you to meet later.'

25

Her back to the door, the girl in Mark's study unwrapped a pink shawl carefully from over her black coat and folded it slowly and took a large envelope from her bag and set it on the coffee table where there was a bottle of red wine on a yellow legal pad. She wore a cream-colored jacket and a narrow dark skirt and polished boots and her hair was pinned back from her face. Mark kissed her on both cheeks, poured wine in two glasses, handed her one. She turned around as she gulped at it and wiped the stain off her mouth before she saw Betsy watching her. Betsy's own shirt and jeans were a mess, but she pushed her hair back, fussed with her collar, and stood at the door. She had slept for hours. When Mark saw her, he gestured for her to come in.

For an instant, in Meryl Briggs and Mark Carey standing close together in his study, Betsy saw a conspiracy. She hesitated in the doorway.

'You know Betsy Thornhill?' he said to Meryl, took her coat from her, turned to Betsy. 'Please sit down, Betsy. I want you to look at something.'

He took Meryl's arm and said, 'Will you show Betsy the pictures, please?'

She sat on the leather sofa. Meryl perched beside her. She took three photographs from the envelope and placed them face-down on the table in front of them.

Betsy said, 'What are they? What's going on?' She could smell the girl's musky perfume.

Meryl looked up.

'You remember I told you how Ketsen liked photographing women?' she said to Betsy. 'Making them over? Do you remember?'

'I remember.'

Betsy reached for the photographs on the table, but Meryl put her hand on them. She said, 'Let me finish first,' and held out her glass to Mark. 'Can I have some more of that?'

'Of course,' he said and filled her glass.

Meryl knocked it back and turned to Betsy again. 'I told you I'd seen pictures of you when I was cleaning up Ketsen's files?'

'Yes.'

'It hit me after you came by my place, but I didn't really think about it until Mr Carey called me,' she said.

'What hit you?'

'The woman in the pictures that I thought

was you, I found them. The pictures, I mean.'

'How?'

It was after Betsy left her apartment in Hoboken that Meryl had remembered, she said. She knew that Bobby sometimes sent his pictures to a fly-by-night art magazine which had recently folded. Meryl knew because she always shipped his pictures. When Bobby died, she went to see the guy who ran the magazine, told him the cops wanted all of Ketsen's stuff. He was OK with it, she said. He didn't care. He had forgotten all about it, to tell the truth.

His studio in Williamsburg was jammed to the ceiling with files, photographs, paper, back issues of the magazine. Looking around, Meryl asked if she could look through his pictures and offered to help clear it up. They cut a deal: Meryl would help him clean up and she could take what she wanted. Whatever had Bobby's name on it, she threw in a shopping bag.

'And?' Betsy stubbed out her cigarette and lit another one.

'I looked for photos of me. I didn't care about the rest, but I took all Bobby's shit,' Meryl said. 'I tossed the rest of it in my closet.'

'Go on,' Betsy said.

'After you came to see me, I thought about

it, not right away, but after, so I went back in the closet and I found these.' She swept her hand over the pictures on the table.

'Why didn't you tell anyone?'

'I didn't want the cops bugging me anymore.'

'You gave me Ketsen's keys, though.'

'That was before I thought about the pictures. You asked, I had the keys, I knew you thought that I did it and I thought the keys might shut you up. You did, didn't you?'

'What?'

'Think I killed him,' Meryl said.

'Can I see the pictures?'

'In a minute. When Mr Carey came to see me, I told him.'

'How come?' Betsy asked. 'Why Mark?'

'Friend of the family.'

Mark, who was next to Meryl on the sofa, put his hand on her arm and said, 'Meryl, dear, would you show them to Betsy, please?'

'Sure,' she said and turned the pictures over, one at a time. 'It's not you, is it?' she asked. 'But it looks like you.'

* * *

Everything was in those images, in the black-and-white pictures that lay on the table next to the glasses of red wine. Betsy had no idea how long she sat and looked without speaking. No one else spoke, either. Somewhere in the big house a clock ticked. The smell of roast potatoes came from the kitchen. Mark coughed briefly, a guttural smoker's cough.

Betsy looked down at the girl in the pictures, at her own daughter all dolled up in fishnet tights and spike heels and a black leather mini-skirt. Franny's black hair was cut short. In one of the pictures she was naked to the waist, bare-breasted, with a young girl's high round breasts, in another she posed on the edge of a bed, naked except for a fur coat draped over her shoulders.

There was no doubt that it was Franny in the pictures. Seeing them, Betsy understood why she had killed Ketsen, but it made her feel criminal, looking. It felt pornographic, staring at her naked daughter.

Abruptly, Betsy got up and knocked the pictures off the table.

'Don't get the wrong idea,' Meryl said.

'What do you mean?' Betsy was still standing. 'I want a cigarette,' she said to Mark.

He found one, gave it to her, lit it.

Meryl said, 'Like I told you before, the women liked it. We all liked it. It's what was so creepy about the whole deal.'

'You liked it?' Her voice came out flat.

'Here's what I didn't tell you exactly because I was too embarrassed,' Meryl said. 'The women Bobby photographed loved it. They wanted to be the opposite of what they were, and he could spot it a mile away, the ones that felt like that. Plenty of them told him to go fuck himself, but the others, he took them out and talked to them and was nice to them, and in the end, they wanted to pose for him. They liked it. We're so programmed, you know, want what we don't have, be like someone else, long legs or puffed-up lips or whatever. It's us.'

'Go on.'

'I let him do those pictures of me you saw before — I wanted those pictures. I wanted to see what I looked like, white, different, so did this one.' She pointed to the picture of Franny. 'I mean, look at her. Look at her face. She's either high or she's getting ready to come, you know?'

It was an animal's response: Betsy crouched low, clutched the pictures, felt her nails scratch the surface; she wanted to rip them, tear them into pieces, burn them, see the images of her daughter disappear. Franny humiliated. Like a solid fist punched into her stomach. These things Betsy touched, these pictures, she hated more than anything she could remember.

Mark held out his hand. She ignored him, threw the photographs on the floor, stumbled backwards, propped herself up against the wall.

'You met her?' Betsy said to Meryl. 'The girl in the photos?'

'I heard from the others. She was pretty, like, drab, you know, at first, and he got her these outfits and she would strut around, and she loved it. Bobby took her shopping. They would do all the make-up places in SoHo and come back with bags and bags of stuff. She adored him. He liked touching her, he would just graze her breasts with his hand right in the studio, let everyone know she belonged to him.'

'Who?'

'Whoever,' Meryl said. 'Whoever was in the studio, you know?'

'When was this?'

'I'm not sure. Last year. Year before. He just saw people for how they were inside, and he liked playing with them. It wasn't even a power thing, not in the conventional sense, not just a head game. It was fun for him. For both of them.'

'Fun?'

'Yeah,' Meryl said. 'Also one of the kids who worked with us, an intern, said she thought this girl was at the studio recently, but there were always rumors and the kids in the office always smoke too much weed, you know. With them you can't trust shit.'

'Recently? When?' Betsy said.

'Yeah. Maybe three weeks ago, give or take.'

'You were there?'

'I was running errands for Bobby that day,' Meryl said. 'You know who the girl in these pictures is, right?'

All the time the two of them talked, Mark kept his mouth shut. He sat and smoked and coughed and made notes on the yellow pad. When Meryl finished talking, he stood and gathered up her coat. The meeting was over.

'Thanks, Meryl,' he said. 'Thank you for coming.'

He put Meryl's coat around her shoulders and her scarf in her hand and kissed her cheek and asked if he could keep the pictures. She nodded. He asked if she wanted a car to take her home, she said she'd take the train.

'Listen, I hope you win,' she said to Betsy. 'I hope no one gets fucked over because of that bastard.'

'Is there anything else?' Mark said.

Meryl stood in the doorway.

'I told you he stole from the World Trade Center wreckage, didn't I? You saw. He stole pieces of metal and called it sculpture. He went down there dressed as a fireman to get pictures. He took pictures of dead people and body parts and, like, sold them as porn.' Meryl's voice was quiet and cold. 'He stole from everyone.'

* * *

'You know, don't you?' Betsy said.

'Yes.'

'When did you know?'

In the dining room, they sat at the table where yellow roses, heavy silver, good glass were reflected in cherry wood. A platter with rack of lamb and roast potatoes had been set down by Mark's Jamaican housekeeper, a bottle of Bordeaux already open. Mark served Betsy and himself. She couldn't eat; she drank wine and smoked; the pictures of Franny stayed in front of her eyes.

Mark put down his knife and fork, and said 'I knew that you had a daughter.'

'Bel told you?'

'Yesterday. And I'm worried about her, Betsy. Bel's not well. I can't get her to see a doctor. I'm scared.'

Betsy felt cold suddenly. 'What's wrong with her?'

'I don't know.'

‘I’ll talk to her. What else?’

Mark said, ‘I had guessed. She told me your girl lived in the building when she was in college, and afterwards, too, some of the time. Remember, I know your mother, I know Eva. You’re a dead ringer for her. It makes sense that you might have a child with the family face. It is your child, in the photographs, isn’t it? Your daughter, is that right?’

‘You didn’t say much when Meryl was here; you were pretty formal.’

He loosened his tie. ‘Sometimes it’s better to just listen.’

‘Yes, yes, OK. Yes, it’s Franny. Yes,’ she said finally.

‘Why don’t we talk to her, then?’

‘I don’t know where she is. I went to Las Vegas because her father lives there and I told Joe and he’ll tell her and I’ll never find her.’ She put her glass down too hard, it rang on the wood surface of the table. ‘I’m sorry.’

‘You don’t need to be,’ Mark said. ‘We’ll find her.’

‘You don’t know Franny,’ Betsy said. ‘I’m not even sure if I want to find her, I mean I do want to find her, I want to protect her, I’m sorry about it, sorry for her, sorry for me.’ She held back the tears, crying emptied you out. But her not letting go made her feel dry, hard, stony.

'You're on my side, aren't you, Mark?' she said and thinking of Franny as the opposition shocked her.

'I'm on your side.' He tapped his long thin fingers on the table lightly. 'It's OK, Betsy, you hear me? This is what lawyers are for. Tell me exactly what you think.'

'You heard what Meryl said. Franny was in some kind of thrall to Ketsen. She let him take pictures of her dressed up like a hooker. He put them on a website, he sent them to a magazine. Maybe she couldn't stop him.'

'Meryl said the women went along with it. Franny liked him doing it.'

'I don't believe that,' Betsy said.

'It still doesn't make her the killer, not necessarily. It's a motive, but it could be a motive for someone else.'

'Like me, you mean?' she said. 'A motive for her mother, is that what you mean?' Betsy said.

'I didn't say that.'

'I'm sorry, I thought it's what you were thinking. There were other women involved with him.'

'Women the witnesses could have mistaken for you?' Mark asked. 'I don't think anyone would confuse you and Meryl Briggs or Franny and Meryl.'

'There were others.'

'Listen to me. It's a very shaky case. No one saw the murder. No one saw anyone kill Ketsen. The witnesses, so-called, all they saw was a white woman in a red coat going into his building at the right time, and possibly going into his apartment. That's it. They focused on you only after the newspapers, after the line-up. In their heads, the woman began to look like you. Or someone like you. Let me tell you a story. May I?'

Betsy nodded.

'After the Twin Towers fell, people who escaped ran outside and saw more horror. Some reported they saw piles of dead cows, legs sticking in the air. What they actually saw were dead bodies, people who had fallen or jumped. Later someone discovered many of them had seen pictures of slaughtered farm animals from Britain during the foot-and-mouth epidemic, and they took the pictures they knew and processed their memory of these with the horror outside the Towers. People do that. I think that's what happened. Your face became known and witnesses put it on the woman who went into Ketsen's that night.'

Mark held up the wine. Betsy shook her head.

'Why was Meryl so forthcoming with you?'

'Her uncle Lincoln Briggs was a friend. I

got him out of jail a few times. He was in the movement. Civil Rights. The 1960s.'

'I remember, you know,' Betsy said. 'I'm old enough.'

'I sometimes forget,' he said. 'Do you believe it was Franny? Tell me.'

'Who else could be mistaken for me? Ketsen was a pig. He used women. Franny is a righteous girl. She would take against you if you offended her. If it's not her, who?'

'Should we have some Calvados?'

'What are you going to do with the pictures?'

Mark reached to the sideboard for a bottle and glasses.

'That's what I've been thinking about,' he said. 'What about this Calvados?'

'I don't want anything else,' she said. 'I want to know how I'm going to climb out of this. I've had six messages on my phone from Frank Dolce. I haven't called him back, he'll show up, he'll be waiting, I know it,' she added. Her voice was panicky. 'Help me.'

He poured himself a drink.

'I need a couple of days,' he said. 'I want you both safe and out of trouble, you and Franny. We don't know where Franny is. What about you?'

'How will you keep us both safe?'

'I have a call in to someone.'

'One of your friends.'

'Yes,' he said. 'He's on vacation, he'll be back at his desk the day after tomorrow. We'll have answers,' he said. 'He owes me.'

Betsy looked at him and saw something like pity on his face.

'You don't believe me, do you?' she said. 'You think I did it, don't you? You think I killed him.'

'I told you, I'm on your side.' He looked at his watch, tossed back the Calvados, pushed his chair from the table.

'Go home now. I'll call a car for you.'

'I don't want to go back to the apartment,' she said. 'Please, Mark.'

'I want you to try to behave as normally as possible.'

'Isn't it a little late for that?' Betsy said.

'It will be just fine.'

'Then come home with me.' She gulped the last mouthful of wine. 'I mean, spend the night.'

Mark reached across the table and took her hand and said, 'Listen to me.'

'I'm listening.'

'That's a very nice invitation but you don't want me.'

'Who said I did?'

'You really don't,' he said.

'Because you're married?'

'Christ no, that's never stopped me,' he said. 'Right now you just want someone who makes you feel safe, and I do that, and you think it's something else, but it's not. I'm a bastard.'

'That's obvious.' She pushed her wine away abruptly and some spilled on her white napkin and stained it red. 'I'm going.'

'I'll get my coat and walk you home. I could do with some air.'

'I can go home by myself.'

She got up and went upstairs to get her bag, hurried back down, went towards the front door. Mark was waiting. He put his arm around her.

'Don't be hurt,' he said. 'You want a nice guy. Someone who pays attention to you and makes you feel good. I don't know.' He looked away. 'I can't do any of that.'

Betsy picked up her bag and jacket and he opened the front door.

'Why not?' she said again.

Mark pushed his hair off his collar, rubbed his eyes, shrugged.

'I don't know how,' he said.

26

Betsy slipped out of her apartment and down to Bel's the next morning as soon as she saw Frank Dolce's car in the street outside. She knocked on Bel's door and waited. There was no answer.

'Bel?'

'What's the matter?' Marie Tusi said, coming up the stairs, wheezing. 'I heard someone banging up here on Bel's door. What's going on?'

'I don't know. She doesn't answer.'

'She doesn't answer the phone either,' Marie said. 'I tried last night and then this morning. She never gave me keys, she wouldn't; I said over and over, Bel, you have to give me keys in case, but she didn't want to. She didn't like me having her keys. Betsy?'

'What?'

'That cop is here again,' Marie said. 'I saw the car outside, big maroon Crown Vic job, right?'

'I'm going up to get Bel's keys,' Betsy said.

'What about the police?'

The pulse, like a tiny clock in her neck, throbbed but she smiled as best she could at

Marie and said, 'It's nothing. OK? For now. Just forget about it.'
'Sure, girl,' Marie said. 'Of course.'

* * *

The green smell of rotting flowers hit her and made her gag as she went into the apartment. Bel's place was always spotless, now the daffodils on the mantel were withered and there was a pile of newspapers on the living room floor.

The room was empty.

'Bel, are you there?' Betsy called in the direction of the bedroom. 'Bel?'

From the bedroom in back came a small noise like a mouse crossing a bare floor. Quietly, Betsy opened the door. Bel was in bed, eyes closed.

'Bel?' She leaned down.

Bel opened her eyes.

'Hello, cara. I get a flu, everyone thinks I'm dying.' Her words were slurred. 'Marie's been talking again, right? She told you I had the flu?'

'I knocked a long time and I got worried so I used the key you gave me.'

'You thought I croaked? Don't be concerned. I'm not going anywhere,' she said, but Betsy saw she was worried. 'Sit down.'

'Let me fix you something,' Betsy said.

'Fine. Make me some tea, OK? Give me a cigarette, will you, sweetheart?' Bel shoved herself up against the headboard. 'On the dresser.'

On the maple dresser was an unopened pack. She gave it to Bel who tried to get the cellophane off. Her fingers shook. She dropped the pack on her chest.

'Do it for me, sweetheart, will you, please?'

Betsy reached down and took the pack, opened it, shook a cigarette out for Bel, gave it to her, lit it.

Bel nodded, took a drag, coughed, smiled. 'Thanks.'

'How long have you been like this?'

'A day or two. It's nothing.' She spoke very softly, very slow. Betsy had to lean down to hear her.

'I'll make tea,' she said. 'Did you eat anything?'

Bel shook her head and closed her eyes and Betsy took the cigarette from her fingers and carried it into the kitchen.

Dirty cups and bowls were piled in the sink, Betsy put the kettle on, washed the dishes, looked out the window and saw the maroon car still parked across the street. Frank would wait outside all day if he had to.

The kettle boiled. Betsy fixed two mugs of

tea and put a slice of lemon on the saucer. On the tray, she placed the mugs and a jar of cherry jam and a plate of ginger snaps she found in the cupboard.

'I like ginger snaps.' Bel was sitting up, smoking. She held up the cigarette. 'See? I can smoke all by myself. I'm fine. Thank you, cara. Thanks. So, sit. I was thinking I'd like to see Venice again. Would you go with me?'

'Of course. We'll go to Venice as soon as you're better.' Betsy sat on the chair next to the bed. 'What happened?'

'I'm not senile, you know. Don't look at me like that. I just had a fancy to see Venice with you. Let me drink my tea.' She coughed, the cigarette still between her lips. 'Where were you?' she added.

'What do you mean?'

'Come on,' Bel said. 'You leave without telling me. You get everyone all worked up.'

'I'm sorry.'

'It's OK. I forgive you. I always do.'

'I know. Is that how Marie knew I was away, you told her?'

'Of course not. I don't include Marie in any of our business.'

'How did she know?'

'She's bloody nosy is how.'

She wanted to tell Bel everything, the way she had when she was a kid and Bel knew all the answers. But Bel was old and sick and when she picked her mug up it shook so badly, Betsy took it away. Bel couldn't help her, not anymore.

'You want to close your eyes again?' Betsy said. 'You've seen a doctor?'

'I'm fine. I am a doctor.'

'Give me a number,' Betsy said.

'Listen, sweetheart, I'm old enough to decide how I'm doing, OK? Fine, not fine, I don't want a doctor. What's Mark going to do about your case?'

'He says he has some ideas.'

'What ideas?' Bel said and then, as if she'd used up her energy for the day and had nothing left to draw on, she sagged back against the pillows, her face gray as cement. Her eyes lost their focus.

Betsy leaned over. 'Bel?'

So softly Betsy had to put her ear next to her mouth, Bel said, 'I could use some sleep.'

'Please tell me what's wrong with you. I can't bear the idea of you not feeling well. I'm going to call a doctor if you don't tell me what's going on.'

'Promise you won't tell anyone. I don't want any doctors. I don't want anything. I don't want you telling Mark Carey, either.'

'Yes.'

'No, promise.'

'I promise.'

'I think that I had a little stroke,' Bel said. 'Over the weekend. Something bothered me. There was noise in the building, someone banging on the radiator or maybe on my door, I couldn't tell. I thought someone was in the apartment here, but that was my imagination, I think, and the room turned orange and went upside down. It was as if I felt hands around my head. That's all I remember. I woke up on the floor. I couldn't find my bag.'

'I'll look.'

'It's gone,' Bel said. 'I looked. Also, I'm not going into the hospital, I don't want them to hook me up to machines and make me a vegetable. They don't let you smoke, either.'

'Let me call someone.'

'You are the someone. I love you. You were always like the kid I'd have wanted if I wanted kids, only better. Betsy?'

'Yes, Bel.'

'It was love at first sight, you know, cara? As soon as I saw you as a baby. You're who I want here. I already saw Franny.'

'When?' Betsy caught her breath. 'When did you see her?'

'Can you find my bag for me?'

'Yes. Where did you see Franny?'

'Here.'

'You imagined it. She's in Afghanistan.'

'Cara, I'm not senile.'

'When?'

'Over the weekend,' Bel said. 'Maybe last week. I saw her. I'd like to sleep a little and we could talk later. Find my bag for me.'

'Try to tell me when you saw Franny. Which day?'

Bel raised her thin shoulders, closed her eyes, slumped back on the messy pillows and said, 'I don't remember.'

Betsy sat in the chair next to the bed and listened to Bel's ragged breathing. She held her knotted hand lightly. Franny in New York, Bel had said. She had seen Franny. She was here, in the building, without Betsy knowing. Or was it only Bel's feverish imagination?

When she was sure Bel was asleep, Betsy got up and went into the living room, looked out the front window and saw that Frank's car was gone. She threw out the dead flowers, looked for Bel's bag, couldn't find it and left her sleeping and went home.

The light on her machine was flashing, and when she played the messages back, there were two from Frank Dolce left for her in the last hour. Four old messages, she discovered, had never been erased: one was from Bobby Ketsen. His voice was still there, a dead man wanting a date.

27

She dialed the phone all day, for hours, relentlessly, as if her life depended on it and she started thinking of Franny as one of the disappeared and herself as one of those wailing South American mothers. Franny was as remote and inaccessible as a hostage held in the Andes. *Frances, call her Frances*, she told herself that afternoon while Bel slept downstairs in her apartment and she sat by her phone, holding it like a lifeline. I'm drowning, she thought.

Again and again, she called London. She called hotels in foreign cities where Franny might be working and had fractured conversations with people who did not speak English or feigned ignorance. A man on the phone in Tehran informed her that he loved New York.

Betsy knew Joe was one step ahead, in touch with Franny, warning her, keeping her safe, the way he saw it. *Change your name. Use another name*, he would tell her. *Don't talk to your mother. Stay away from your mother. Your mother is a killer.*

Franny was gone, but she had been in New

York. Meryl said she had heard the kids at Ketsen's office talk about Franny. She had been there. The kids at the office were always high on weed. Bel had seen Franny, but Bel was old and sick. Did the cops know about Franny? That she existed? Did Frank know?

The phone in her hand, she sat for hours, redialing numbers on the phone with the chipped mouthpiece, wondering what information the cops had, what Frank knew. She picked balls of lint off the bedspread, and smoked and made calls.

* * *

'Your pineapple is rotten.'

Frank Dolce looked around the kitchen and then sat down and folded his hands over each other the way he always did.

She lifted the fruit off the fridge where it had sat for a week and tossed it into the garbage.

'I don't know why,' she said. 'It's bloody cold in here. The pineapple, I mean. It shouldn't go bad like that when it's cold.'

'Where were you?' he said.

'I went to Las Vegas.'

'You lied to me.'

'I'm sorry.'

'You should have been straight with me about it, Betsy.'

'I didn't do anything,' she said. 'You know I didn't.'

'We're running out of possibilities on this Ketsen thing, and I'm leveling with you, but you don't level with me. We have the picture that looks like you. We have the witnesses. The line-up. Then you run off to Las Vegas without telling anyone. It doesn't look good,' he said and took the coffee she handed him. 'I'm sorry, Betsy. There are just no other suspects, except you. Christ, I'm tired.'

She listened to him and felt calm. A lethal calm she figured was impenetrable had enveloped her. Her mind moved forward. Franny seemed unreachable. But Betsy would find her and get a plane, wherever it was, she'd find her.

Frank didn't know. He didn't mention Franny. She had to be sure, it was what she needed, the single piece of information: *did Frank know that she had a daughter?*

'I'm sorry, too,' Betsy said. 'I'm really sorry about Las Vegas.'

'I felt lousy when I heard.'

'Heard?' Her voice rose. 'What do you mean, *heard*? How the hell did you hear? You knew I went?'

He nodded.

'Then why did you ask me?'

'I hoped you'd tell me,' he said.

'Who told you?'

He was silent.

'It was Joe,' she said.

'Yes.'

'How did he find you?'

'I don't know. It's not that hard if you know the case you want to talk about. He seemed to know your address. Maybe he called a couple of precincts downtown. You were married to this guy? He sounds like a freak.'

'We weren't married.'

'I gave you a lot of rope,' Frank said. 'I knew you were lying when you were on the phone. You said you were here.'

'Did I?'

'You let me believe you were here.'

Betsy got up and looked in the fridge for a beer. Joe wouldn't tell Frank about Franny. Joe would protect his kid, wouldn't he?

'What did Joe tell you?' she said. 'He's nuts, you know,' she added. 'He sits out there on the desert and he's so ripped from the dope he smokes he doesn't know what he's doing, Frank. You're right, he is a freak.'

'I didn't like the sound of him. I had to listen anyway.'

'What did he say?'

'Can I have a glass of water while you're up?'

She closed the fridge and turned on the tap.

Out of the blue, Frank said, 'Don't do it.'

'Don't do what?'

Betsy filled a glass and gave it to Frank who drank it in one gulp. She sat down at the table next to him.

'I told you before,' Frank said. 'Mark Carey.'

'How come you have it in for Mark?' she said. 'Because he represented people who called the cops pigs once upon a time. Is that it, Frank? I mean you hate him because he was an old leftie or something?'

'He hustles everyone. He knows people and he uses his connections.'

'So?'

'I don't know.'

'What don't you know? What is it, Frank? What's really wrong with Mark Carey?'

His face was sorrowful and he said softly, 'I can't compete with him.'

Without any warning, he got off the chair and slid onto his knees on the kitchen floor and put his arms around her waist. Betsy, not knowing what to do, sat stiff as a board.

Frank said, 'Don't put yourself in harm's way like that. I'm afraid for you. Please.

Please, let me help you.' He looked up at her. 'He only takes loony-tunes cases, terrorists, scum like that. He's defending some Al-Qaeda shit-brain. You hear me, Betsy? You use Mark Carey and everyone knows you're guilty. I'm trying to help you. I can get you a good lawyer.'

'Everything's fine now, Frank. Honest.'

'You like him, don't you?' Frank looked at her. 'You'll go with him in the end. I know that. He'll make it so comfortable, you won't be able to resist. Never mind. There's no point in me hanging around here anymore, is there?'

'I don't know, Frank,' she said softly. 'It depends why you were hanging around here in the first place.'

'I have to go. I'm sorry for the way I acted.'

'Did Joe say anything else?'

Frank looked puzzled. 'What do you mean?'

'Never mind,' she said.

Seeing him on the floor, she felt the sterile calm that had hung on her fall off. Betsy slipped off her chair and sat on the floor next to Frank. She put her head on his shoulder, he put his arm around her.

'Don't go,' she said. 'Let's just talk, OK. Tell me a joke or something. Would you? Come on, take off your jacket, OK?'

He took off the leather jacket, put it up on the chair, put his arms back around her.

'I acted like a jerk just now,' he said.

'You didn't,' she said. 'You really didn't. I always wanted a man who got down on his knees for me.' She smiled. 'Like in the movies, right?'

On the floor of the kitchen that smelled of pineapple, they sat and rocked. She leaned up and kissed him on the mouth.

'Let's go in the bedroom,' she said.

All he knew was the way she tasted when he kissed her back and he got up and followed her.

* * *

They took Bel to the hospital later that day. Betsy found her crumpled in a corner of the bathroom and called 911.

At St Vincent's, they put Bel in intensive care. Visitors were not allowed. After Marie, who had showed up, went home, Betsy lurked in the corridor outside the intensive care unit. Bel was eighty-four and frail, the doctor said. Betsy could wait if she wanted, but there wasn't any point. Even Bel lied about her age.

For what seemed like hours, in the same black jeans and sweater she'd put on that morning, Betsy sat on an orange plastic chair in the hospital waiting room. She counted the chairs in the row and picked up a battered copy of *Newsweek* and read it without understanding a word. She knew that Bel being sick was connected to her and to Franny and Ketsen's murder. Someone had hurt Bel. Someone had scared her. Someone who was connected.

She tried to mourn for Bel, but all she did was cry for herself. She sat in the corridor at St Vincent's and listened to the sound of the nurses' rubber-soled shoes on the floor and wept without making a sound. Bel had worked at the hospital all her life; Aunt Pauline, too. Both the women who showed her how to be alive were gone. Both gone now.

Mark showed up that evening and sat on the chair next to hers.

Betsy said, 'Bel's going to die, isn't she?'

'I don't know. That's up to her. It's in her will. She was the first person I ever knew to make a living will. Make her own decision about who pulls the plug and how to go,' he said. 'But she was more alive than almost anyone I ever knew.'

'They won't let me in to see her. They say I'm not family, Mark. Which is bullshit. Make them let me.'

'I'll try. I'm listed as next of kin. She was

afraid her sister would show up and do something stupid. They always call me first if anything happens.'

'I think someone terrorized her.' Betsy leaned back against the wall.

'Who?'

'I don't know. She said she'd seen Franny recently, but that's all she said.'

'If Franny went to her, it would be privileged. Bel's a doctor. Right now, whatever Bel knows is locked up inside her head. We'll have to wait. She's in a coma,' he said gently. 'I'm really sorry, but I have to go now. It's just for tonight and tomorrow. I have to go to Washington. Betsy?'

'What?'

'Can you go away for twenty-four hours while I'm gone?' Mark said, buttoning his coat. 'Just leave town quietly.'

'Why?'

'I want you to vanish, make yourself scarce. Nothing melodramatic, either. Just visit a friend. Don't tell me where you're going so I don't have to lie, just go. Can you do that?'

'Tell me why.'

Mark turned up his collar. 'I don't want this case to go any further. I don't want them to indict you. I don't want you talking to Frank Dolce.'

'Will they arrest me?' she said.

'Not if I can help it. But go away. Out of the city. And not to Las Vegas, please. Do you have someone? You could go to a hotel if you don't. I could give you some money.'

'I have someone. What about Franny? I can't find her.'

'Give me a day,' Mark said. 'You have my cell phone number?'

'Yes.'

'And you'll do it?'

'When should I go?'

'Now,' he said. 'Go tonight. Are you sure that you've got a place to go?'

'I have a place,' she said, turned abruptly, walked down the hospital corridor, then started running.

PART FOUR

28

Penn Station was nearly empty by the time she got there. Betsy bought a ticket from a machine. Electrical wires dangled from the ceiling and half-built walls resembled ancient ruins. Late commuters slumped against the wall or squatted near the floor, half asleep, leafing through their newspapers, drinking coffee from paper cups; one man sipped at a beer in a paper bag. A cop watched a homeless man looking for a place to settle down. The air was dank and fetid and stank of bad coffee and commuter sweat.

Leaning against a wall, she buried her face in a magazine she had bought and waited for her train. There had been more pictures of her in the *Post* that afternoon and the idea someone would recognize her in the station scared her. Betsy zipped up her black ski jacket and thought about the red coat and the day she bought it in London to celebrate her new face. A lost planet. Long gone.

In the copy of *Gourmet*, she tried to lose herself in the pictures: frozen mousse and ice creams and sorbets and fruit — lemon, peach, key lime, mango, pomegranate, pear. Had she ever cared so much about photographs of fruit?

As soon as her train was announced, Betsy ran down the platform, looking for an empty car, stumbled in, put her bag on the seat, sat next to the window.

Four black women, heading home to Long Island from a shopping spree in the city, entered, glanced at her, strolled to the far end, piled their bags on a seat, sat down and began laughing. They passed a box of Dunkin' Donuts. Otherwise the car was empty.

Magazine over her face, Betsy closed her eyes. The train shunted out of the station. The seat was hard. She tried to relax against it, tried to nap, but she could only think about Franny. Frances Thornhill. Her kid. Her daughter. She was a kid herself when she had Franny. Franny was an easy child and beautiful and sweet. Hard to believe she was real, she was so lovely. She laughed all the time and slept through the night.

'Ticket.'

Betsy opened her eyes and gave the conductor her ticket and he punched it and gave it back, barely looking at her.

The past few days, there were times Betsy was unsure if Franny had killed Ketsen after all, but not once she saw Meryl's photographs. It would have made Franny nuts, Ketsen sending out those pictures of her.

The photographs floated in front of Betsy. She imagined the scene in the studio, it was a world she knew by heart: a make-up woman hovering over Franny, her bag by her side, laying out cosmetics on a pink towel on an aluminum trunk. On a chair, Franny, looking in the mirror, seeing Ketsen behind her watching the transformation. Egging her on, posing her, the clothes, the fishnet tights, the leather skirt. Take off your top, Franny. Try the fur coat. Go on.

In the train window that was covered with grime and graffiti etched in the glass with a key, she saw her own face. She saw Franny's face take over her own and herself as her daughter, and the train rattled on through the ugly suburban landscape.

* * *

'Who is it?'

'Ma?'

'Who's there?' The querulous voice, unsteady with age, called out. 'Who is it?' She sounded aggrieved, as she always did, but fainter now, the voice wispy and slow.

Betsy heard the uncertain steps inside. She

crossed her arms over her chest and bent her head. The taxi she'd taken from the train station pulled away and left her alone on the front steps in the dark. Her feet were cold.

'It's me. Betsy,' she said. 'Mary Elizabeth.'

It was a year since she'd seen her. The last time, her mother was in the hospital with a broken hip and Betsy visited.

There had been times, after her father died, when Betsy was in college and felt lousy, she went home. She would lie on the settee and her mother would fix sardine sandwiches on buttered Kaiser rolls. King Oscar sardines out of the rectangular red can, and the two of them would eat and watch TV and share a cold beer.

Bad times when she got pregnant and Franny was born. Years when they didn't talk much, her and her mother. Finally, she'd made peace with the old lady. Got to like her, admired the resilience that kept her going no matter how her body turned on her, pieces breaking, hip, ankle, wrist, this woman who had been such a beauty.

Betsy wasn't crazy about the house, though — the dark prim rooms, tightly upholstered furniture.

'Ma?'

'I'm coming,' she said. 'I'm coming. I'm not deaf.'

There was the sound of bolts and locks and, slowly, the door opened. In the doorway, stood her mother in a green silk bathrobe.

Eva Thornhill leaned on a stainless steel cane and peered out at her daughter. In her seventies, she was still handsome, the crisp cheekbones, the fine skin. Her brown hair — she got it colored religiously every month — was held in place with hairspray. Behind the thick glasses, the once intense blue eyes were cloudy with cataracts; she fumbled with the door: Eva was going blind.

'Come on if you're coming,' Eva said. 'It's late.'

'I'm sorry if I woke you up.'

'I can't sleep. You know that. I never sleep. You knew I couldn't sleep, so you felt it was fine to arrive at any hour. Didn't you?'

It was one of her mother's complaints that she couldn't sleep until three or four in the morning, that she never slept. It had been her complaint since Betsy's father died.

'I'm sorry,' Betsy said.

'Are you coming in?'

'Is it all right?'

'Of course, it's all right. You're family, aren't you? You're welcome,' she said. 'I've been expecting you anyways,' Eva said. 'You should have called. You didn't have to send me information through Bel Plotkin.'

'I tried.'

'Did you really?'

'I'm sorry. Bel's sick.'

'Is she? I'll light a candle.' The sarcasm was heavy, but Eva had disliked Bel for years.

Betsy followed her through the door and into the front room. It was unchanged. The settee that her mother re-covered with the same gold fabric every three years was still in front of the fake fireplace with the two matching armchairs on either side and a low glass table with the bowl of silk flowers between them. On the mantelpiece was the framed picture of Betsy's father, young, in his police uniform, and another of her at her first communion. The little girl in the frilly white dress and corkscrew curls seemed a complete stranger. Nothing of the baby who had died when Betsy was seven. After the funeral was done, nobody ever mentioned Betsy's sister.

'Where's the picture of Franny?' she asked her mother.

'I keep it in my bedroom.'

On the opposite wall was the print of a Renaissance Madonna that had hung in her mother's house all Betsy's life. For years, Eva believed it was valuable, a rare find that she alone could have spotted at a tag sale. When Betsy was in college, she persuaded her mother to let her take it into the city and get it valued.

The woman in the velvet headband at Sotheby's told her the print was a piece of worthless junk, a page cut from a book, the book itself without value and Betsy, gleeful, went to her mother's and delivered the news; it took years until Eva forgave her.

'You should have come here right away. You got my messages?' Eva said. 'Did you know I was in the city?'

'No.'

'I went to that cockamamie building on Cornelia Street. I waited for you.'

'When?'

'Sunday,' Eva said. 'Two hours I sat with that woman, Marie Tusi.'

'She never said anything.'

In the front room, Betsy helped her mother into one of the chairs, then leaned down and kissed her cheek.

'Are you hungry?' Eva asked.

'No. Thank you,' Betsy said.

'Sit down, then.'

Betsy sat on the edge of the settee.

'Take your jacket off. I assume you're staying.'

'Is that all right?' Betsy said. 'I'd like to stay over a couple of nights, if you don't mind.'

'You can stay as long as you want.'

'Thanks.'

Eva looked at her. 'Did you kill him?'

'I don't believe you'd ask me that.' Betsy sat back, exhausted, against the unforgiving gold fabric.

'I have to ask you. I'm your mother. I need to know what to do.'

'What do you mean what to do?'

She knew, though. Her mother meant the church. She would talk to her God about it, or maybe the priest, or some statue at St Agnes'.

'No, Ma,' she said. 'I didn't.'

'Good.'

Leaning forward, Eva peered through thick glasses at her daughter. 'What did you do to your face?' she said. 'You look good.'

'Thank you.'

'Don't sound so surprised. I can still see some things. I approve, you know, this surgery business. I would do it myself if there was any reason anymore. Old stinks.'

The skin on her mother's hand, when Betsy held it, was dry as paper and covered in brown spots.

'How are you, Ma?'

'I don't sleep,' she said. 'Are they sending you to jail?'

'Of course not.'

'Your father had some friends if you need

help, attorneys, also someone in the city. I could find his name. You need money?'

'No, thank you.'

'You're welcome.'

'That's very nice of you,' Betsy said. 'Thanks.'

'You don't have to thank me. I'm your mother. I don't know, maybe we should have talked more,' she said, half to herself.

'We did talk. Not so much when I was younger. Later we sort of talked. Didn't we?'

Eva settled back in her chair, removed the thick cataract glasses, held them between her fragile hands.

'When your father died, you didn't let me talk to you about it,' she said. 'I wanted to talk, you just shut your door.'

'I was a kid.'

'You weren't that young. It was lonely around here after Michael passed.'

'I'm sorry,' Betsy said. 'Can I smoke?'

'Let me have one,' Eva said. 'You're surprised? I decided I needed a vice. There are some cigarettes in the box on the mantel.'

The box contained a half-smoked pack. Betsy got it, sat on the brown tweed carpet next to her mother's chair, lit cigarettes for both of them. Eva took three small puffs, crushed the cigarette out in a shell-shaped ashtray on the table. She tightened the belt on her bathrobe, put her glasses back on.

Betsy looked up at her. 'Would you mind if I went to bed? I'm a little tired, Ma. If you don't mind, I'd love to get some sleep.'

She was fifty-one years old and sitting on her mother's carpet, asking permission to go to bed. Eva nodded.

'Shall I take my old room?' Betsy said.

'No.'

'Why not?'

'Take the little guest room at the end of the hall upstairs. The bed is already made up.'

She was too tired to argue.

'Get yourself some juice, if you want,' Eva said. 'There's juice in the icebox. There's a bottle of Jack Daniels in the cupboard if you want a real drink.'

'Thanks, Ma. It's OK. I don't want anything. I'm fine.'

'Take some juice. It's good for you. You'll get dehydrated. It's bad for your skin.'

'Thanks again. For letting me stay,' she said and bent down to peck her mother's cheek. 'We'll talk in the morning, OK?'

Eva looked up.

'I told you you don't have to thank me. I love you. Take some juice up with you,' she said. 'Give me a kiss goodnight.'

Betsy kissed her, picked up her bag, went through the arch that separated the living room from the hall.

To the right were the stairs up to the bedrooms, to the left the kitchen door. On the wall was the cuckoo clock Eva brought back from a trip to Austria once, long time ago. Long time. Betsy leaned down and unlaced her Timberlands and took them off.

From the kitchen came familiar noises: a tap dripping; the hum of the old fridge; wind off Long Island Sound that rattled a loose window. Something else.

Listening to the elusive noise, Betsy stopped, boots in her hand. Again she heard it: the scratching of a pencil, a faint cough. There was somebody else in the house.

29

Sometimes, Frances Thornhill wore dark blue sweatpants and a faded black T-shirt to sleep in. She had them on now, sitting in her grandmother's kitchen, intent on the crossword puzzle on the table in front of her. A triumphant little smile flickered over her face as she licked her pencil and filled in the squares.

Shifting her weight, she tucked one foot under her. On the table was a glass of apple juice, half drunk. She had woken out of a sleep so deep she didn't know where she was, then realized it was her mother's old room. It spooked her, lying in the room that was her mother's when she was a kid, and Franny had come downstairs to the kitchen. The solid kitchen door was shut; there was only the faint sound of the cuckoo clock and, from time to time, the sound of voices: Gran talking to herself, Franny figured. Or the TV.

Her short dark hair was tied back from her face with a red cotton scarf. On her feet were the thin terry scuffs Gran had put out for her, no socks, and she could feel the smooth wood of the kitchen floor under her feet. She untied the scarf, smoothed her hair with her fingers, then fastened it again.

From the airport, she'd come straight to Gran's. She liked the old woman. She liked her toughness, her resolve, the way she refused to depend on anyone, even her silly faith and, most of all, that she was a repository for family stories, especially about Grandpa Mike who died before Fran was born.

Everyone said she looked like Gran; there was a bond that was almost visceral. Gran never asked much, just offered her food and a bed and received Frances' birthday gift of a little Russian icon with the half-smile that indicated pleasure. Franny liked old people in general. They told her stories and made her feel useful and she felt they deserved her attention.

Gran still called her Franny. To tell the truth, Franny thought of herself that way, even though she insisted everyone else call her Frances. What a fucking pain in the ass I am sometimes, she said to herself and chuckled.

Betsy was something else. Betsy needed more. She was a needy woman. Frances had always thought of her mother by her name.

'Mummy,' she'd practiced saying when she was little and at school in London. 'Mummy' she said back then because she wanted to be like the other kids. Her best friend, Rima, told her that 'Mummy' was what people said. *Mummy*. My Mum. Franny found it embarrassing.

All the time she was growing up in London Rima had lived next door with her father, Max. Their back gardens were side by side. Max and Betsy put a gate through from one to the other, there were shared barbecues, Christmases, school breaks; it was almost ruined for them, the way Betsy and Max pushed the girls' friendship. Not to mention Betsy and Max falling into the sack together a couple of times when they got drunk.

She liked Rima, trusted her. It was Rima she'd run into on the street in London when she went to her mother's house a few weeks earlier to get some old textbooks she'd stored in the basement. Rima who dragged her home and made tea and told Fran about Betsy's face.

Afterwards, Franny found pictures in Betsy's bedroom.

As a kid, facelifts alarmed her. They repelled her now. This need to be younger was disgusting, Franny thought. People were dying of hunger and Betsy spent money on fixing her face and what for? Because silly Vicky did it? So she could take more stupid pictures of fruit, then show the pictures on the telly? Because Tom Mason wasn't exciting enough? The way Franny saw it, Betsy, so self-absorbed, never understood how good and decent and kind Tom was.

Franny was judgmental and she knew it about herself and it was a lousy trait, but there it was, she thought: it's who I am.

'At least you laugh about it. Some of the time,' Rima had said to her once. 'At least you know what a pain in the ass you are.'

Hard to by-pass her feelings about plastic surgery, though. In her work Fran met women who were abused, raped, executed for wanting an education. She met women who had had their babies torn out of their bellies. She had been to the site of the World Trade Center and seen the body parts. It revolted her the way women like her mother fixed themselves because they turned fifty. The places she went, most women never got to fifty.

She stretched and yawned and went to the fridge and pulled out a plate with a piece of coconut cake on it, stuck her finger in the icing and licked it. The plate in one hand, she shut the fridge, sat down and ate hungrily.

Joe had called her and warned her about Betsy. 'Your mother is crazier than ever,' he said. 'Lost the plot. Gone nuts. Looking for you, sweetie. Keep out of her way, OK?'

She was already on her way to Gran's when he called. Now, she finished the cake and leaned back and pulled milk out of the icebox.

Her mind drifted. There was the guy she'd met in the hotel in Islamabad who worked for Food Aid. She liked him and it made her blush slightly and she tipped back the milk carton and drank from the waxy lip.

Suddenly, Fran looked up. From the living room came the sound of more voices and she listened, edgy now. She tried to go back to the crossword, but her concentration was broken. The voices got louder. There was someone with Gran in the other room. She looked at the back door.

Slip away, Fran told herself. Get out while you can. Disappear. But where could she go at midnight in Rockville Center Long Island with only a buck in her pocket and her bag and shoes upstairs? She calculated the possibility of leaving before the inevitable conversation with Betsy, whose voice was distinct now.

What was the point in talking things over? You did what you did and so did everyone else.

'You always say that,' Rima said once. 'You

always say, It is what it is.'

Franny had laughed and said, 'Isn't it?'

* * *

'Why did you want to be me, Betsy?'

Franny was standing by the fridge. To Betsy, so desperate to find her, it seemed both shocking and completely predictable finding her here. She looked good, she looked better than Betsy remembered, tall, thin limber, pretty, the dark hair tied up with a red kerchief. It startled her when she realized it was over a year since she'd seen her kid.

'Did you say something?' Betsy asked. 'I came to get some juice.' It was the only thing she could think of. 'I was thirsty.'

She tried to hug Franny who stiffened and turned away as if to study the clock over the sink.

'The juice is in the icebox,' she said.

'Thanks. How are you, sweetheart? You look good. I like your hair,' Betsy said and at the same time she saw the two of them reflected in the kitchen window.

Two tall, pale women, her in the black sweater, Franny in a black T-shirt, both with short dark hair, stood watching themselves caught in the window with a ledge where a cactus stood in a terracotta pot.

Slowly Franny turned around and stared at her mother, then said softly, for the second time, 'Why did you want to be me?'

Her back against the sink, she tossed some snapshots on the table.

'I found these pictures of you in the house, in London,' Franny said. 'And how freaky was that, you looking like me, like Gran when she was young. The family face, she always said it, right?' She paused for breath. 'Why, Betsy? What for?'

Inside her shoes, Betsy felt her toes curl, tense, rigid. On the table were the pictures Franny had taken from the house in London. The clock ticked and the kitchen was drenched in fallout from the tension.

'Franny, sweetie, I don't mind that you took the pictures from my room,' Betsy said.

'My name is Frances, OK? Frances Michelle Thornhill, and if you think the apple doesn't fall far from the tree, well, not this apple, OK?' She crossed her arms over her chest. 'Did you ever wonder why I didn't use your name professionally? Why I made myself just Frances Michaels. Did you?'

'I never thought about it.'

'You wouldn't. I've always hated Franny, it was something you wanted because of some book you read and thank God for Gran who wouldn't let you call me Zoë, but you made me Franny. It's a really stupid name.' She spoke with a nasal London drawl, but her accent was screwed up because of Betsy and the years she'd spent at college in New York and on the road. 'I can't believe what you did to your face,' she said. 'Well, say something, then.'

'What do you want me to say?'

'I don't know.'

'You knew from the pictures about my face?'

'Rima told me. You could have told me yourself.'

'I thought you'd disapprove. Rima could do it better. She's your best friend.' Betsy fumbled with the cigarettes she'd brought from the living room.

'There's been something weird about you for years, the way you were interested in my friends or my music. You thought you were still some kind of rock chick, didn't you? You were always wanting to be this goofy good-time girl. You wanted to suck up all the oxygen there was. You were so in denial you didn't even get it.' She looked at her mother. 'Please don't smoke in here.'

Tossing the pack on the table, Betsy said, 'I didn't ever want to do anything that would hurt you. Maybe I didn't pay attention always. I was a kid when you were born and I made it all up as I went along, but I never ever wanted to do anything that was bad for you.'

'Hard to believe,' Franny said. 'You never liked the way I did things. I wanted to cut my hair, you didn't like it. You hated my clothes. You nagged me about my posture and my friends. You'd have liked it better if I was some idiot Bridget Jones person obsessed with men and diets and stuff.'

'Franny, everybody goes through it, I mean mothers wanting their kids to stand up straight, that kind of shit.'

'Frances.'

'Sorry.'

'When I was little all you did was take my picture. I remember, you made me pose for you all the time.'

'You were a beautiful child,' Betsy said.

'I hated it.'

'Hated what?'

'Being beautiful. I felt like your fruit.'

'What?'

'I felt like one of your pieces of fruit, something you made an object of for taking pictures.'

'You knew how ravishing you were, though, didn't you?'

'How could I avoid knowing it when it's all anyone ever said to me from as early as I could remember. Egged on by you, probably.'

'Why didn't you tell me?' Betsy asked and sat down at the kitchen table.

'I tried. God knows. You could never bear a confrontation. You disappeared up your own ass so long ago it was like you were your own junta. And stop saying you're sorry, it's like a guilt trip you lay on everyone, you just give in and apologize. Part of the charm offensive, is it, Betsy? Part of the way you get people to do things for you? The way you get your men? Do you understand how much I hated all that food in the house? You were obsessed with it. The whole bloody thing, the food culture, all those TV shows and books and people starving and you and your friends hunting down some obscure ingredient while people are starving.'

'Like pigs for truffles?' Betsy smiled.

'Everything's a joke with you.'

'Sometimes it makes life easier. Why don't you sit down?'

'I don't think life is supposed to be easy, it's not the point really, is it? I mean you got your face cut up so you could make a big splash on telly taking pictures of fruit?'

Voice still low, Betsy said, 'Is there more?'

Franny was on a jag now, a binge, all the words she'd never said spewed from her.

'There's plenty more,' she said. 'It was fine.

We went our separate ways, it didn't matter anymore. I didn't take any money from you, did I? I mean I got a scholarship to university and then I earned my keep.'

'I wouldn't have minded helping you. I expected to help you.'

'That's the point. I didn't want your help.'

'We talked. We were always in touch. You called. I called. We talked about stuff. Didn't we? I was there for you.'

'It didn't seem that way to me,' Franny said. 'You talked and I let you because you hated confrontation and after a while it was fine, we talked and I never said anything that mattered.'

Betsy kept silent. In the hall, the clock struck twelve-thirty. Franny sat down on the opposite side of the table, then leaned her arms on it and stared into Betsy's face.

'Why were you hunting me?'

'I wasn't hunting you. I wanted to see you.'

'It was horrible, Joe calling, other people calling, you leaving messages. You were hunting me. Why?' The voice that had been cool and hard wavered and Franny's eyes filled up.

How can I ask her, Betsy thought to herself. How can I ask her about Ketsen. She was afraid to ask. I'll go to Frank, she thought. I'll tell him about Franny and the photographs. It was a motive, the photographs would drive any mother to confront the guy who took them. I'll take the rap. Frank will believe me.

Franny wiped her eyes with her fist.

'Look,' she said. 'I just want a life of my own, OK?' She glanced at the ceiling. 'I have to go upstairs,' she said. 'I can hear Gran. She might need help.'

* * *

'Do you want a drink? I want a drink,' Franny said coming back into the kitchen.

The fury had subsided. In the cupboard over the stove, she found the bottle of Jack Daniels her grandmother kept for special occasions.

'Yes,' Betsy said.

Franny took a pair of milky-blue glasses down and poured the whiskey in them.

Betsy took the drink and said, 'Is Gran all right?'

'I tucked her in.'

'How long have you been here?'

'Since last night. I always come see her around this time of year, her birthday, my birthday, you know? What difference does it make? Listen, Betsy, you want to tell me what you were doing with Bobby Ketsen?'

It was out now. The words could never be unsaid. Bobby Ketsen. Betsy waited, trying to understand what Franny knew.

'I missed your birthday. I'm sorry.'

Franny said, 'I mean I don't care, but just out of curiosity. I never even told you I knew him.'

'He gave me a ride from the airport. It was a coincidence.'

'It took me a while to find out that you got involved with him, God knows why or how, and then everyone in London is going, ohmigod, oh it's so terrible, who could believe Betsy Thornhill would do a thing like that? Me, I believed it.'

'Believed what?'

'Look, you want me to say it? I know you killed Bobby Ketsen. Oh, don't let's pretend, Betsy. It was all over the place, in all the papers, everyone knows.'

'He was your boyfriend. I'm sorry he's dead, but I didn't kill him. You can't believe that.'

'Why ever not?' Franny's words were cool. 'If you've been to Rwanda and seen the way people who knew each other hacked their neighbors' heads off with a machete, if you went to Bosnia like I did, where kids who played together a week earlier slaughtered each other, or Afghanistan where they stoned a women to death because an eight-year-old boy accused her of adultery, you'd believe anything. Americans are always so shocked when bad things happen or anyone doesn't like them. Boo-hoo, they're like babies, or they were until the Trade Center. And you with how you can't stand violence, you put your hands over your eyes at the movies like a ten-year-old. It's all bullshit. You were pretty handy with a knife when the time came. I don't know why you did it. Maybe you got involved because he liked the way the Thornhill women look and he dumped you or you wanted that part of my life, too, and you couldn't get it, so you whacked him.' She laughed. 'Whacked him. My mother whacked a guy.' For a few seconds, Franny laughed, hysterical but icy.

'Stop it,' Betsy said. 'I didn't kill him.'

'You're the most unreliable witness I ever met. You lie to yourself all the time.'

It was what Joe had said to her, Betsy remembered. It wasn't true that she lied to herself. Was it?

'If you knew it was me, why did you disappear?'

'I didn't disappear,' Fran said. 'I just didn't answer the phone. I knew the police would get round to talking to me if they knew where I was and I didn't want to tell them I knew you did it or they'd put you in the slammer.' She laughed. 'It would upset Gran. Anyway, I'm not that cynical. You're my mother, my mummy, aren't you? I love you, don't I?'

'You're a cold woman,' Betsy said.

'I learned from the best.'

'I didn't kill him. I didn't kill him and I never wanted to hurt you.'

'Well, Betsy, you know what the road to hell is paved with, don't you? I need some air.'

* * *

It was freezing out and there was no noise except for the wind. On the stone patio was a white wrought-iron table and three chairs. An umbrella was folded and lay on the ground up against the side of the house next to a black metal barbecue set and two folding deckchairs. There was a light glaze of frost on the grass. A fence that separated Eva Thornhill's house from her neighbor's — there was still a light in one of the bedrooms — was painted grass green.

Drink in hand, Franny sat on one of the white garden chairs.

'It's cold out. You're only wearing slippers.'

'Jesus, Betsy, you could turn *King Lear*

into a domestic sit-com, couldn't you? Don't you ever think about anything except food and clothes?'

'Will you tell me about Bobby Ketsen and you?'

'Fuck you.'

For a while they sat in the garden and Betsy smoked and Franny pulled her knees up under her chin. In the house on the other side of the green fence, the lights went off.

In the dark, it seemed easier to talk and Betsy said, 'Where did you meet him?'

'You want me to tell you this shit to help you out, right?'

Betsy nodded.

'OK, that's fair. That's at least bloody honest. I met Bobby at NYU first where he gave a photography seminar. He was a teaching assistant. He helped out in a school in Harlem and he recruited me and some other people,' she said, glancing up at her mother. 'I met him and he seemed interested in things I cared about, so we started seeing each other once in a while. Maybe we met half a dozen times. That was way back, you know, nine, ten years ago when I was still in college. Then about a year ago, I met him at the airport.'

'What airport?' Betsy's mouth was dry.

'JFK. I was coming back to New York after

Christmas in London and there he was and he offered me a ride.'

'Into the city?'

'Yes.' Betsy was freezing.

'What's the matter with you? You're shaking.'

'I'm cold, that's all,' Betsy said. 'Was it accidental, him offering you the ride?'

'Of course not. I mean it was an accident us meeting at the airport, but I already knew him. I told you that. I don't know what you mean, accidental.'

'I was thinking about somebody else,' Betsy said.

'You usually are. You want to hear about Bobby or not?'

Betsy nodded.

'He wasn't the first guy I fucked if that's what you want to know,' Franny said. 'You thought I didn't do guys, didn't you? You thought I was some kind of neuter, didn't you, or a lesbian like Bel and Auntie Pauline? Anyway, I fucked Ketsen. So we had this thing for a while. He seemed like he wanted to help people.'

'He took your picture.'

Franny looked up, startled. 'How did you know?'

'You want me to be straight? OK, I saw the pictures he took of you. I didn't guess.'

Her voice quiet and bitter, Fran said, 'You know everything about me, don't you?' She got up and started towards the kitchen door.

Betsy put her hand out to stop her. 'Don't go.'

Franny sat down again. 'So what did you think about the pictures, then, Betsy? I mean you're a bloody photographer, aren't you?'

'I don't know what to say.'

'I loved it, you know. It was brilliant. I actually enjoyed thinking about you and your pictures, all that, what did Max always call your stuff? Gastroporn. He always said you could make people want to fuck a vegetable. I figured you'd be really surprised, me posing like that when you had decided I was some zealous little do-good geek that never had a man because that suited you, you'd be the glamorous one in the family, wasn't that it?'

Betsy shook her head.

'He didn't abuse me. He didn't make me do anything. I loved it. It was fun because I made him pay.'

'How?'

Franny said, 'For every bloody picture he took, I made him give money to something I cared about, you know. I soaked him plenty. I was always into causes, right? I was a whore for the righteous, you're thinking. You're right. Me, I could come for world hunger.'

'You weren't thrilled about it when he put your pictures on the web, though, when he gave them out to some magazine?'

'You know that, too?'

Betsy nodded.

'How?'

'I met his secretary.'

'Meryl?'

'Yes.'

'Poor Meryl. She was so hung up on Bobby. I never met her, but I heard. I heard from a few people I kept up with.'

'People who knew Bobby?' Betsy asked.

'Jesus, am I talking to myself? Yes.'

Betsy's mouth was dry and she swallowed hard and said, 'Where were you the weekend before last?'

'Where was I? Why do you care?'

'I wanted to talk to you.'

'Come off it. I was in London, then I flew to Pakistan.'

'I called London. And Pakistan.'

'Maybe I didn't feel like talking.'

Slowly, Franny got up off the chair and wandered across the yard. The half-frozen grass crackled under her feet. For a few minutes, she walked in circles, she made a figure eight on the lawn and then, winded, leaned on the green fence. After a while, she turned slowly back to Betsy.

'You think that I killed Bobby,' Franny said. 'That's it, isn't it? You think I killed him and they think it's you because you look like me now.' She emitted a small brittle laugh that hung with her breath on the frozen air. 'It's really funny, isn't it? Betsy? It's why you've been hunting me, isn't it? You could imagine me killing someone.'

'You said anything was possible. You said any of us could do anything. I love you. I don't care what you did.'

'You're my own fucking mother,' she said. 'You killed Bobby Ketsen for whatever reason, but you made yourself believe that I did it.' She pushed her hands through her hair. 'You convinced yourself, didn't you? You're crazy, you know that.'

Betsy got up and tried to hug Franny who pulled away.

'So where does that leave us?' Franny said and started laughing and couldn't stop even when tears streamed down her face. 'It's pretty funny, don't you think?'

Betsy put her hand lightly on Franny's arm and said, 'What are we going to do?'

'I don't know about you, but I'm going in to have another drink.'

* * *

For a while, both of them exhausted from talking, they sat in Eva's kitchen and drank the old woman's Jack Daniels and listened to the cuckoo clock when it popped out of its hut on the half-hour. Betsy went upstairs and got a blanket and put it around Franny's shoulders.

'Fran? Sweetie?'

Half asleep, she looked up and said, 'What?'

'Was it that awful? You hated your life in London when you were a kid that much?'

'I hated it.' Franny pulled the blanket around her and pulled her feet up under her and clasped her arms around her knees.

'I'm sorry. But it got better for you afterwards?'

All the anger gone, Franny said, 'It got better when I went to New York. I got off the plane and I felt free, you know? I felt I could be anyone and no one would stare at me and I could start over.'

'I know how you feel.'

'You do?'

'Yes.'

'Listen, I brought my own baggage with me,' Franny suddenly said. 'Like all kids. You're born with stuff. Your parents never think about that, but you just are who you are. I hated the way I looked because it made me different so I got angry and peevish and it took me years to unload the chip. I know that.'

'I didn't protect you in some way I could have?'

'You didn't have to take my picture all the time,' Franny said. 'I don't want to talk about that anymore.' She looked tired, vulnerable, young. 'Why did you do that to your face?'

'A whim,' Betsy said. 'I wanted a change. Tom saw this old picture of me and said I looked like a real dish when I was young. You start thinking about it, you see all the women who've done something and you read the magazines and other people tell you how great you'd look, and, I don't know. I think I wanted it for a long time. Before I had the surgery I kept looking in the mirror and seeing my mother's face. I told myself all kinds of shit to justify getting it done.'

'And when it was done?' Franny asked. 'What did you feel when you looked in the mirror then? Don't lie.'

'You want the truth?'

'Sure.'

'I loved it. It was exciting. It was like starting over. It was like you felt when you got off the plane in New York to go to college and you could unload some of the past.'

'Would you change it back if you could?'

As if to protect it, Betsy's hands went to her face and she turned away and walked to the sink, examined the cactus, stared out of the window, wanted to answer but couldn't because she didn't know the right answer. When she looked back, she saw Fran had fallen asleep.

* * *

For what was left of the night, a couple of hours, the blanket over her, Franny slept at the kitchen table. Betsy sat and watched her. The scene at the airport came back again: it was Franny Ketsen had seen when he saw her, it was Franny he wanted. He wanted Franny, he got Betsy, and it set off the events that led to his murder.

Or did it? Would Franny have killed him anyway? Would things have moved forward in the same way without her, without Betsy? She could have stayed in London, never seen Bobby Ketsen, the world would have continued on its murderous course without her knowing that he existed, had lived or died. Would it?

Franny had taken the photographs from the house in London, she knew about Betsy's face and how much they resembled each other. Franny knew she was in New York.

Knew she could get away with it because it would all fall on her mother, all the shit in the universe pouring down.

Betsy could never ask. If Franny said she didn't kill him, she could never ask. It didn't matter, either. Her daughter slept, her head on the table. Arms folded under her, dark hair messy, she looked like a child. Betsy would take care of her. The airport, the day she took a ride from Ketsen, was where it had begun; it would all end in this kitchen on Long Island. The cuckoo came out again, it was five in the morning.

The image of a busy road floated into Betsy's mind. She saw traffic roaring towards them and Franny stepping out into it and she saw herself step in front of her daughter.

While Eva was still asleep, Betsy would pack and Franny would pack and they would take the car and go to the airport. She had most of Pauline's cash with her, it was in her bag, and she'd buy Fran a ticket and give her money and put her on the plane, then she'd go to the police, to Frank Dolce and tell him it was her. It didn't matter, so long as Franny was safe.

In her mind, Betsy ran into the road and stood in front of her daughter as the traffic came towards them.

30

It was after seven when a smudgy gray light came up over the backyard. Franny was still asleep. Betsy, who had dozed briefly, woke up and saw the clock. She put her hand on Franny's shoulder.

'Fran? Get up. Come on.' Betsy wanted to get out before Eva was awake, it was already late. From upstairs came the sound of boards creaking, Eva's cane, water running. The toilet flushed.

There were footsteps on the stairs. Eva was coming down, slow, hesitant, the footsteps irregular, the breathing loud like a rattle.

When Eva pushed open the kitchen door, Franny blinked, rubbed sand out of her eyes and looked up.

Eva said, 'I want some coffee.'

'I'll get it,' Betsy said.

Eva sat at the table.

'I'm taking Fran to the airport,' Betsy said. 'I'll get your coffee and we'll get dressed and then I'll take your car so I can drive her.' She didn't ask her mother's permission.

Fran blinked sleepily and said, 'What are

you talking about?'

'No,' Eva said. 'You can't do that.'

Betsy filled the old stainless Farberware pot with water and coffee and plugged it in. She turned off the tap and said to her mother, 'Excuse me?'

'You're not taking Frances to any airport,' Eva said.

'We'll get a cab, then.'

'No.'

'What?'

Eva pulled up the collar of her green silk bathrobe and said, 'Sit down.'

Betsy said, 'There's a flight to London. She can make connections there.'

Franny was silent.

'Here's what you're going to do,' Eva said, cleaning her glasses meticulously with a handkerchief. 'You're both going back into the city and talk to the police. I'll call a lawyer if you decide that's what you want. You're going to figure this out, and if you don't, I'm going to call the detective who's been leaving me messages night and day and who showed up here already.'

'What was his name?'

Eva fished a card from her pocket.

'Detective Dolce,' she said.

'When was he here?'

'Sunday. After I got back from the city.'

'You didn't tell me,' Betsy said. 'How did he find you?'

'He knew your father was a cop, he knew your name. I didn't see the need to tell you. I assumed you would do the right thing, which is what you're going to do,' Eva said. 'Otherwise, I'll call him and tell him you're both here. I'm sick to death of all of this. I want this cleared up. I'm too old and too tired. We'll have our coffee and you'll both go and get a few hours' sleep and then change your clothes and I'll call you a cab. You can get the train into the city.'

'No,' Betsy said.

'It's the right thing.'

'I'm bloody sick of doing the right thing in order to satisfy you,' Betsy said. 'This is for me and Franny to decide. Frances, I'm sorry.'

Eva turned to Betsy and said, 'Did you tell her about Bel Plotkin?'

Her voice tinny with fear, Franny said, 'What about Bel? What's wrong with Bel?' She clawed at Betsy's sleeve. 'Tell me what's going on.'

She hadn't told Franny about Bel. She knew she'd want to see her, she'd insist on going to the city and the cops would pick her up.

'I didn't want you to worry,' Betsy said. 'Bel's had a stroke. She's in the hospital. I was going to tell you this morning. There's nothing you can do for her.'

'Bel had a stroke and you didn't tell me?' Franny said. 'You didn't think I'd care?' She got up. 'I'm going into the city. She's at St Vincent's?'

Betsy nodded. 'They think she'll make it.'

'Think? You don't understand, I have to see her. My God, if Bel dies and I don't see her, it will be unbearable for me. You don't get it.' Hurriedly, she made for the door. 'You're coming or what?'

'Wait a while.' Betsy reached for her arm.

Franny twisted away. 'I can't,' she said.

Trying to buy time, Betsy said, 'Why not?'

'I love her is why.'

'No.' Betsy put out her arms as if to keep her from walking into the middle of a car wreck. 'No. I don't think you should go.'

'I'm going,' she said. 'You can come or not come. I'm going upstairs to take a shower and get my things,' she added and, holding the blanket like a cape, pushed open the kitchen door.

Eva Thornhill looked at her daughter and granddaughter, then noticed the photographs that were still on the kitchen table.

'The family face,' she said. 'Goddamn it to hell.'

* * *

'Drop me at St Vincent's,' Franny said in the cab on the way downtown from Penn Station. 'Then we'll go see the police. Which precinct?'

Stalling, hoping for time, trying to think of a way out, Betsy said, 'We could both use some sleep.'

'I'd rather get it over with.'

'I'll call a cop I know and we'll go in tomorrow.'

'You're friends with a cop?'

'He's an all right guy.'

'Fine, then call him now. Stop stalling.'

Her phone was in her bag and Betsy got it and dialed Frank. His machine was on. She left a message, then tried his pager.

A few minutes later, while the taxi stalled in traffic and Betsy stared out of the window, Frank called. He was at his mother's in Bay Ridge. It was her seventieth birthday. He'd meet them in the morning at the station house. Sure, he said. Nine was good. Sure. Yes. He sounded pleased that she'd called. It made him happy. He'd be there early and bring coffee.

'I'll come to the hospital with you,' Betsy said.

'I'd like to see Bel alone, if you don't mind.'

Betsy nodded. 'I'll drop you and go home. I could make some supper for us.'

Franny fidgeted with her bag. 'Look, Betsy, I'm not really ready for us to be so freaking cozy if you don't mind, I just want to get this done. I'm not angry anymore, honest. I'll get a bite with Marie.'

'Marie Tusi?'

'Yes.'

'I'm sure she'll be glad to see you,' Betsy said.

'Marie was good to me when I was at school here. Her and Dev both.'

'I'm sure she'll make something nice.'

'That's not really the point, is it?'

'I'll make up the sofa for you and you can bunk down there whenever you get in.'

The cab sped down Ninth Avenue until the driver, seeing a red light, slammed on the brakes and Franny was thrown against Betsy.

'Excuse me,' she said as if her mother was a stranger, then moved back to her side of the taxi and turned her head towards the window.

* * *

The red light on the answering machine was flashing when Betsy got home. The answering machine she'd bought nearly two weeks earlier to fend off Bobby Ketsen's calls. *Have dinner with me, Betsy*. He planted a landmine, they tripped on it, all of them; it exploded.

She tossed her bag on the floor, dropped her ski jacket on a chair and played back the messages, including one from Mark Carey. Back tomorrow, his sonorous voice said. If you're picking up you're messages, Betsy, I'll be back tomorrow.

It was Mark she needed. She called and left a message for him. Mark would know what to do for Franny. Why was Fran so eager to talk to the cops? Betsy asked herself, and took off her boots because her feet were killing her.

She had a blister on her left foot; she ran the tap in the bathroom sink, hoisted her sore foot into it, let it soak, then stuck on some Band-Aids. She put on slippers and got clean sheets out of the closet and made up the sofa in the living room for Franny.

After she ate something, Betsy would go to St Vincent's. In the kitchen she made a peanut butter sandwich, ate half, drank some Diet Coke. When she called the hospital, she got the head nurse on Bel's floor who told her Bel was sleeping.

No visitors, the woman said to Betsy. She had a low raspy voice and sounded overworked and short-tempered. No visitors, she said again. Doctor's orders.

Was Franny there? Betsy asked. Was there a young woman with Ms Plotkin? Bel Plotkin, she repeated herself. She was impatient but the nurse, distracted by noise in the background, cut her off.

Fretful, Betsy tied up the garbage bag and lugged it down to the can on the sidewalk.

The weather was warm again. A light rain fell. From across the street, a waiter Betsy recognized emerged from the Spanish bar and waved at her. At the restaurant next door, a delivery man hauled dirty linen to a truck. Two teenage boys leaned against the wall of the house two doors down, shared a cigarette and a comic. You could feel the first brush with spring.

For a minute Betsy stood, smoking on her stoop, then tossed her cigarette into the gutter and went back upstairs. Her head hurt. Her stomach lurched. It was coming to an end. One way or the other, it would be over tomorrow at nine in the morning. Over or just beginning. Betsy felt tired in her bones. She went in the bedroom and sat down on the bed, still in her clothes, and fell asleep on top of the covers.

⋆ ⋆ ⋆

The luminous dial on her clock pointed to three. Three in the morning. Betsy turned over, saw her door was open. The light was on in the living room.

On the sofa, covers over her head, Franny was asleep, one white arm trailing out of the blankets, fingers grazing the floor. Her breathing was deep and even. Betsy turned off the lights and tip-toed back into her room where she took off her clothes and got into bed and lay on her side and watched the clock.

It was raining hard out, rain pounding on the roof. Adrift in a half-sleep, she felt detached from herself. Cars swished through the wet streets.

People were drowning. In a huge bucket of frozen pink daiquiris, toy cars sank, little plastic figures tumbled out of the cars, out of buildings, sank in the pink liquid. The outside world seemed crowded with toys and toy figures, all in danger of drowning. Then she looked at the huge plastic cup of pink slush and saw her face floating in it, but her face was a photograph and it was Bobby Ketsen taking her picture. Her new face. Falling through a hole, she struggled to the surface, reaching, clutching, pushing. Help me, she said out loud and the sound of her voice, and of somebody weeping, woke her up.

31

Nearby, someone weeping. Muted sobs. Somebody trying not to cry, hold it back. An explosion of tears followed. Someone who was not an experienced weeper.

Betsy thought: *Bel's dead*. The crying came from the living room, she heard it the same time she saw the lights outside. Red and blue lights flashed in the early-morning dark and pulled her completely out of sleep. She swung her legs over the side of the bed and stuffed her feet in a pair of sneakers. She reached for the light.

Naked, she grabbed sweatpants and denim shirt off a chair and put them on and went into the living room. Wearing a faded gray T-shirt, Franny was huddled on the sofa, crying as if her heart would break and her ribs crack.

'Is it Bel?' Betsy said, hurrying to the window. 'What is it? Franny? Sweetheart?' Her own heart thudded. 'Is it Bel? Did the hospital call? What's the ambulance doing here? Franny?'

Betsy sat at the end of the sofa and put her hand out and Franny took it.

'It's not Bel,' she said. 'I saw her. She's going to make it.'

'What is it?'

'It was my fault.' Franny wiped her nose with the back of her other hand.

'What was your fault?'

'Bobby Ketsen,' Franny said.

Betsy put her arms around the girl who leaned against her. She had killed him, she needed her mother. To Betsy, holding her, Franny felt thin, fragile, scared.

'I'm sorry I'm such a sniveling wreck,' Franny said. 'I loved her. She was really good to me and she cared so much, and now she's dead and it's my bloody fault.'

'Her? Fran, sweetie, I don't know what you mean.'

'Marie.'

'Marie Tusi?'

'She's dead.'

'What do you mean dead?' It was what she had asked Frank Dolce when he told her about Ketsen.

'I made her do it.' Franny started to cry again.

Betsy held on to her, felt Franny's heart pounding, smoothed her hair, rubbed her back.

'Marie went out without taking her meds, it was raining, she was petrified, she started running. She couldn't breath. She just fell on the side-walk and I couldn't help her.' Franny paused. 'Can I have some water?'

'I'll get it. You called the ambulance?'

Franny nodded. Betsy got her a glass of water and waited while she drank it in two gulps.

'Thanks.'

'That's OK. You want me to make coffee?'

Franny shook her head. 'Could you just sit with me?'

'As long as you want.'

'I'm so sorry I was horrible to you at Gran's. I'm sorry. I'm sorry we never talked more. I'm a bloody awful human being, I really am and I'm sorry. I've kept everything in for so long, I was so afraid to tell anyone about Bobby and the photographs and what a jerk I was, it all got to me.'

She looked up at Betsy and in her face, Betsy saw the little girl who could make your heart turn over with her looks.

'You're not awful,' she said.

Franny sat cross-legged on the sofa.

'I got back from the hospital,' she said. 'I stopped at Marie's, she was waiting for me, Dev was away and she had fixed those short-ribs. She butchers her own meat. Something didn't feel right, she was asking me about the case and saying how you were probably guilty of killing Bobby. She wanted it, that you did it. She wanted it really bad, I could feel it, but I just ate and let her talk and I was so tired I came upstairs and went to sleep.'

'Go on,' Betsy said.

'I woke up around six and something bothered me, and I'm not sure what it was, maybe it was seeing Marie fixing supper, seeing her with a knife in her hand, and I don't know, it just bugged me, and I went downstairs and woke her up.'

'What did you say?'

'I said, I need you to tell me the truth. I can't let them arrest Betsy for something she didn't do. She's my mother.'

'You're saying it was Marie who killed Ketsen?'

'She wanted to take care of me, she thought she was a better mother than you.'

'She knew about the pictures?'

Franny shrugged. 'I guess I must have said something. She said I told her and she went to see him and he wouldn't give her the photographs. He was drunk out of his head. An easy target. She had the knife.'

'She got the pictures?'

Franny shook her head. 'That's the awful thing. It was for nothing.'

'Did she set me up?' Betsy said.

'I don't know that either.'

Franny picked up a pack of cigarettes from the table near the sofa, offered them to her mother.

'You probably need one of these,' she said.

A picture of Marie floated into Betsy's mind: the big bony woman in the window, watching the streets, seeing the cops come and go. Or inside her apartment with the big gray computer on the dining room table, a bowl of wax fruit, the Naugahyde Barcalounger where Dev sat to watch the wall-size TV. Through the door she heard people in the building enter or leave, heard the mailman. Whenever Betsy came in or went out, Marie knew. Had known.

Franny said, 'I told her we'd go to the police together, you, me, her. We'd fix things for her, we could say it was self-defense, that she went to Bobby's and he hit her — we could say he was a violent guy, that he hit women.' Franny gulped the water. 'We talked and she told me she did it and I could see the panic on her face. Before I could do anything, she went out in her pajamas and started running. I went after her, but she just dropped.'

'Her asthma?'

Franny nodded.

'I went and got her inhaler, but it was too

late. She was just lying in the rain in the gutter in those flannel pajamas and the rubber boots.' Franny hesitated. 'It's my fault.'

'It's not your fault. You made her tell the truth. You saved my ass.'

'You're welcome. I couldn't let them put you in jail,' Fran said. 'The food would have been horrible.' She went on. 'I think Marie was with Bel when she had the stroke. I think she might have frightened Bel.' Franny got up. 'Can I take a shower? The cops and EMS people are still downstairs waiting for Dev to get home.'

'Franny — I mean Frances — '

'I don't care that much, you know. I was just making a thing out of it.'

'Of what?'

'What you call me.'

'Take a shower,' Betsy said and added tentatively, 'I'll make us some breakfast if you want.'

Franny scraped her hair back from her face, smiled. 'I'd really like that a lot.'

* * *

It was over. Frank came by and shook hands with Franny and they sat together and she told him her story and showed him her passport. It was routine, Frank said. Just checking where she'd been the Saturday night Ketsen was murdered, same as he had checked everyone involved. Friends in London told Frank Franny had been with them Saturday and there was no US entry visa in her British passport until days after Ketsen was dead.

Frank spoke only briefly to Betsy and kept his expression official, though his eyes were veined with red. He's been drinking, Betsy thought. Or maybe it was because Mark Carey showed up and kissed Betsy on the cheek.

He let Frank take charge. He leaned against the wall and listened to what Frank said. It didn't matter. Mark's presence dominated everything and Frank Dolce felt it.

They went downstairs to the Tusi apartment that still smelled from the short-ribs and tomato sauce. Dev had returned and he sat motionless in the tan Barcalounger in the living room. Until now, he had been spry and animated, but his head was sunk on his chest and he waited for the cops to leave so he could mourn for Marie by himself.

The Tusi apartment was crowded, Dev sitting silent, Betsy and Franny in the doorway with Mark, Frank and a couple of uniformed cops in the kitchen.

In Marie's kitchen, Frank found a Japanese knife with a twelve-inch blade. Dev confirmed that he'd brought it back in '45, on his way home from the war in the Pacific. It was a souvenir, an old sushi knife, but Marie liked it for butchering meat because it was easy to use. There would be tests, Frank said. Forensics would compare it to the wounds in Bobby Ketsen's neck.

It made Betsy gag, seeing the knife and imagining how it had been used, seeing it in Marie's big capable hands, thinking of her slicing at Ketsen with a chef's dexterity.

Franny was quiet and confident and talked softly to Mark who put his arm around her. She wasn't scared. She had seen worse. Franny had seen people slaughtered with knives.

* * *

It looked, over the next seventy-two hours, as if Marie Tusi really had killed Bobby Ketsen. There was evidence, not perfect, Frank said, but good enough. Probably OK, he said; some partial fingerprints at Ketsen's place matched hers; the unidentified voice on his answering machine could have been her voice. Her voice was on her own answering machine and they made a match.

'Why would Marie put the knife back in her kitchen? Why not throw it away?' Betsy asked him when they met up at his station house, him and his partner, Jimmy Grant, Betsy and Franny, all sitting around in the bleak room with paper coffee cups, like characters in a play.

'Maybe she was worried her husband would see it was missing, and she knew no one would ever look in her apartment. Why would we? Why would anyone connect Mrs Tusi to any of this? I didn't see it, neither did Jimmy,' he said loud enough so his partner could hear.

Jimmy Grant looked sour because Frank had made the case and he got up and left the room.

It was the same room where Betsy had sat before, she realized, after the line-up. Betsy wore a gray suit with a skirt and her good boots and a string of pearls. Franny, a neat tweed jacket buttoned over a white shirt, had her suitcase with her.

A few minutes later, Mark Carey hurried in, his hair disheveled, his coat unbuttoned. He apologized. He was late and he was sorry and he tossed a yellow pad on the table and put his briefcase down and took out cigarettes. He passed them around, then shook Frank Dolce's hand.

'You never told me you had a daughter,' Frank said softly to Betsy. 'She has a different name from you.'

Betsy said. 'I couldn't involve her. It was my problem.'

'You want to take me through it one more time, why this middle-aged Italian lady would knife this guy?' Frank said to Franny and turned on his tape recorder.

She told her story while the others smoked and listened.

'It was for me,' Franny said. 'Marie thought she was protecting me. I should have understood long ago but I didn't until I saw her with a knife in her hand. I'm sorry. I really am.'

'You think she was some kind of nut?' Frank said.

'I never thought so. She used to cook for me when I lived in the building. She was nice to me.'

'Betsy?' Frank stubbed his cigarette out in a coffee mug.

'Yes?'

'You never suspected this?'

'Of course not.'

'So you feel sure it was Mrs Tusi?' Mark said.

'Sure enough,' Frank said. 'We'll see, of

course. There are plenty of loose ends, but for now, I think that's about it.' He got up and shook hands with Franny.

'I talked to your friends in London a second time,' he said. 'In case they mention it. You have good friends.'

'Yes,' she said. 'I'm lucky.'

'Well, thank you,' he said. 'You look a lot like your mother, you know.'

When Franny and Mark left the room, Betsy hung back. The smell of cigarette smoke was thick in the room.

'Frank?'

'What?'

'There's something else, isn't there?'

'A kid came in, a hacker Mrs Tusi knew. She got him to shut down Ketsen's website where he posted the pictures of women he took. You'll go to Mrs Tusi's funeral?' Frank said.

She knew there was more, didn't ask. She said, 'I'll go to the funeral.'

'Would you like me to be there?'

'I don't know, Frank. Why would you want to?'

'Close a door,' he said.

'Make it tidy?'

'Yes.'

'I'll let you know when it is,' Betsy said. 'The funeral.'

'I never thought it was you. I told you. There was nothing I could do to stop you being obsessed, but I was never close to arresting you.'

'My transparent life?'

'Yes.'

'I was pretty crazy,' Betsy said. 'Did you ever figure out why Marie destroyed the Irving Penn photographs at Ketsen's? The picture with the onion?'

'Maybe she was furious. Maybe she wanted to hurt Ketsen even after he was dead by messing with his photographs, his stuff, the pictures he did,' Frank said. 'I don't really know. There are always loose ends. Sometimes we just settle for what we get.' He looked mournful. 'Anyway, the pictures were fakes.'

'What do you mean?'

'He made them up,' Frank said. 'His lawyer went in to look over the contents for probate and get the damage appraised. It turns out Ketsen made them himself and told everyone they were Irving Penns. He was a congenital liar. Nothing is what it seems, right, Betsy?'

* * *

They stood out on the street near Frank's station house, her and Franny. From the stables next door came the smell of horses and two mounted cops emerged and clopped away while they watched.

At the curb, Mark Carey looked for a taxi.

Franny said, 'I feel awful. I mentioned to Marie I wanted the pictures Ketsen took, but I never asked her directly. She ran with it. She was obsessed.'

'Who will rid me of this turbulent priest, is that it? You mention it, she picks it up and runs with it,' Betsy asked.

'That's pretty tough.'

'I'm sorry. Did you really think I killed him?'

Franny shook her head.

'For a while I believed it, but why would you? Unless you got involved in some weird thing with him, but I didn't believe Bobby would bother with you.'

'Why not?'

'Truth?'

'Sure.'

'You're too old. He liked fresh meat.' She looked at Betsy. 'What? You're insulted. Listen, until I saw your new face in person, I couldn't know how young you looked. I just thought if it was you, what was Bobby doing with somebody's mother? Betsy?'

'Yes?'

'Last night at Gran's, I like that you

wanted to ship me out and keep me safe and be a good mother.'

'I meant it.'

'Hey, it's over,' Franny said, then, out of the blue, hugged her. 'I like you better for all of it. We said something to each other that mattered, you know, after all. It's weird, isn't it?'

'What's weird?' Betsy asked.

'The murder never had anything to do with your face at all, or anyone's face, just a bunch of stupid pictures.'

A taxi had pulled up and Mark stood by it and said, 'What about some lunch?'

Franny smiled. 'Thanks. I've got a lot to do before the plane goes tomorrow. It's an early flight, I'll get a room at the airport.'

'Can't you stay a few days?' Betsy said.

'I have a job. But maybe Easter,' Franny said. 'In a few months.'

'I'd like that a lot.'

A cab stopped and Mark handed Franny her bag and she said, 'Thank you.'

'You're welcome.'

Leaning out of the taxi window, Franny looked at her mother.

'We'll talk soon,' she said. 'I'll call. You know something? The face is pretty nice.'

'Yeah?' Betsy laughed.

'After all,' Franny said. 'You look like me.'

32

'I'll walk you part way.' Mark took her hand and she could feel the pigskin glove against her skin.

'What about lunch?'

'Not today, Betsy, but thanks. I have a plane to catch.'

She took her hand away from his and shoved it in her pocket where there was a crumpled ten and two singles.

'Send me a bill,' she said.

'Don't be silly,' he said. 'Anyway, you can't afford me.'

'Thanks.'

'I did it for Bel. She's better. She'll be OK. I think this thing with the murder, it really upset her. She's more vulnerable than she lets on. Take care of her until I get back.'

'Did you see her? Did you talk to her?'

'I went, but I couldn't get in. She was still sedated. Sleeping around the clock. The doctor's a friend and he says it will take time, but she'll be ninety-five percent.'

'Another friend.'

'What's bothering you, Betsy?' Mark

stopped in the street and put his hands on her shoulders.

'The police picture. Marie Tusi didn't look like me.'

Mark put his hand on her shoulders. 'Listen to me. It happens. I told you, people see a woman and a red coat, it's night, the cops are too eager, the papers get hold of it. It was Marie Tusi. There's plenty of evidence. Motive. I believe it. Marie's dead. It's over.'

She looked at him, tried to keep her voice steady. 'When will I see you?'

'Betsy, dear, you don't want to see me unless you're in trouble. And you've had enough trouble for a long time. If you want a good man, try Frank Dolce. He's a decent guy. Hard to believe for a cop, but he is.'

'You mean he'll take care of me, is that it?'

'Don't be hard on him,' Mark said. 'He already has.'

'What do you mean?'

'Never mind. I'm just tired, darling. I'm getting to be an old guy.'

She said, 'Where are you going?'

'Maine,' he said.

'What's in Maine?' she said as they got to Seventh Avenue where he would turn off at St Luke's Place.

'My house,' he grinned. 'My wife. Some rest as these things go, I hope. A bit of music.

Take care of yourself.'

'When will you be back?'

'Don't worry. I'll be back. I'm there if you need me,' he said and kissed her cheek and without glancing at the light, crossed the street.

* * *

The Tusi place was empty when Betsy passed it on her way upstairs. A cop stood outside the door and told her Dev had gone to his brother's place upstate in Utica.

In the apartment, she dropped her bag on the table and took off her jacket. Her red coat hung over a chair and she felt in the pocket for a pack of cigarettes and found the crumbs of the Kit-Kat she had eaten the day she went to Al Kovlovski's garage. In the bedroom, she took off her suit and put on jeans and the worn denim shirt. She dropped onto the living room sofa with a magazine and was too tired to read.

Sunlight poured through the windows and she fell into a half-sleep. The phone woke her, but it was a wrong number.

In the morning, she'd start again. Betsy kneeled up on the sofa, leaned her arms on the window sill and looked out. She'd start on her new book. She'd take a job shooting chickens because it was work and she liked work. There was a volunteer group helping people who were still in trouble from September 11. People in trouble, their apartments still wrecked like Frank Dolce's, needed photographers to document the damage. She'd sign up. She'd invite her mother into the city, see a play, eat some dinner. Maybe call Frank, too.

It made her flush, thinking about Frank, going to bed with him. It had been good.

It was all OK now. Bel would come home and they'd laugh together and Betsy would take care of her. The doctor, when Betsy got him, said Bel was out of the woods but still weak, sleeping, no visitors for at least twenty-four hours more.

The craziness dropped off her. Betsy felt herself climb out of a stifling suit of anxiety and fear. It occurred to her, staring at the ceiling and the patterns the sunlight made, that she had been out of her mind. Ketsen's messages made her nuts, she over-reacted, the appearance of the cops alarmed her, Las Vegas made her panicky. The more she scrambled, the worse it got. She built herself her own trap, clambered in, heard it snap shut. In her mind she traced the events.

Franny. The insane conclusion it was her own child who killed Ketsen was the real madness. Franny who loved Marie Tusi but confronted her for her mother's sake. Betsy's sake. It was over.

It turned dark and Betsy sat in her window and picked at the peeling paint on the sill and smoked and felt light as a feather again, the way she felt when she first arrived on Cornelia Street and took possession of the apartment.

Behind her on the table was the CD player. Betsy stretched her arm back, punched the button, returned to her window perch. Sinatra sang 'Moonlight in Vermont'.

* * *

Sinatra still on, Betsy found the police image of her face and stuck it on the fridge door with a magnet in the shape of a carrot. To remind herself, she thought. To remember how you could fall off the known world through a hole and come out crazy. The sketch looked out at her from the fridge door. In the kitchen mirror, she examined her face, surprised she still looked young.

It was late, but she felt wide awake. The building was empty, Dev away, the Tusi place vacant, Bel in the hospital. The apartment on three had not been occupied since Betsy arrived on Cornelia Street. The whole building was hers. She took Bel's extra key, opened her door and padded downstairs in her socks.

Bel was coming home soon. She was coming back and Betsy wanted to clean the place for her and she unlocked Bel's door and opened it.

Methodically, Betsy opened all the windows in the apartment. In the kitchen, she bagged what garbage remained, tied the plastic bags and set them against the door. She pulled on a pair of green rubber gloves, knelt on the floor, took out a red plastic pail and a can of Ajax and a sponge. For an hour, the radio turned full blast to an oldies station, she scrubbed the floors and listened to the Beatles.

The kitchen and bathroom finished, she vacuumed, dusted, arranged Bel's photographs on the mantel and her records on the shelf. She moved on to the bedroom where she stripped the bed and bundled the sheets up to take to the Laundromat around the corner. She made the bed with fresh sheets, and punched the pillows to fluff them.

Bel's closet was a mess, shirts and skirts falling off hangers, shoes tossed in at random. It was as if Bel, normally so neat, had become too weary to bother.

One at a time, Betsy removed the

garments. She sorted them, folded the shirts, put the skirts back on hangers. A framed poster hung on the wall next to the closet. It was a picture of Venice in the snow and it was crooked. Betsy took it off the hook to dust it. Behind it was another cupboard, the door flush with the wall. Betsy put the poster on the floor.

The cupboard was filled with storage boxes that contained summer clothes and hats and medical books and files with Bel's tax returns. Betsy removed them and wiped them clean. In the back, stowed out of sight behind a box of beach towels, was Bel's medical bag. It was the bag Bel had asked her for the day she sat with her.

The bag was black leather, battered and scarred with use. Sitting on the floor, the green rubber gloves still on, Betsy unfastened it and opened it and, idly, poked around inside, then closed it and put it on the bedside table.

Half an hour later, she was standing by the kitchen window, a cigarette on the sill, polishing Bel's silver. A wooden block with four kitchen knives on the counter caught her attention.

Marie used a kitchen knife to kill Bobby Ketsen. Marie had sprained her wrist the same week he was killed. Before he was murdered. Her wrist was sprained bad before he died. Bel had mentioned it when Betsy arrived in New York. Days after he was dead, Marie still struggled with the garbage. Which wrist? Betsy tried to remember.

She reached for the phone and remembered Bel was not allowed calls or visitors. She was sedated. Sleeping around the clock, the doctor had told Mark. Would Bel ever be well? well enough to tell her story, tell what had happened? Did Bel's status as a doctor allow her to protect even a murderer who confided in her?

Out of the blue Betsy thought: Franny had seen Bel. She said she had seen her and they'd talked and Betsy asked herself how Franny managed to talk to Bel when Bel was fast asleep and even Mark not allowed in.

Without knowing what she was looking for, or that she was looking, Betsy went back into the bedroom and took the medical bag off the bedside table. She sat on the bed and opened it again, pulled off her rubber gloves and, one at a time, removed the items inside: stethoscope, bandages, plastic vials of pills. At the bottom of the bag was a notebook and she removed it and underneath was a hammer. It was out of place. It wasn't with the other instruments, but shoved into the bottom.

Betsy picked it up and looked at the small heavy hammer with a triangular head, the kind doctors used to test your reflexes. Idly, Betsy crossed her legs and tapped her knee and her foot jiggled.

Getting up, she planted her feet apart on the floor, weighing the hammer in her hand, she swung it to get momentum. It was small. If you used it right, it had plenty of heft; if you got momentum, you could stun someone. You could do damage if you got it right. Easier to use a knife afterwards.

Quietly, she put it back in the bag, closed Bel's door and locked it, then sat down in the armchair in the living room, the medical bag in her lap, and waited.

33

She heard the lock and watched as the door opened.

'Hi.'

Betsy looked up. 'Hi.'

'You weren't upstairs. I thought you'd gone out.'

'I was cleaning Bel's place for her. You have a key?'

'I've always had one. Bel said I should keep one in case I ever needed to crash here or something.'

'You had Marie Tusi's key, too?'

'Sure. I was the surrogate kid in this building.' Franny attempted a smile. 'Everyone loved me, all these women, no kids.'

'I see. Sit down, if you want.'

Franny sat on the edge of the sofa and glanced anxiously at the bag in Betsy's lap.

'Bel asked me to get her bag for her,' Franny said. There was a film of sweat on her forehead. 'You found it.'

'Yes. I thought you had a plane in the morning,' Betsy said. 'You were going to stay out at the airport.'

'I decided I'd stay with a friend in the city,

then Bel asked me to get her bag, she was worried about it, and, I don't know, I thought I better check on you, you looked a little freaked-out today, you know?' Her words tumbled over one another.

Betsy said, 'That was nice of you. You'll go to London first?'

'Yes.'

'You have really good friends there, don't you, people who stick up for you when things are tough, like Rima?'

'Sure. Yes.'

'The kind of people you were with two weekends ago, like you told Frank Dolce. Can I get you anything? Cup of tea? Or coffee?'

'I'm not sure I have time. Yeah, maybe a quick one, sure. Thanks. Tea would be nice.' Her eyes never left Bel's bag.

'Let's go upstairs.'

Betsy put Bel's bag on the chair and the two of them, her and Franny, went up.

In her kitchen, Betsy filled the kettle and Franny sat at the table, stiff and edgy, her blue duffel coat still on. On the refrigerator was the police sketch.

'Let me just get this tea,' Betsy said. 'I won't offer you food.'

Franny was restless. She pushed her hair off her forehead. She leaned on her arms, then sat back and crossed her legs. She drank the tea and watched Betsy and played with the yellow mug.

'The hospital said Bel wasn't allowed any visitors,' Betsy said. 'The doctor said she was sedated and sleeping. Even Mark Carey couldn't see her.'

'I don't remember them saying that.'

'Were you looking for something special in Bel's place?'

'You mean besides her bag? I don't know what you mean,' Franny said.

'You could tell Bel anything, couldn't you? She was a good doctor, wasn't she? She would never break a confidence. You trusted her.'

'Yes.'

'Were you in love with Bobby Ketsen?'

Franny put the tea down. 'What are you talking about?'

'I asked if you were involved with him, really involved.'

'Do you believe in evil?'

'I don't know.'

'I believe in it,' Franny said. 'I think there are people who are purely bad. I think they're born bad and they grow up and they never change. Bobby was like that.'

Franny got up and emptied the rest of the tea in the sink and stared at the sketch on the door of the fridge and went to the window.

You were in love, weren't you? Betsy thought. You couldn't stand it because you were attracted to scum, you loathed what he brought out in you, that was it, wasn't it? She wanted to say it, she opened her mouth and then closed it and looked at her watch.

'It's late,' Betsy said. 'You probably want to get going.'

'Is that all right?'

'You don't need my permission. It's fine. You're all set? You have everything you need? Money? Passport? You were always organized. I know that. You used to have two passports, didn't you? Franny? Like most journalists? So you could go to countries at war with each other?'

'Yes,' she said.

Betsy thought: Franny had an American passport. She had dual nationality. She only showed Mark one of them, the British passport, the one with the US visa that showed she had only arrived after Ketsen was dead. She thought it and she kept her mouth shut.

'One more thing.'

'What?'

'I think you should get Bel's bag and take it with you,' Betsy said. 'Take it to the hospital if you want.'

'I'll do that.'

Franny got up and buttoned her coat and Betsy kissed her on the cheek.

'By the way,' Franny said. 'Did you look in Bel's bag? I mean, nothing was missing, was it?'

'I never looked,' Betsy said. 'Take care of yourself.'

The door shut behind Franny. Slowly, Betsy wandered to the kitchen window and looked down at the street, watching for Franny who emerged from the building. It was dark out, but light streamed from the restaurants onto the sidewalk. Suddenly, a crowd of people, a wedding, a party, came out of the restaurant next door and Franny was caught up in the throng.

Betsy tracked her as she hurried up the block. She pushed the window open, leaning as far out as she could and realized something was wrong. The figure she had been following wasn't Franny at all. It was somebody else.

Other titles published by
The House of Ulverscroft:

HOT POPPIES

Reggie Nadelson

A murder in New York's diamond district. A dead Chinese girl with a photograph in her pocket. A plastic bag of irradiated heroin in an empty apartment. A fire in a Chinatown sweatshop. The worst blizzard in New York's history. These events conspire to bring ex-cop Artie Cohen out of retirement and back into the obsessive world of murder and politics that nearly killed him. The terrifying plot uncoils first in New York — in Artie's own back yard — then in Hong Kong, where everything — and everyone — is for sale. An Artie Cohen Mystery

BODY OF A WOMAN

Clare Curzon

Called to investigate the death of a young woman found dumped in woodland, Superintendent Mike Yeadings and his Thames Valley CID team find the body in exotic evening dress, her face covered by a feathered, bird-featured mask. Yeadings realises he had once briefly encountered her, in quite normal circumstances. This was Leila, the dutiful if undervalued wife of Professor Aidan Knightley; owner of a little gift shop in a quiet Buckinghamshire town; devoted to her two teenage step-children; on good terms with her neighbours. The circumstances of her death seem totally alien to all who knew her.

COLD HANDS

Clare Curzon

A dead body is found on a railway line — a straightforward suicide, or something more sinister? When the dead man is identified as a customs officer investigating counterfeit currency, it seems like more than just a coincidence. Superintendent Mike Yeadings is suspicious, so he sends his undercover team, including DI Mott and DS Zyczinski, to Fraylings Court and the heart of the operation